Let Us Prey

Jordan Falconer

 Mindancer Press

Bedazzled Ink Publishing Company * Fairfield, California

978-1-934452-71-4 paperback
978-1-934452-72-1 ebook

Cover art
by
C.A. Casey

Mindancer Press
a division of
Bedazzled Ink Publishing Company
Fairfield, California
http://mindancerpress.bedazzledink.com

For Tammy . . . Who just won't ever let me give up . . .

For Tammy . . . Who just won't ever let me give up . . .

ACKNOWLEDGMENTS

For Casey and Claudia who end up making me look much better than I actually am.

PROLOGUE

Michelle "Mitch" Coopersmith stared at the scruffy fifteen-year-old girl standing in front of her. Two inches shorter than her six feet, the girl had wild, dark brown hair, clear skin, and strong bone structure. She also had the most beautiful, sky blue eyes Coopersmith had ever seen. Unfortunately, they were narrowed with rage, directed at her, over a trivial weekly test.

"Therese," Coopersmith said, gritting her teeth, "for starters, stop yelling at me. Second, the reason why you lost two marks on this test is because the question says, 'show working,' and you didn't do that. All you gave me was the answer."

"Give me the fucking marks," Therese Monkhouse said. "The answer's right, and any moron can do it in their head."

Coopersmith narrowed her eyes as her temper shifted off its normally even keel. "I'm going to try this again. One, stop yelling at me. Two, if you want to get anything out of me at all, stop swearing at me. Push me again, and you'll get an after school detention for it."

"Try it and see what happens. I'll say whatever the hell I like to you. You're just another useless fucking bitch on a power trip."

Coopersmith inwardly flinched. She took a deep breath to calm herself. "Therese, I give up. We aren't getting anywhere with this. The mark stands. I'm sorry you don't like it but that's just the way it goes."

She turned on her heel and left the fuming Monkhouse. She strode into the staff room, thankful that it was the start of her free fourth period. Gabrielle McCann, Monkhouse's English teacher, immediately waylaid her.

"Are you all right?" McCann asked. "Had a run in with Monk?"

Coopersmith nodded, temper still simmering from their brief—and loud—interaction.

"Sit down," McCann said, pushing her toward an empty spot at one of the large, deserted lunch tables.

McCann got her a cup of coffee and sat down across from her. "Is this your first run in with Monk?" she asked.

Coopersmith nodded. "Why is she still in school? Why haven't they expelled her yet or at least taught her some manners? Has she ever done this to you?"

McCann gave her a rueful grin. "She's only tried it on me once. I don't get yelled at very often." She sighed. "Monk's home life isn't the best. She's just never learnt any better. She's got a near genius IQ, so she doesn't find her classes very challenging. I always give her extra books to read, and she loves reading them. If you want the best out of this girl and some peace in your classes, be gentle with her. Discipline won't work, so you've got to try something else to reach her."

Coopersmith's jaw dropped. "You've got to be kidding me. Why should I pander to her bad behavior?"

"Michelle," McCann said patiently. "The very first time I met this girl was when I got stuck minding afternoon detention. You know why she was on it?"

"I'm sure this is very interesting, so why don't we save it until later?" Coopersmith pushed her coffee aside and prepared to stand up. "I've got—"

"—to listen to a more experienced colleague for a moment or so," McCann said, smiling. "Monk was on detention because she was late to school because I think someone had beaten her half to death—it was probably her mother although I have no proof—and she had to walk to get here. She could only do it slowly, so she was late. When her substitute teacher pulled her up for it, she gave the unfortunate woman both barrels and ended up sitting around and talking with substitute teacher after school. The sub thinks you'd be a good role model for Monk because you're a stronger and more complex person. You also have a lot in common, believe it or not."

Coopersmith flinched. "Her mother beats her? Why didn't you report her?"

McCann shook her head. "I didn't find out about it until she'd almost healed, and by then it was too late. She's going to get it tonight." Her blue eyes were serious. "I saw Sister Constance snag her after the two of you finished your conversation."

Coopersmith shook her head and grimaced. "Her mother beats her?"

"Yes, her mother beats her. Monk's problem is not bad character—take a good look into those stunning eyes of hers, they're very gentle—it's a total lack of control brought on by no guidance. No one has ever tried to teach her how to interact with other people. Try. She's worth it. She has an amazing sense of humor, is very smart, and under that rough exterior is one of the sweetest people you'll ever have the privilege of meeting."

Coopersmith shuddered, unable to imagine spending more than five seconds around Therese Monkhouse. "That's fine, but what the hell could I possibly have in common with her?"

McCann shrugged. "You like to read, don't you? Ever read this book? No? Then why don't you?" She pushed a copy of H.G. Wells's *War of the Worlds* toward her, smiling. "Look. Trust me. Just think about it, will you?"

Coopersmith gazed into McCann's sincere and kind blue eyes and nodded. "All right, Gab. I'll try it your way. What's the worst thing that could happen? I could get my star pupil to actually listen to me?"

McCann gave her a genuinely pleased smile. "That's the spirit."

Coopersmith drained her coffee and stood. She felt calmer. "Thanks, Gab." She patted the honey-haired teacher on the shoulder. "Guess what I gotta do now?"

McCann raised her eyebrows in question.

"Mark more weekly tests."

They exchanged glances and laughed as Coopersmith headed to her cubical.

Coopersmith, on recess patrol around the Year Ten courtyard four days later, stopped and stared at the two girls speaking softly to a group of girls. She knew them by sight but not by name.

"—And I heard that she just got sprung from hospital."

"Yeah, I know. I heard Monk is behind bars for that one."

The two speakers turned careful, speculative eyes on her, and continued to whisper behind cupped hands while the others strained to hear.

The girls all seemed to be looking at her and exchanging whispers as she walked passed them.

Coopersmith went looking for McCann after recess finished. She finally found her hiding at her desk marking English essays.

"Hi, Gab," Coopersmith said quietly.

McCann looked up and gave her a broad grin. "Hi, Michelle. What can I do for you?"

"Cut right to the chase, huh?" Coopersmith grinned. "Why is everyone staring at me?"

"Who's staring at you?"

"Looks like half of Year Ten."

"Perhaps they think you're beautiful?" McCann said, grinning.

Coopersmith felt herself blush and rolled her eyes. "No, I don't think that's it."

McCann patted the seat she had in her cubicle. Coopersmith sat down, staring at the mess that McCann referred to as a desk.

"Well," McCann said. "Rumors fly at the speed of light in a girls' school. This particular bunch is talking about how Monk hospitalized you and is now in prison awaiting trial."

Coopersmith raised her eyebrows in astonishment.

"Ah," McCann said. "That little gem was started by Catrina Walsh and Cathy Daniels."

"Are they the two Year Ten girls who look like they could be on the cover of schoolgirl Vogue, but have the eyes of Jack the Ripper and his pet dog Slasher?"

"That's good," McCann said between snorts of laughter. "That would be them."

"How can anyone believe anything that stupid?"

"You're in school with a bunch of horny, underage girls. Stupid doesn't really enter the equation. Only spite does."

Coopersmith shook her head. "No kidding." She sighed.

Two days later, at the end of the last period of the day, Coopersmith dismissed her year ten maths class with a silent sigh of relief. It had been a quiet and easy lesson.

Monk had sat silently through the class with her eyes downcast, drawing patterns on her desktop with her forefinger between bouts of copying example problems from the blackboard. She looked miserable, often at the point of tears, and she flinched when even her friends talked to her.

Coopersmith was worried about her, but couldn't think how to approach her without starting an argument. She leaned back in her chair, chewing her lip.

Slowly the classroom emptied out, except for one student who sat with an almost unnatural stillness.

Therese Monkhouse.

"Therese," Coopersmith said quietly. "Something wrong?"

Monkhouse gave her a wry smile. "Perhaps I should be asking you that."

"Pardon?" Coopersmith asked.

Monkhouse slowly and painfully got out of her seat, and Coopersmith suppressed a flinch. She walked over to Coopersmith's desk and dropped her backpack before it with a sigh.

"Bloody thing is heavy," she muttered, staring at it, lost, for a moment or so. She looked up at Coopersmith, intense, sky blue eyes sad. She blushed. "I'm sorry."

Coopersmith raised an internal set of eyebrows. "What for?"

Monkhouse looked down and shifted from foot to foot. "For yelling at you. For being rude to you. I didn't mean it to happen like that. I just got mad, that's all," she whispered.

"Therese?" Coopersmith said softly. "Look at me."

Monkhouse's head stayed down, her face a mask of tension.

"I don't bite," Coopersmith said gently. "C'mon now . . . look at me."

Monk looked up, pale as death, hectic spots on her cheeks. Her eyes swam with unshed tears. "Yeah?"

Coopersmith gave her a kind smile. "Forgiven."

A sliver of hope entered Monk's mesmerizing blue eyes. "Really?"

"Really," Coopersmith said, heart lightening at the relief in Monkhouse's eyes.

"Thanks," Monkhouse said softly. "Miss Coopersmith?"

"Yes?"

"Could you please call me Monk? I hate being called Therese."

"Sure, Monk."

A comfortable silence hung between them for a moment or so.

"I have to go and catch my bus," Monk said. "I'll see you tomorrow?"

"No worries," Coopersmith replied easily. "Can I ask you to do me a favor?"

Monk stared at her evenly. "Okay," she said after another moment of silence.

"If you ever want to blow my head off like that again, could you please give me fair warning? Like, 'Miss Coopersmith, I'm getting mad at you'?"

"Why?"

"Because I'm asking you to do it."

Monk stared at her, intense, blue eyes curious. "All right." She smiled.

Coopersmith stood and began packing up her books, Monk watching her closely.

"Penny for your thoughts, Monk?" Coopersmith asked.

"Is that Miss McCann's copy of *War of the Worlds*?" She pointed to the battered paperback on Coopersmith's attendance folder.

"Yup." She glanced at Monk. "Just finished it. Good book, huh?"

Monk nodded, spark in her eye. "Not bad. But I'm more an H.P. Lovecraft fan."

Coopersmith grinned. "You like reading horror?"

"Yeah. Do you?"

Coopersmith widened her grin. "Sure. I love old horror movies as well."

Monk laughed softly. "So do I. I love 'em. Ever seen Max Shrek's version of Dracula? The silent movie version?"

"Oh, yeah. I've seen it."

"I've come to suck your blood," Monk said in bad, nameless, eastern European accent. "Although I've never understood why a vampire needs to announce that? Isn't it obvious? And they never exactly knock on people's doors selling bibles, now do they?"

Coopersmith laughed. "That was good. I have no idea. How difficult is it for the good guys to spot a vampire? And then to wonder where it sleeps during the day, although there's fresh cemetery dirt on the castle floor and a big coffin in the dungeons? And they're standing on it?"

"I know," Monk said, rolling her eyes. "Hello? How can you have a distant family member, who has the same name as someone who died hundreds of years earlier, who hates sunlight, and honestly not wonder? It ranks right up there with the dumb blonde taking her clothes off while there's a heavily breathing maniac in work boots stomping around the deserted house."

Coopersmith nodded and grinned. "Said girl gets bonus points for running out the front door naked while all her neighbors are at home."

They laughed.

"I don't suppose you've seen the old Frankenstein movies?" Coopersmith asked.

Monk grinned. "Yes. How on earth could you miss the big guy staggering around in platform shoes holding his arms out for balance?"

"There's one line in one of those movies where Victor Frankenstein actually says, 'you have a civil tongue in your head. I know because I sewed it there myself.'"

Monk laughed. "You're kidding me."

"Nope. Keep an ear out for it."

Coopersmith led the way out of the classroom, Monk trailing behind her. By the time they reached the door to the staff room, they were slinging movie quotes back and forth and laughing loudly.

"Miss Coopersmith?" Monk asked, wiping the tears off her face.

"Yes?"

"Do you mind if I borrow Miss McCann's book? I don't have anything to read while I'm waiting for the bus. I already finished my English novels."

"Your bus doesn't take that long to come, does it?" Coopersmith asked.

"Yeah, it does." sighed Monk sighed. "If you look to the left as you go out the front door, all the skeletons in *Saturday Night Fever* poses are the people on my route that died waiting for the bus."

Coopersmith snorted laughter. "How about we keep each other company, then? I'm on bus duty this afternoon."

Monk gave her a shy smile. "Thanks. I'd like that."

Coopersmith dropped her books off at her neat desk and walked down to the bus stop with Monk. By the time Monk's bus came, and they parted company, the seeds of an easy, close friendship had been planted.

CHAPTER ONE

Fucking bitches, Monk thought sourly. *It's the first day of school, and they're already being a pair of prize arseholes.* She sat on a wooden bench, leaning against the dark red brick of the school auditorium and watching her most hated enemies approach. She shifted back slightly, trying to escape the hot Australian sun beating down on her unprotected head.

Catrina Walsh and her sidekick Cathy Daniels walked by, casting furtive glances back at her and giggling. Cathy finally shot Monk the finger and glared at her.

Monk snorted. *Idiots. They really do believe they're better than everyone else.*

"Morning, Monk. I recognize that look."

She blinked at the corona outlining the tall figure standing in front of her.

Monk grinned. "Morning, Mitch. You're looking a little worse for wear, aren't you?" She swung around and stretched luxuriously as her math teacher dropped a little awkwardly to the seat beside her.

"Yeah," Coopersmith said, cautiously stretching her long legs out in front of her and wincing as she did so. "Oh, my aching body." She carefully rubbed her left knee.

Monk leaned forward, concerned. "Still hurts, huh? Ice pack help at all?"

"Not much. I think the bone's bruised. It'll heal." Coopersmith sighed. "So what are you up to?"

Monk glanced at Coopersmith, saw the gentle concern in her vibrant green eyes, and felt all of her irritation slip away. "About five ten." Coopersmith mock frowned. "I'm not up to anything, really. What are *you* up to, troublemaker? How come you're here so early?"

Coopersmith grinned, showing her straight, white teeth. "I came here just to see you, Petal. My little jewel. My little cupcake. The center of my universe, the—"

"Oh, please. Uncle. Damn." Monk laughed.

"Okay, okay, I'm really here because of parking. More shade and closer by."

"That certainly makes sense," Monk said.

Coopersmith winced as she shifted her bruised knee.

Monk flinched and grimaced. "You want me to carry your stuff up to the staff room, or are you okay?" Coopersmith shook her head, and Monk grinned. "You gonna make it up the stairs okay with your walking frame?"

Coopersmith nodded, grinning, and then raised an eyebrow with a teasing spark in her eye. "Are you calling me old?" she asked in her best teacher's voice.

Monk snorted. "Sorry. Aged? Debilitated? Archaic? Antediluvian?" She gave Coopersmith a wide, fake smile.

Coopersmith tried to frown, but gave up and laughed softly. "That was good. Anything else you'd care to add?"

Monk leaned forward. "No, ma'am." She stretched out the words.

Coopersmith tried to look outraged and failed miserably, so she gave up and laughed instead. "You'll keep, Monk, you'll keep. You're such a brat."

Monk grinned and joined in her quiet laughter.

Coopersmith's eyes grew more serious. "Really, what *was* that look for?"

Monk frowned, a little confused. "What look?"

Coopersmith smiled gently. "The one you were wearing when I walked up."

Monk remained confused for a second. "Oh. That. Nothing, really."

Coopersmith glanced at Catrina Walsh and Cathy Daniels. "Those two. Talk to me, Monk."

"Nothing, just basic school girl politics. Don't worry about it," Monk replied, shrugging. She gave Coopersmith a crooked reassuring grin.

Coopersmith sighed and shook her head. Her gaze flickered at Catrina Walsh and Cathy Daniels, disapproval lurking in her eyes. She sighed and reluctantly got up. "You'll let me know if you need anything?"

Monk inclined her head and smiled. "Always."

Coopersmith hefted her backpack onto her shoulder and grabbed her briefcase. "Okay, then, I'll meet you after school and I'll give you a lift home."

Monk felt her spirits lift. She watched Mitch head toward the stairs near the auditorium as a tide of nameless emotions flooded through her and left peace in its wake.

She settled back against the warm auditorium wall. She started when a backpack thudded to the ground beside her. She yawned mightily, stretched, and grinned. "Howdy, Fletch, how are you?"

Fletch grinned, shaking straight brown hair out of her eyes. "I would be better if it wasn't for this hell hole."

Monk grinned more broadly. "Morning, Sister, how are you?"

Fletch gave a theatrical groan. "Nice. That fucking prank is *never* going to work on me."

Monk flashed her best diffusing grin. "I'm not kidding. Hello, Sister Constance, how were your holidays?"

Fletch started when a bony hand descended onto her thin shoulder. She glanced up and froze when she saw Sister Constance.

Sister Constance, known as Saint Hatchet Face to the students, opened her puckered mouth to berate Monk.

"Give us a break, Sunshine," Monk said. "It's Monday bloody morning, and quite frankly it's too fucking early to get pissed about anything." She bit her lip.

Fletcher closed her eyes and sighed. She shook her head and pinched the bridge of her nose.

"You two get yourselves into my office right now," the old nun thundered. She glared at them.

They exchanged glances, stood, and trailed behind Sister Constance. They soon found themselves outside the school office, on the hard bench, worn smooth by the years of backsides that had graced it.

Fletch played with the hem of her skirt. Her hands shook. Monk watched her curiously, arms folded across her chest, long legs idly stretched out in front of her, comfortably crossed at the ankles.

"Relax, it'll be fine," Monk said.

She watched the hallway full of milling, confused Year Seven girls, junior teachers, and girls from other grades trying to get to their first period classrooms.

One young woman, a new teacher, caught her roving eye. The teacher was taller than the six-foot Coopersmith and not much older than Monk. She had long, straight, shining black hair that cascaded to her waist, a willowy frame, and the most perfect bone structure Monk had ever seen. It made her arrestingly beautiful to look at. Her piercing gray stare fastened onto them for a moment, blasting them with intense, swift scrutiny, and then slipped away, much to the flustered Monk's relief.

"—fucking mouth shut."

"Huh?" Monk said. "Relax, will you? It'll be fine. I'm in more trouble than you are, and I'm only going to be yelled at."

"Like I said, if you had kept your fucking mouth shut, neither of us would be sitting here! Hatchet Face would have told me off, and that would have been it. Instead, you open your bloody mouth, and we both fall right in." Fletch snarled, glaring at her.

Monk grimaced. "I know. Sorry, Fletch."

Suddenly Coopersmith stood before them, holding her books and attendance folder, focused on Monk. "God, Monk, what are you doing out here? Please don't tell me you're here to see Sister Constance."

Fletcher stared at her, round eyed.

Monk sighed and tried to smile, but failed. "Sister Constance."

Coopersmith looked as though she had just bitten into a raw lemon. Monk frowned at the principal.

Coopersmith gave her a brief, reassuring grin, and then turned to Sister Constance. "Sister. How are you this morning?" she asked, smiling.

Sister Constance glared at her and then pounced. She pointed a bony finger at Monk. "You, young lady, will keep your dirty language to yourself, and will not speak until spoken to first." She rounded on Coopersmith. "I'll thank you not to be speaking to the students like that. Don't you have a class to teach?"

Monk narrowed her eyes and frowned. She was on the brink of standing up for all three of them when Coopersmith squared her shoulders and towered over the old nun.

"Yes, of course. I have things to take care of." She turned and flashed a sympathetic grin at Monk. "I'll see you in maths, young lady." She turned and gave Sister Constance a face full of hair and then strode down the corridor. Sister Constance coughed and spluttered in her wake.

Monk struggled to contain a snort of laughter.

In the midst of the milling youngsters, Angela Michaels, an

acknowledged school bully, swung a vicious punch that connected with a thin and colorless blonde girl in Year Nine. The younger girl uttered a brief cry of pain and fell backward. The tall, black-haired woman who had captured Monk's attention earlier, got there at the same time as Coopersmith. She grabbed Michaels and threw her to one side as Coopersmith awkwardly caught the sobbing, flailing victim.

Michaels tripped over her feet and landed on her behind on the green painted concrete. Coopersmith, off balance, slowly dropped to her good knee and leaned over the wet-eyed young girl and carefully supported her, making sure nothing worse than bruising was wrong with her. The girl had the beginnings of an impressive black eye. The brunette leaned over them both, Michaels forgotten. Monk watched them closely, not at all at ease with the vulnerable position Coopersmith had put herself in.

Michaels rapidly recovered her equilibrium and looked as though she was going to pummel Coopersmith. She leapt to her feet, threw several frightened first years aside, and crept up behind the kneeling Coopersmith. She pulled back her foot to give Coopersmith a vicious kick in the kidneys. The number of milling, craning girls around Coopersmith and the brunette gave Monk the seconds she needed to make it into the mêlée.

Monk and Fletcher ran forward at the same time, dodging juniors. Monk grabbed Michaels under one arm, Fletch under the other, and their forward momentum threw Michaels against the brick wall with an audible thud.

Michaels grunted as the air left her chest in an explosive rush, and all the fight went out of her. She stared at them venomously. Monk returned the stare and then looked at Coopersmith to make sure she was all right. Coopersmith was staring at her, slightly shocked, and Monk felt a blush.

Sister Constance stormed up behind them. "That's enough, all of you! Get to your classes!" she roared.

Silence descended as all the girls stilled and waited to see what would happen next.

"Get to your classes. Now!" Sister Constance shouted. She pushed girls none too gently down the hall.

Monk and Fletcher remained, holding onto Michaels. Monk shot a baleful glare at Michaels, and the two locked eyes in a battle of wills that lasted until Sister Constance snuck up behind Monk.

"Thank you, Miss Monkhouse and Miss Fletcher. Miss Fletcher, you are excused. Miss Monkhouse, you are on afternoon detention for your disgusting, foul mouth. Good deeds do not excuse your past behavior." She pointed at the brunette. "You will be supervising."

The brunette, who had been watching the proceedings with great interest, looked as though she wanted to protest. Coopersmith shot her a warning look and gave her head a quick shake. The brunette's mouth closed with a snap.

Monk quivered internally. "Shit," she mumbled, sighing. She slumped her shoulders and could feel Coopersmith's eyes on her, but kept her eyes trained on the faded green floor. She could not face the disappointment and gentle reproach she knew would be there.

Sister Constance whipped around and glared at her. "Make that two weeks. Anything else to add?"

"No, Sister," Monk said, smiling coldly, glaring at the old nun. She felt her temper flare and forced it down, highly aware of Coopersmith's proximity.

Sister Constance turned, snakelike, on Angela Michaels. "You, young lady—if you can even be called that—get into my office."

Mr. Smith, one of the school's physical education teachers, jogged up behind them, whistle swinging on his blindingly white polo shirt. With a quick word of thanks to Fletcher and Monk, he took the squirming Michaels toward the principal's office.

"Well? What are you all waiting for? Go to class," Sister Constance said to the milling juniors. Some of the older girls quickly moved out of her way.

Sister Constance pushed the stragglers toward their respective rooms. Fletch spared the morose Monk a sympathetic glance as they were swept toward the auditorium and their rapidly approaching orientation assembly.

Monk's new chemistry teacher, Miss Wells, was waiting for her class outside the science labs. She sat on the benches outside the end lab, eyeing each girl appraisingly as they walked past.

"Morning, Miss," Monk said with a smile as she came to a halt before Wells.

Wells remained silent long enough for Monk to begin fidgeting.

"Who are you?" Wells asked, folding her arms in a gesture of arrogant confidence.

"Therese Monkhouse. Monk," Monk said coolly.

Wells stared at her. "I've heard about you. Am I going to have trouble with you this year?"

Bully, Monk thought, biting off an angry retort. "No, Miss."

"Good." Wells smiled. "And wipe that look off your face."

Monk narrowed her eyes and glared at Wells.

Miss Wells met her glare with glittering, light brown eyes.

"Good morning, Miss Wells," a tall redhead said as she approached them. She was wearing a neatly pressed uniform and blazer with a small pin on it.

Wells ignored her.

The girl's smile faltered. She turned to Monk with a cautious smile. "Hi, Monk."

Monk turned to her and smiled, ignoring Wells. "Hi, Jackie." Some of the stiffness left her shoulders.

"Good morning. And you are—?" Wells ignored Monk and smiled at Jackie politely, a gleam in her eye.

"Jackie Sharp," the girl said, smiling automatically in return.

Wells grinned broadly, odd, yellow eyes glittering. A quick sliver of dislike shot through Monk.

"Well, Jackie Sharp. You're the school captain. How about you keep Therese company this year? I can only hope that your influence rubs off on her." Wells's tawny eyes pinned Monk in an unforgiving stare.

Jackie's expression remained neutral. "It would be my pleasure, Miss Wells."

Wells eyed her for a moment, apparently on alert for signs of deceit. She gave them both a cold look. She turned away, opened the door, and allowed them to enter the room. The other girls in their class milled around the doorway.

Monk and Jackie calmly and quietly headed toward the back of the room, but Wells stopped them. "You two sit in the front row next to the windows."

Jackie and Monk exchanged disbelieving looks. Monk led the way to their assigned seats. "Un-fucking-believable. I haven't had this happen to me since I was twelve."

"Yes, it *has* happened to you since you were twelve," Jackie snapped. "Miss Coopersmith did it to you a couple of years ago, remember? Now, if you keep your mouth shut, maybe we'll make it through this ordeal, okay?"

Ouch, Monk thought. *I wasn't expecting that. Jackie doesn't have a reputation for being a bitch, and I didn't exactly ask for that, so I wonder what's up with her? Wait—I can only think of one other reason for this. Maybe it's not a mood thing, maybe she just doesn't want to associate with me.* She slipped her stoic mask back into place.

"I hadn't intended to say anything." Monk studied her hands. "Look, why don't you just ask her at the end of the class if you can move? I reckon she'll let you do it. You don't have to be stuck with me if you don't want to be."

Jackie looked closely at Monk. "Err, Monk," she began, then stopped and took a deep breath.

Monk sighed, gazed at her, and waited for her to speak. She wondered what Jackie would throw at her next.

"No, and I'm sorry I wasn't very nice. It's not you, it's this class." Jackie looked at all the girls. They were a large clique of Catrina Walsh's and Cathy Daniels's friends. They loathed Monk and ignored them both.

Monk nodded. Wells, judging by her chattiness with Daniels and Walsh, had taken as strong a liking to them as she had taken a dislike to Monk and Jackie. This year was probably going to be hell for them both.

Monk nodded and waited for her to go on.

"I'm not sure I'm very comfortable here." She leaned forward and said in Monk's ear, "I'm also not sure about Miss Wells, but I'm starting to think I really don't like her all that much."

Monk studied her, weighing her. "You're afraid of me, aren't you? You're afraid that Wells is going to pick on you because my slime now covers you, too? That's fine, I understand. I only ask that if you bail, please do it now."

Jackie blushed, looking stung. "Why are you being such a bitch? What *is* your problem?"

Monk smiled. "Take it easy. I'm okay once you get to know me. I'm just being honest. I'm also the friendliest face in the room, unless you want to sit with Catrina Walsh, Cathy Daniels, or an associated crony."

Jackie sighed, and her shoulders slumped in defeat. "That's honestly not it, but I had noticed that."

"Please don't stress about this. I know you want to stay under

Wells's radar. I do warn you, that no matter what I do, I'm going to be a magnet for this woman's temper, and you may get caught in the backwash. That being said, I promise I'll keep my mouth shut and work. I don't want trouble either." Monk smiled. "I don't mind if you want to hide behind me because of all that. I'm strong enough to put up with whatever stupid shit she wants to dole out."

Jackie smiled. "Then I guess it's time to do the two musketeers thing."

Monk chuckled softly and held out her hand to the surprised Jackie, who took it without hesitation. "I apologize, if I offended you. I promise to behave myself."

Jackie grinned ruefully. "Accepted. I apologize for flying off the handle at you. All for one and one for all, right?"

"Thank you." Monk grinned. "*Le roi est mort, vive le roi!*"

Just at that moment, Wells strode to the front of the room, arrogantly leant against the teacher's bench, and stared out at the class appraisingly. "For those of you who haven't met me yet, my name is Miss Wells, and I'll be taking you for chemistry this year. Let's begin, girls, with the absolute basics. Can anyone tell me what an atom is?"

Monk put up her hand.

Wells's smile turned predatory. "All right, Therese. Give it your best shot."

"It's the smallest part of a chemical element that can take part in a chemical reaction."

"*That* was your best shot?" Wells asked. "It's missing some . . . *elements?*"

The class giggled, and Jackie frowned. Monk tensed.

"Which ones?" Monk asked calmly.

Jackie gave her a barely perceptible smile.

"Um, how about the part that actually answers the question?"

Monk looked confused. "That *did* answer the question."

Wells glared at her. "*Don't* talk back to *me*, Therese." She folded her arms, matching Monk's stony gaze. "If you don't know the answer to a question, kindly keep your mouth shut."

Monk held her tongue.

"I get it," Wells said after a moment of silence. "You're offended now, aren't you? You thought you were the best in the class, didn't you? Well, you're obviously not." She gave the rest of the class a conspiratorial look. She looked pointedly at Catrina Walsh and Cathy Daniels. "I think it's time for the real talent to come out, don't you?"

Jackie's eyes widened.

Monk remained silent as she felt the color rise in her cheeks.

"Cat got your tongue, Therese?" Wells asked sweetly. "Grow up. You don't get to be top of the class unless you make an attempt to study and learn the material. Something you've obviously never bothered to do."

Monk's jaw tensed.

Jackie shifted in her seat.

Wells rounded on her. "Miss Sharp, I put you next to Therese in the hopes you would teach her some manners. You're not doing a very good job, are you?"

Monk gaped. *What the fuck is she picking on Jackie for?*

"Excuse me?" Jackie asked, politely.

"I see. Not very bright either, are you? Well, why don't you keep sitting there looking idiotically attractive beside your . . . *friend*." Wells nailed Jackie with a forbidding stare.

"Jackie is *not* my keeper, Miss Wells," Monk said.

Wells's stare swung onto Monk and blasted her. "Shut up, Therese. When I want your opinion, I'll give it to you."

Jackie stole a quick glance at Monk, cringing.

Monk knew her eyes burned with anger for Jackie.

"I'm sorry," Jackie whispered. "I'm so sorry."

"It's okay," Monk replied.

For the next forty minutes, Monk tried to keep as quiet as possible and noticed that Jackie barely made a sound. Wells took every opportunity she could to criticize them. Monk tried to ignore it, and Jackie hid behind her.

The bell finally rang, signaling the end of the period, and Wells tossed her chalk onto the teacher's bench. "I'll see you tomorrow, girls. Read chapter two of *Basic Chemistry* for class tomorrow." She turned to Monk. "Make sure you read it, Therese, and do try and learn it, will you?"

Monk glared at her.

Catrina Walsh and Cathy Daniels exchanged whispers and giggled at her.

Wells smiled and strode out of the science lab.

Monk blew out a breath. She had a pounding headache. "Well, that certainly could have gone a bit better. Are you sure you want to sit next to me in class? I'm only causing you grief."

Jackie looked pale and exhausted. "No." She sighed. "She doesn't seem to like me any more than she likes you. We're both in trouble, I think."

Monk nodded. "I know. Are you all right, though? She was really, really, really nasty to you."

"So? She wasn't exactly Mother Theresa to you either, you know."

Monk laughed, despite herself. Jackie gaped at her for a second, and then joined in her laughter. They laughed loud and hard with an edge of hysteria from their draining tension.

"God, she's such a bitch, isn't she?" Monk wiped the tears from her eyes.

Jackie nodded. "Oh, yeah." Her expression turned serious. "You're in trouble in this class, aren't you? Do you need to change classes?"

Monk sighed. "I guess so, but I don't think it's anything I can't handle. When it comes to assessments, the teachers don't mark their own class's work. They mark someone else's. I'm stuck here."

Jackie looked relieved. "So Wells can only get picky on class tests that don't matter?"

Monk nodded. "Yup. Besides that, I can't change classes. The other one doesn't fit my schedule, which is why I'm in this one to begin with. I have no choice." She paused. "Besides, I don't think I want to leave you here by yourself. That was too much to handle alone."

They walked out of the science lab together, and Jackie turned to Monk. She looked as though she wanted to say something but faltered to a stop. "Look, . . . ah . . . thanks . . . I guess I'll see you in class tomorrow?"

Monk nodded, giving her a broad grin. She was starting to like the school captain. "Sure. Have a good rest of your day."

Jackie grinned. "You too, Monk."

Monk headed toward her homeroom with a heavy heart. Roll call was only fifteen minutes long, but instinct told her that it would last an eternity before the freedom of recess and an hour and a half of bliss in math with Coopersmith.

"Hi," a soft voice said beside her.

Monk looked around, distracted, and saw one of the new girls.

"Hi," she said.

"I'm Vanessa Lightman." The tall, blonde girl with watchful brown eyes held out her hand, and Monk took it.

"Therese Monkhouse. Monk."

They reached the door of the classroom, and Lightman pushed it open so they could both enter.

Monk walked through the door of the classroom into sudden and intense silence. She looked around to see what had everyone's attention. Her spirits crashed to earth at the sight of her hated chemistry teacher sitting with negligent ease behind the desk at the front of the room.

The other thing that caught her attention was the empty desk for two directly in front of Wells.

Fuck, Monk thought. *Here we go again.*

Lightman's brow contracted, and she stared back and forth between Monk and Wells as they squared off. She followed Monk to the empty desk in the deafening silence.

Wells gave a sarcastic smile. "Nice of you to join us, Therese." She nodded toward Lightman. "Who's your little friend?"

Monk gave Lightman a swift glance. Lightman's eyes narrowed in outrage at Wells's rudeness. Monk opened her mouth to speak.

"Pardon me?" Lightman said, coming to a halt. She stared coldly at Wells, hands on hips. "Little friend? If you want to know my name, why don't you just ask me?"

Wells looked surprised for a second, and then her expression hardened. "I wasn't talking to you." She pinned Lightman with a ferocious stare.

Lightman snorted. "Yes, you were talking *about* me instead, weren't you? I'll tell you what, why don't I tell you what my name is, since it's *my* name? I'm Vanessa Lightman." She gave Wells a cold smile. "Would you like me to spell that for you, or do you possess sufficient literacy to identify it on the roll?"

Wells's face darkened, tawny eyes flashing. "Shut that mouth of yours, Vanessa Lightman, or you'll be paying Sister Constance a visit."

Lightman did not look impressed. "Maybe I'll be doing it anyway, *Miss* Wells. I'm sure she'd like to know all about you."

Wells leaned forward. "Get out of my classroom," she said in a dangerously quiet voice. "I don't think I really want to have you around all year, so I'll race you to the principal's office." She zeroed in on Monk. "You. You." She paused. "Therese, why don't you spend your time out in the corridor? If you can't arrive to roll call on time, then I really don't want you in here."

Monk felt a fleeting moment of elation. Kicked out of class without having said one word, she picked up her backpack and trailed behind Lightman as they left the room. The silence was still deafening, and Monk noticed that while most of the girls looked as though they wanted to punch her, some of them looked shell-shocked, unable to understand what had just happened.

Out in the silence of the hallway, Monk sighed in profound relief. She dropped her backpack onto the faded green, concrete floor, and fell cross-legged beside it.

Lightman stared down at her, as though she had taken leave of her senses. "Are you really going to stay here?"

Monk frowned. "Of course. What else am I supposed to do? I'm already in enough trouble with her as it is."

Lightman looked at her in disbelief. "Do you always do what you're told to do?"

Monk gave her a confused look, and then remembered that Lightman was probably the one person who had no idea her big mouth had already scored her an afternoon detention. "No, of course not. But I just don't want to pick a fight with her. I just want to make it through my last year of school."

"You *are* aware that she's being unreasonable?"

Monk nodded and smiled ruefully. "Oh, yeah."

"Then why the hell are you putting up with it?"

"It's safer for me to pull my head in. I can't argue with her. I'm already skating on thin ice around here."

"That seems like such a piss poor reason." Lightman cocked her head and studied Monk.

"It's not. It's as good a reason as you can get." Lightman looked disappointed, so Monk continued. "Look, it's a long story, and one day I'll fill you in on it. Just not now." She gave Lightman a curious look. "What about you? You just ripped Wells a new arsehole in there. You're going to be in really deep shit for that, you know."

"If she's going to stand there and be a stupid bitch, I'm going to be the first person to tell her all about it." Lightman gave a strangely carefree laugh. "Besides, I really don't think she's going to give me any shit."

Monk stared at her as though she had grown another head.

Lightman started walking with negligent ease down the hallway. "I don't really expect you to know this, but the name Lightman should ring a bell with the hierarchy in this fine learning establishment. My mother owns Lightman Industries, and she's filthy rich. She spent a lot of money to get me in here—and keep me here—on short notice. I think the teachers here will have been told to treat me with kid gloves."

She turned around and walked backward so she could wave to Monk. "I'll see you at lunch. I think it's time to have a quick chat with Mr. Collins." She turned around and strolled down the hallway, whistling softly as she went.

Monk spent recess sitting in the hallway outside her homeroom, thinking. She couldn't understand what she had done to deserve Miss Wells's ire. Yet it didn't matter in the long run. She simply had to survive her final year of high school.

She wished she could shift to the other class but there was no way she could shuffle the rest of her schedule around. She sighed. She would simply deal with each day as it came, and chemistry was over for today.

Monk was so occupied her thoughts on how she could deal with Wells she didn't notice that recess had passed and third period had begun. She grimaced as she pushed herself up off the hard concrete and tried to stretch her aching and stiff body.

She went into the classroom, sat in her seat by the window, and gazed out at the blue sky above.

"I was rather hoping I'd see you. I rushed like no one's business to make sure I made it here before anyone else."

Monk turned and felt her blood run cold with dread.

Coopersmith leaned casually in the doorway, holding onto her books with perfect ease, idly flicking the pen in her hand. Her eyes were kind and gentle, as always. "Don't look at me like that. I'm not going to bite you."

Monk firmed her chin and tried to relax.

Coopersmith walked across the room and dropped her books on the teacher's desk. Her vivid green eyes stayed on Monk as she squatted in front of her desk and rested her chin on her stacked fists.

"Trust me. Don't be so afraid of me. You don't have anything to prove to me. I know you didn't do much to deserve the detention you got." She straightened so she was kneeling, took Monk's cold hand, and squeezed it. She gave Monk an encouraging smile. "It doesn't matter what you did or didn't do around St. Hatchet Face. She gets an idea into her head and flails around, not really caring what happens to anyone in the process." She paused and then glanced at the door. "You're my friend, and I really like you. I'll help you in any way I can, so stop stressing about your mother, all right?"

Monk relaxed her tense shoulders and sagged as a wave of relief washed over her.

Coopersmith's eyes were warm and gentle. "Feel better?"

Monk blinked away her tears. "Yup." It was all that she could manage. She focused on Coopersmith's gentle compassion and her horrible morning with the chemistry teacher from hell slid away a little. Her clash with Sister Constance also receded. She wanted to tell Coopersmith everything, but she held back.

Coopersmith held her gaze for a little while, eyes sympathetic as the backwash of Monk's distress continued.

Coopersmith got back to her feet and gave Monk an easy, mild smile. "Just relax and let everything go for a couple of hours. You're with me now. I'll take us back to my place after school, make us dinner, and we can talk. Just remember, there's no problem so sticky, or solution so horrible, that lil' ole Mitch won't help you out."

Monk laughed softly, and Coopersmith grinned.

"Better."

Coopersmith made her way to the front of the classroom. She leaned against the desk, long legs crossed in front of her, greeting each of the girls as they trickled in from their morning break.

CHAPTER TWO

Monk felt stupid as she approached the auditorium for afternoon detention. She was sweating, and her uniform clung to her uncomfortably.

A group of about eight or so juniors sat outside the hall, talking and looking tense. Angela Michaels, aloof and alone, sat off to one side. Her arms were crossed, and she was hunched over, studying the ground and frowning. Monk was amazed that Michaels was still in school. She had been sure Michaels would be on suspension.

Monk picked a bench in the shade, and sat, sighing, thinking about her day. Coopersmith had steered clear of calling on her during their double math period, allowing Monk to collect herself. She felt a surge of love for her maths teacher.

A shadow passed in front of her closed eyes, and a sultry voice called for their attention.

"C'mon, girls, into the auditorium. Now."

Monk opened her eyes and found herself exchanging interested gazes with the beautiful woman she had seen in the morning. Her eyes were arresting. They were color of a stormy sky, framed by long eyelashes and perfect, pitch-black eyebrows. Her expression was openly friendly, and Monk took an instant liking to her.

The teacher gave Monk a grin that lit up her eyes. "That includes you, young lady."

Monk gave her a broad smile. "Okay, no problem, I'm on my way." She stood and shouldered her backpack. The tall teacher eyed Michaels coolly, and Monk caught an intoxicating whiff of her expensive perfume.

"Angela Michaels, get yourself into the auditorium. Now."

Michaels stared at them scathingly for a moment. She got up, her expression insolent. She sauntered into the hall behind the rest of the group.

The teacher gestured gracefully toward the doors. "After you."

"Thanks." Monk inclined her head and walked into the auditorium, aware of the teacher close behind her.

The girls were all sitting in the seats close to the door they had entered, and the teacher, all of about six-four, if Monk was any judge of height, went over to them and held up a hand for attention.

"Good afternoon, girls. Welcome to after school detention. For those of you who have never been a party to this mysterious ritual, this is how it works. Normally, you would be sitting in these seats, writing lines—of my choosing—for the next hour. Not this afternoon. We're going to do something more interesting." She gave an arch smile that made them straighten. "You're going to sweep the auditorium."

She pointed a long arm to a ragged collection of brooms that leant against the rear doors of the auditorium. "Go ahead, ladies, grab a broom and get to it."

The girls, some veterans of afternoon detention, grumbled and moaned.

"Like hell we are," Angela Michaels said. "You can't do that."

The teacher smiled. "Actually, I checked with Sister Constance. I most certainly can, and I am." She waved a hand and nodded toward the brooms. "Get moving."

Monk sighed and dropped her bag on the nearest seat. She took a step toward the brooms, but a soft voice behind her said, "Not you. Stay put."

Monk froze.

"Fucking bitch! We'll *see* who has to sweep the motherfucking floor," a soft voice said from across the auditorium.

The tall teacher stiffened. "Freeze, Angela Michaels."

The junior flipped her off and kept sauntering toward the back of the hall. All the other girls stopped and stared, round eyed, at the interaction.

The teacher motioned swiftly for Monk to sit, and then strode toward Angela Michaels. Monk sat on the edge of a seat and swiveled around so she could watch.

Michaels slammed into the ten inches taller teacher. Undeterred, she put her hands on her hips and glared at the teacher defiantly.

The teacher said something that Monk couldn't hear, and then Michaels turned and pointed at Monk, furious. The teacher listened to her tirade for another moment or so. Finally, she said something else to Michaels, grey eyes flashing, and the junior dropped her head and went to the group of girls, feet dragging.

The teacher watched her as she picked up a broom and started pushing it around with a negligence that was astounding, even for someone unwillingly performing a task. The teacher shook her head and grinned ruefully as she walked toward Monk.

Monk gave her a curious look.

The teacher motioned for Monk to join her at the stage, and Monk did so with confidence she did not feel.

"Hello," the teacher said, with a broad grin. "You're the crazy senior who decided to play chicken with the principal this morning. What's your name, brave soul?"

Monk tried not to stare at her beautiful, lush body. "I'm Therese Monkhouse. Please, call me Monk." She gave the young teacher a charming grin. "So you're the crazy teacher who decided to drop kick Angela this morning. What's your name, brave soul?"

The teacher grinned. "That's interesting. I'm Therese Warland. Please, call me Miss Warland."

Monk relaxed a little. "All right, then. So why have you singled me out from work, Miss Warland?"

Warland smiled. "You're quite a rarity. I'm sure seniors almost never end up on afternoon detention." She cocked her head. "Accordingly, I suspect you really don't belong here."

"Really? How do you figure? I think I earned my place here."

"Perhaps so, but I think you're too old for this kind of punishment. How old *are* you?"

"Eighteen. How old did you say you were?" Monk inwardly winced and wished she could take back her question.

Warland gave her a curious look, and an interested gleam shone in her eyes. "Twenty-two."

Monk nodded toward Michaels. Her performance with the broom had not improved. "You know you're going to be in trouble with Angela Michaels, don't you?" She gazed at Warland, admiring her easy confidence.

A small smile played about Warland's ruby lips. "Do I look like I can't handle her?"

Warland pulled herself onto the stage with an ease that was born of her height. She patted the stage next to her, and Monk grinned and jumped up with lithe grace. Warland smiled back at her.

"Well," Monk began slowly. "I don't think it's a question of your not being able to handle her, it's a question of how much damage you're going to have to clean up before you catch her."

"What do you mean?"

"That." Monk pointed toward the end of the hall. All the girls had stopped working, and were watching a shoving match going on. Michaels was pushing a young Year Seven girl with flame-red hair, and the girl was pushing her back, red-faced and dismayed. "Don't get me wrong, I'm sure no one here minds not doing lines, but now Michaels is armed. She's a complete psycho."

Warland cursed softly. "Hey! Knock it off!" Her voice echoed through the auditorium. She slid off the stage and walked toward them. Monk tensed and slid off after her.

Angela Michaels smiled coldly, eyes on Warland.

Warland came to a halt in front of the two of them, hands on hips, and although Monk could not make out the words, it was clear that Warland was angry.

Halfway through Warland's lecture, Michaels deliberately turned to the Year Seven girl that she had been tormenting and pushed with all her might. The redhead tripped over the bristles of the broom she had been leaning on. She landed on her behind with a yelp.

Monk jogged toward them.

Warland glared at Michaels and helped the red-headed girl up. Michaels hefted the broom and aimed for Warland's head.

Monk sprinted across the auditorium, leapt over the last of the seats, and launched herself at Michaels. She crashed into her a second before her blow landed on Warland. The broomstick bypassed Warland's head, hit her back and shoulders instead, and knocked her forward and into the red-headed girl.

Michaels roiled beneath Monk and struggled to throw her off. Michaels managed to get one arm clear and threw a savage, wild punch at Monk. Her fist glanced off Monk's shoulder and slammed into the side of her neck, leaving Monk gagging and spluttering long enough for Michaels to slip out from under her.

Michaels turned toward Warland and viciously kicked her in the ribs. Warland grunted and doubled over, stunned. The red-headed girl, shaking with fear, leaned toward Warland, as Michaels pulled her foot back and aimed another savage kick at Warland.

Monk stumbled to Michaels and hooked an arm around her neck. She dragged Michaels backward.

An unusually strong hand grabbed her by the scruff of her neck and tugged hard. Michaels slipped out of her grip, whirled, and lunged at her. Monk grunted as long, ragged fingernails tore through her shirt, gouging into the soft skin of her chest just below her collarbone, leaving deep grooves of broken skin, blood, torn uniform blouse and flying buttons.

Someone threw her backward. She tripped over a chair, fell onto her back, and hit her head. She hissed in pain as she rolled over and slammed into the floor, shoulder first. She grunted and laid there for a moment, eyes closed, unable to move. The gashes in her chest were a blaze of pain, and she could taste blood in her throat.

"You really are a ferocious little brat, aren't you, Therese?"

Monk's spirits sank. It was Wells. Wells had thrown her onto the floor.

Monk coughed and pushed herself to her knees, dizzy from the impact of her head on one of the hard seats. "I didn't do anything, Miss Wells. Angela Michaels started it."

Wells's yellow eyes pinned her mercilessly. "It doesn't matter which one of you started it. You're both as bad as the other." She grabbed Monk by the arm and ensnared Michaels.

Monk glanced around, looking for Warland. Her heart sank. Warland sat on the floor, dazed. She apparently had not noticed Wells enter the room.

The red-headed girl was alternating between concerned stares at Warland and worshipful glances at Monk. The other girls simply stared at them, eyes wide with shock.

Monk, aching and bleeding heavily from the gouges in her chest, allowed Wells, who was much stronger than her wiry frame suggested, to drag them toward the rear doors of the auditorium.

Wells turned around to the red-headed girl. "Freeze. You're coming with us. You're in on this too, aren't you?"

"No, Miss Wells." She looked at the floor, coloring.

Just beyond them, Warland shook her head, much to Monk's relief.

Warland focused on them, and her eyebrows shot up. "No," she finally managed, getting to her feet. "It's neither of their faults. Angela Michaels took a swing at Kilkenny here, and then me. Monk pulled her off of me."

Wells eyed her appraisingly. "That's as may be, but I still need to tell Sister Constance about this. It doesn't matter who started it. No one should be throwing punches at all."

"That's true, Miss Wells, but I think Kilkenny and Monk can both be excused for being involved in this." Warland turned her attention to Angela Michaels. Michaels had settled down, but still had the aura of a tightly coiled snake, ready to strike at a moment's notice. "There's something bad wrong with you."

Wells waved a dismissive hand and attempted to brush her aside. "I think we'll let Sister Constance make that decision."

Monk's heart sank even further.

Warland stood stiffly, piercing gray eyes boring into Wells. "Yes, we will, Miss Wells, but I'm the one in charge of detention, so let me deal with this. Would you mind taking over?" She did not wait for Wells to respond. "Kilkenny, you're with us."

Without really knowing how it had happened, Monk found her arm out of Wells's strong hands, and in Warland's. Warland's grip was much gentler than Wells's.

Warland let go of Monk when they reached the auditorium doors, but kept a firm grip on the eerily silent Michaels. She eyed Monk, concerned.

Monk pulled the shredded remains of her blouse closed to satisfy some modicum of modesty. She could feel blood trickling down her body and grimaced. They left the auditorium, Kilkenny silent beside them.

They tramped the corridor until they were outside the principal's office. Warland, pale and strained, looked at Monk closely, concern in her gray eyes. "Are you going to be okay for a minute or two while I see Sister Constance?" She glanced at Kilkenny. "Consider yourself dismissed, Kilkenny. I think you've done your dash with detention this afternoon."

Kilkenny nodded tensely. "Thanks, Miss Warland."

Monk sighed, sagging slightly. "I'll be fine until you get back."

"I have you under my fingernails," Angela Michaels said in a soft and venomous voice.

They stared at her, repulsed.

Michaels held up her hands, displaying her fingernails. They were bloody and chunks of Monk's chest skin stuck out from beneath them. She put her middle finger into her mouth with chilling calm, and her cheeks indented as she sucked the skin and blood out from under her nail.

"That's more than enough from you," Warland said softly.

Monk screwed up her face in disgust, mirroring Warland's expression. Kilkenny shifted uncomfortably beside them.

Warland, with no particular gentleness, grabbed Michaels and dragged her into the office. She looked back at Monk. "Stay put, I'll be back in a second."

Monk nodded and slumped wearily on the bench, closed her eyes, and felt her chest throb.

Kilkenny dropped to the seat beside her. "Uh, you're Monk?"

"Yeah. You're Kilkenny?"

"Yeah. Thanks for saving my and Miss Warland's necks."

"You're very welcome," Monk said, smiling.

"Um . . . Are you all right? Your chest looks bad."

Monk looked down and sighed as she tried to pull the flaps of her ruined and bloody shirt closed. "I'm all right."

"I'm sorry."

Monk gave her a surprised look. "Whatever for?"

"If it hadn't been for me, you'd still be fine."

"I don't know how this could possibly be your fault. Honestly. Don't worry about it. I'll heal." Monk gave Kilkenny a gentle smile. "You tripped. Are *you* all right?"

Kilkenny grinned. "Nothing a rubber cushion won't fix."

Monk burst out laughing. "Thanks," she said, quieting in fits and starts. "I needed that."

"Well," Kilkenny said. "I'd better go. I have to go and get my bag from the auditorium."

Monk heard the fear in her voice. "I'll get it. I have to go and get mine as well. Which one is it?"

Kilkenny looked as though she were ready to burst into tears, but her entire body relaxed. "It's the black and silver Reebok with the ankh on the zipper. It's close to yours."

Monk nodded. "I'm gone. You want to wait for me? Just tell Warland I'll be back in a couple of minutes."

Kilkenny nodded.

Monk levered herself to her feet with a sigh and headed back toward the auditorium. Once there, she put her hands on the closed wooden doors and steeled herself.

She sighed. "Show time," she said softly and pushed the doors open.

All the girls that were a part of detention stood in a row before Wells. Wells was sitting on a seat back with her feet on the seat in front of her. She frowned when she saw Monk.

"What are you doing back here, Therese?"

Monk forced herself to move quickly, despite the throbbing in her chest. She walked over to the side of the hall, spotted her backpack and shouldered it, flinching as pain knifed through her chest.

"What? Don't feel like talking, Therese?" Wells asked coldly.

Monk looked for Kilkenny's backpack. Her hands shook.

Footsteps came up behind her. She closed her sweating hand around the straps of Kilkenny's backpack, just as a strong hand grasped her shoulder and tugged.

Monk felt the cuts in her shoulder tear further and yelped as she was spun around to face her chemistry teacher.

Miss Wells, looking furious, stood before her, a row of blank-faced girls just behind her. Hatred radiated from Wells in cold waves, and Monk struggled not to shuffle from foot to foot. She tensed her muscles, preparing to fight her way back out of the hall, and met Wells's tawny eyes.

"How's your little mate, Kilkenny?" Wells asked softly.

Monk's shock at the question was quickly overwhelmed by her temper. "Leave her alone," she ground out. "She's just a kid."

They glared at each other.

"Is everything all right in here?" a voice asked from the doorway.

Wells broke the stare and faced Coopersmith.

"We're fine," she said in clipped tones.

Monk took the opportunity to slip away from Wells, break through the wall of girls, and head toward Coopersmith, whose eyes widened when she saw the blood on Monk's uniform.

"Where do you think you're going, Miss Monkhouse?" Wells snarled.

"With me," Coopersmith replied coolly, staring at Wells.

"She can go with you when she's finished here."

"No. Now." Coopersmith's stare blasted Wells with icy disregard. "She's coming with me."

"I *am* finished here," Monk said to Wells with quiet dignity. "You sent me to Sister Constance's office, didn't you? Isn't that where I'm meant to be?"

She walked out of the hall, Coopersmith behind her, leaving a silent and furious Wells in her wake.

She began walking back to the office, grunting in pain as her backpack strap dug into the cuts on her chest. The thin scabbing broke open and fresh blood trickled down her chest. Coopersmith pulled her to a halt.

"Monk," she said, eyes glued to Monk's shredded blouse. She started to hold out her hand to Monk, but stopped. "What happened to you?"

"Angela Michaels."

Coopersmith muttered an oath and frowned. "We have to get something on those cuts before they get infected."

"I'm fine."

"No, you aren't," Coopersmith said sharply, emerald eyes troubled as she gazed at Monk. "Were you really headed back to the office?"

Monk nodded and held up Kilkenny's backpack with her good hand. "I have to give this to Kilkenny and apologize to Miss Warland for leaving. She asked me to stay put."

"Why wasn't Kilkenny headed back to get it herself?"

"She didn't want to go there. I volunteered because I'm not afraid, and I had to go there anyway."

"You want me to carry it?"

Monk shook her head. "I got it."

Coopersmith nodded. "Fair enough. But after we've dropped off her bag you're coming with me."

"Okay," Monk said as they continued down the corridor.

They rounded the corner and saw Warland standing beside Kilkenny.

"Monk?" Warland asked. "I could have gotten those for you, you know."

Monk shook her head. "If you do that for me she wins. That's not going to happen." She smiled but it didn't touch her eyes. "Besides, you're not my slave girl." She gave the wide-eyed Kilkenny her backpack.

Kilkenny's thin shoulders sagged in relief. "Thank you."

Monk grinned at her, despite herself. "No worries."

"I'll see you tomorrow," Kilkenny said to all three and hared off down the corridor toward the library.

"We have to take care of your chest," Coopersmith said. "C'mon. We're going to the sick room."

"Okay, let's go," Warland said, holding up the keys to the science prep room.

A couple of minutes later Coopersmith was gently pulling Monk's backpack off her shoulder and dropping it beside her own on the carpeted floor of the sick room.

"You're going to have to take your shirt off," Warland said, studying the front of Monk's ruined blouse.

Monk felt herself blush.

Coopersmith grinned. "We're all girls here."

"And we promise not to stare." Warland mock leered at Monk and pushed her back so she was sitting on the table behind her.

Monk grinned. Both teachers radiated concern despite their banter.

"All right, all right, I'll give you both a cheap thrill at my unappealing K-Mart underwear," she shot back, undoing the last two buttons of her shirt and opening it. She glanced at them apologetically. "Not much point in taking this off. It's not working for me anyway."

Warland hefted a bottle of peroxide and a handful of cotton wadding. "This is gonna hurt like hell no matter which way you slice it."

Monk's chest throbbed dully, and she nodded.

Coopersmith, on her undamaged side, slipped an arm around her trim waist and took her good hand. "You're allowed to swear, Monk."

Warland poured the peroxide onto the cuts, and Monk buried her face into Coopersmith's neck, moaning with pain. The bolt of pain that tore through her robbed her knees of strength, and she squeezed Coopersmith's hand convulsively.

"Oh, God," she moaned. "That hurts."

"I know," Coopersmith said, tightening her arm around Monk's back.

Tears of pain slipped through Monk's tightly-closed eyes. She was dimly aware of the scent of Coopersmith's perfume and her willowy body.

Monk felt the pain radiating down her arm and took several shuddery breaths. "Shit."

"I know," Warland said, pushing the gauze against her damaged chest.

"Ouch," Monk said, almost regretfully pulling away from Coopersmith.

Warland leant forward and began to tape the gauze down.

"What happened to your back?" Coopersmith asked, frowning at Warland's bloody shirt. She hooked a finger onto Warland's collar and pulled the shirt off her back.

Warland's back was a mass of bruising and smeared blood. Monk and Coopersmith exchanged glances.

"Your back looks as bad as my front," Monk said, putting her ruined shirt back on again.

"I know," Warland said. "I feel it."

Coopersmith sighed. "Does someone want to tell me what happened?"

"I don't really have time to talk," Monk said. "I have to get home."

"I can give you a lift," Coopersmith said. "'Fess up, Monk."

Monk looked at Warland. Warland shook her head.

"Okay, this is what happened," Monk began, and told Coopersmith an edited version of what had happened *during* detention.

Coopersmith sat back on the table when Monk finished and chewed her lip thoughtfully. "Odd." She gazed at Monk. "Do you want me to step in?"

Monk shook her head, tears threatening to break her composure. "I'll be all right."

"Monk," Warland said. "I think there's probably more going on here that you're not telling either one of us. That's fine. Just remember, I'm on your side. If you need my help, all you have to do is tell me when, and I'll be there."

"Same goes for me," Coopersmith said quietly.

Monk stared at both teachers. "Thanks."

Warland exchanged a glance with Coopersmith. "I have to get back to detention. I'll see you both tomorrow, all right?"

"Sure," Coopersmith said and left, Monk in tow.

"Are we headed back to your place?" Monk asked once they were in Coopersmith's car and underway.

"Yep," Coopersmith said. She glanced at Monk and gave her a half grin. "I didn't think you really meant you wanted to go back to your place."

Monk nodded. "You'd be right."

They lapsed into silence for the remainder of the drive back to

Coopersmith's apartment. Monk was exhausted. It had been an emotionally draining day. Her chest hurt abominably, and all she wanted to do was relax for a little while.

Finally, Coopersmith pulled into her assigned underground parking space. They got out of the car. Monk hissed as she put her backpack on her shoulder.

"Hurts bad?" Coopersmith winced. She gently caressed Monk's broad shoulder and took her backpack from her.

Monk sighed and nodded, leaning into her touch.

Coopersmith led the way to the elevator and pushed the button.

"Okay, Mitch, 'fess up," Monk said. "What's the matter?"

"Are you all right?" Coopersmith asked, unable to keep the pain out of her voice. "And what is the deal with Terri Warland?"

"Warland . . . she seems to be becoming a friend." Monk met Coopersmith's eyes and gave her a gentle smile. "I'm all right. Just shredded and sore."

Coopersmith closed her eyes and sighed. "Just be very careful with her."

"I would never do anything to deliberately hurt you. I'll be careful, don't worry. I never talk about you."

Coopersmith smiled. "You don't have to say it, I already know it." She was silent for a moment. "Just keep in mind one thing about Terri—she's a teacher, and she's going to have the same problem with you that I do, and it's the one of walking the line between friendship and teacher. You should keep that one quiet as well."

Monk nodded in understanding. She closed her eyes and sighed.

She felt Coopersmith lean forward, felt Coopersmith's hands gently cup her face.

Monk opened her eyes and was almost nose to nose in an intense stare with Coopersmith.

Monk nodded, and was fuzzily aware that she was being pulled into Coopersmith's arms. She tightened her arms around Coopersmith's lithe body, holding her close, inhaling the wonderful fragrance of her perfume, relishing the solid feel of her beloved maths teacher. The moment was exquisitely sweet. Something she had craved all day. The pain in her chest slipped away for a precious few seconds.

It seemed to last for no time at all and for an eternity, but finally Coopersmith let her go and straightened.

Three quarters of an hour later, they were sitting down to steak and vegetables, courtesy of Michelle Coopersmith. Monk wore one of Coopersmith's old tee shirts, amazed at the faint trace of her perfume that wafted up from it. It was at once sweet and comforting. For the first time all day, she relaxed, and was finally able to talk about what had happened.

"Okay, so spill," Coopersmith said. "What's happened to you today? Why were there pieces of you coming off after recess? I know it wasn't only detention. And you still haven't given me a real blow by blow of what happened during detention."

"Well," Monk began, after a moment's pause. "It began like this . . ."

Monk told Coopersmith everything about what had happened to her in chemistry, roll call, and the episode with Lightman. She finished with being in detention and thrown over a set of seats by Miss Wells.

Coopersmith allowed her to finish, and then pushed her knife and fork aside, dinner only half finished. Her eyes were troubled and filled with sympathy. "I really don't know what to say. Are you sure about this? Do you want me to step in?"

Monk skin crawled at the prospect of Coopersmith being anywhere close to Wells. "Fuck. No. Stay away from her. She's an ugly, vicious bitch. You say anything to her and she's going to make trouble for you as well as me. I'm safer than you are. Don't go anywhere near her. She's *my* fucking problem. Promise me. Please. Promise me."

Coopersmith eyed her curiously. "I'm a big girl. I can take care of myself."

"So am I," Monk snapped. "Or so you keep saying. Let me go and deal with this on my own. I can do this. You always ask me to trust you, and now I'm asking you to trust me. I've learnt a lot from you, and I'm not going to do anything stupid."

Monk held her cutlery in a white knuckled grip. She looked at her hands and forced them to relax. She smiled, although she kept her intensity.

"I'm only asking you for the one thing you've always given me. Your friendship. Sometimes I'll be upset and I'll ask you to listen, no more."

Coopersmith was quiet for a moment, eyes flickering with sympathy and anger. "I promise. Whatever happens, I'll be right there for you. Even if you don't want me to openly stand beside you." She smiled, took Monk's restless hands, and caressed them. "Just remember, I can help you, and I'm willing to do it. It's okay to lean on me."

Monk felt a tear in her eye, mostly from crashing up and down another emotional roller coaster. Coopersmith put her arms around her.

The gentleness of the act shattered Monk's barriers, and she sobbed into Coopersmith's chest. Coopersmith held her for the longest time, letting her cry herself out, gently stroking her hair.

She gently kissed Monk's shaggy crown. "It's all right. I'm right here with you, just like always. I won't let you go through this by yourself."

Later that evening, Coopersmith pulled up in front of Monk's house. She looked at Monk, flinching at the torn shirt and drying blood.

Monk gazed at her, remembering the soft scent of perfume, the feel of her arms. A surge of emotion left her trembling. "Thanks. For everything."

"No worries," Coopersmith said. "I'll see you in school tomorrow."

"Sure," Monk said, shutting the car door and painfully shouldering her back pack.

She returned Coopersmith's wave as the Pathfinder flipped a neat U turn and headed back down the street.

Monk knees shook as she turned toward the house. A familiar surge of loathing and fear welled inside her. Her mother's and father's cars were in the driveway.

She went into the house. It seemed deserted, but she heard soft voices as she approached the kitchen. Her parents and older sister, Jean, were sitting down to dinner.

"She's inconsiderate and rude," her mother said. "When she gets home she's in trouble."

"She's a bitch," Jean said. "She always was."

"Maybe we should ask her why she's late?" her father said. "Maybe there's a reason for it."

Monk walked into the kitchen, and they all turned to stare at her. "Hi," she said into the deafening silence.

Her mother shot out of her seat and gave Monk an openhanded slap that left her reeling.

Her father quickly got up and left, Jean almost forcibly in tow.

Monk touched her throbbing cheek and could feel her face flush with shame. "What was that for?"

"You know perfectly well what it was for." Her mother glared at Monk, and her eyes widened when she noticed the ruined school uniform. "What the hell did you do to your uniform? Those things aren't cheap!"

Monk gaped at her, feeling like a deer caught in headlights. She didn't want to respond, but her mother seemed to be expecting her to answer. She decided on the truth. "I got clawed by a school bully."

"You were in a fight? Figures. What the hell did you do that for?" her mother asked, glaring at her.

"I didn't start it."

"Liar. I don't believe you. Of course you started it."

"I didn't start it," Monk said, backing up a step, hating herself for showing her terror. "I was trying to help someone."

" 'I didn't start it,' 'I was trying to help someone,' " Mrs. Monkhouse mimicked savagely. "Bullshit. I'm tired of endlessly hearing your poor me-ing. You open your mouth, and all that comes out is whiny, self-righteous crap. Nobody wants to hear that shit. Of *course* you started it. You keep forgetting I know you better than you know yourself." She crossed her arms and glared at Monk. "You're lying. I don't even know why I bothered asking you. You couldn't tell the truth if Jesus was standing next to you asking for it. No one believes anything you have to say. I'm sure what really happened was that you put on airs and got thumped for your trouble." She clenched and unclenched her hands. Her eyes flashed. She lunged at Monk and backhanded her again. "Go away, liar. Get out of my sight."

Monk clutched her face, and her mother lashed out again and shoved her.

"I said, *get out of my sight.* Come out of your room again this evening, and I'll fucking kill you!" her mother screamed.

Monk, shaken, bolted to her room and shut the door behind her with a sigh. She was sure her mother was telling the literal truth about killing her.

An unbidden image of Coopersmith flitted through her mind, and she felt humiliation for having sought comfort. She should have gone straight home from school after detention. She was terrified of her mother and cursed herself for her weakness. *I hate talking. Every time*

I open my mouth, something bad happens to me. Tears spilt down her cheeks, and she forced herself to stop crying.

The lump in her throat made it hard for her to breathe.

She glanced at her watch. It was seven-thirty, and she was exhausted. She slipped off her ruined uniform, left it in a pile by her desk, and slid into bed. She was asleep moments later.

CHAPTER THREE

Lunchtime the next day found Monk in a new uniform blouse, courtesy of Coopersmith. She had been pale when she had seen herself in the mirror, and she felt listless and slightly ill. She had gotten precious little sleep. She had spent the night living through a series of the worst nightmares she had ever had the displeasure of experiencing. She couldn't remember specifics but they all involved Coopersmith and Wells, and they all finished badly for Coopersmith.

She left her fourth period classroom with a sigh of relief. Girls jostled past her as she made her slow way toward the senior area and her accustomed seat. It was empty, and she scanned area, looking for her friends. She checked the second and third floor balconies to see if they were on their way down. She spotted Lightman, who leant forward, balling and relaxing her fists in what seemed to be rage. The target of her anger was hidden in the alcove that led to the landing at the top of the stairs. Suddenly Lightman took a step back and seemed to be forcing herself to relax.

Wonder who she's talking to? Monk thought. *Or talking at more like. I don't care what her mother does for a living, I reckon her neck is on the chopping block if she doesn't get her mouth under control.*

Lightman threw up her hands in a dismissive gesture and turned with a shrug. She looked down and saw Monk looking up at her. She waved

Monk returned her wave and pointed at her accustomed bench, and Lightman gave her a thumbs up.

Monk collapsed onto the bench with a sigh. A backpack hit the ground beside her moments later, and a body fell heavily onto the seat.

Monk gave the grinning Lightman a curious look. "What happened to you yesterday? Did you end up going to see Collins?"

Lightman stretched languidly in the seat next to Monk and yawned. "Oh, that. Well, yes, I did get to Collins's office, but he wasn't there. I tried again today, but he wasn't there again. You got kicked out of roll call, didn't you?"

Monk nodded.

"I really don't know why you put up with that woman's shit," Lightman said.

"I don't think I really have a choice. I'm on detention after school for the next two weeks, and I'm fucking lucky Wells isn't taking it."

Lightman stared at her. "How the fuck did you manage that?"

"I was kind of involved in a fight with a junior, and Wells caught us at it."

"Was it Angela Michaels?"

Monk nodded. "You've heard of her?"

"Yup. I heard she got suspended last night, and it's not terribly likely she's going to be coming back to school any time soon. They're deciding on whether or not to expel her. I don't think it looks good for her."

"And it's about bloody time they noticed she was a fucking psycho." Monk whistled appreciatively. "Although I must admit yesterday was extreme, even for her." The ragged tears in her chest throbbed dully. She studied Lightman. "So what's the story? Who told you?"

Lightman smiled archly. "I have my sources."

Monk waited for her to continue, but Lightman stayed silent.

Monk cleared her throat. "All right. So what happened to you at lunch yesterday?"

"I got put on lunchtime detention."

"What on earth did you do to score that one?"

"I called McCann a bitch."

"Why?"

"Because she plays favorites in class, and that drives me nuts, so I told her so. Unfortunately, I ended my sentence with the words, 'you bitch.'"

Monk stiffened. She liked McCann. "Is that how you got booted from Corpus Christi?"

"How do you mean?"

"By calling teachers names. Did they finally get sick of it?" Monk asked.

Lightman shot her a look that was an odd mix of friendly and hostile. "Well, no, it wasn't. What makes you think I got booted from good ol' CC?"

"You told me yesterday your mother paid a lot of money on short notice to get you enrolled here. That means you got booted, doesn't it?"

"You got me. Yes, I got booted. Why? I got caught, sans clothing, with one of the teachers."

Monk, sensing a lie, was instantly on guard, but Lightman looked sincere. She tried to put aside her wariness. "Who spotted you?"

"Unfortunately, it was the principal. It was after school, and in her classroom, and we didn't think we were going to get caught. But we did." Lightman shook her head. "I don't really want to talk about it. I think I was in love with the lady in question. I haven't been able to reach her, thanks to my mother." She flinched and stared at Monk anxiously.

Monk accepted this without judgment. She understood the sentiments perfectly. "So I take it you cut roll call today to go and see Mr. Collins?"

Lightman relaxed, and the spark of fear in her eyes was extinguished. "Yes. You don't care if I slept with a woman?"

Monk almost laughed, but restrained herself. "No, I couldn't care less. Doesn't faze me at all. I can understand where you're coming from."

The relief and gratitude in Lightman's eyes was almost palatable. "You have no idea how glad I am to hear you say that."

Monk smiled and shrugged.

"I guess this means we can go girl watching together." Lightman wiggled her eyebrows.

Monk became still.

Lightman grinned. "You ignore your hormones, don't you?"

"I don't pay much attention to them, no. They're not real useful when it comes to dealing with people."

Lightman stared at her, shocked. "*Au contraire, ma chère.* They're pretty much what dictates how you interact with other people. Besides, what would you say if I told you I thought you were cute? One little haircut, and you'd be stunning."

Monk's temper flared. "Drop it, Lightman. Firstly, you couldn't possibly find me cute, simply because I'm not. Secondly, yes, I know I need a haircut, and it's going to happen on the weekend. Thirdly, I don't like to treat people as though they were pieces of meat."

Lightman opened her mouth and closed it with a snap, thanks to

Monk's warning look. She shrugged after a moment. "Being attracted to someone is *not* treating them like a piece of meat. What's her name?"

"She doesn't have a name, simply because she doesn't exist."

"Ah, ha! Now I have it. She does have a name, but she doesn't love you back so it's to hell with the way you feel, right? But you'd crawl ten miles through a desert to sweat in her shadow anyway, wouldn't you?"

"Just fucking drop it, will you, Lightman?" Monk labored to control her temper. "You don't want to talk about your ex, and I'm not pushing you on it, so don't push me on this. I have no deep and dark secrets. Believe it and move on."

Lightman's smile died. "Relax. I'm sorry, I really didn't mean to piss you off. I'm just curious, is all."

The bell rang, signaling the start of fifth period, which was modern history for Monk.

"Well, Apology accepted." Monk got up and began walking away and then looked back. "I'll see you tomorrow, okay? I've got some stuff I have to do."

She walked off toward the block of classrooms beneath the library, not waiting for Lightman's response.

Monk arrived at the science labs late in the afternoon, heart hammering with dread at the prospect of another chemistry class with Wells. The gouges in her chest hurt abominably.

She walked into the almost empty lab and saw Jackie Sharp. The school captain's books were open on the bench in front of her. She was staring off into space, twirling her pen between her fingers with an absentminded precision that Monk admired.

"Hey, Jackie. How are you doing?" she asked with a grin.

Jackie looked up at her and smiled. "Oh, hi, Monk. I'm good. How are you?"

"I'm fine, I guess. How come you're in such a good mood?" Monk asked.

"It seems I owe you a huge vote of thanks."

Monk tried to look appreciative, but felt confused. "How so?"

Jackie gazed into her eyes. "For sticking up for my sister."

"Huh?"

"My sister. Detention yesterday. Kilkenny," Jackie said patiently. She laughed softly at Monk's surprised expression.

"Kilkenny?" Monk said. "Kilkenny is Kilkenny Sharp, your sister?"

"Yep." Jackie became a little more serious. "She told me what happened in detention yesterday. It seems you saved her neck, and also Warland's."

Monk blushed. "I dunno about that."

"And had another run in with Wells."

Monk sighed. "Well, that part is true, anyway."

"She said that Angela Michaels took a chunk out of you."

"Well, she has a tendency to take a chunk out of everyone."

"Are you really all right?" Jackie blushed and shifted in her seat. "Kilkenny told me about the gouges, and she's bound to ask me this afternoon."

Monk grinned. "Tell her I'm fine." She paused. "May I ask why she's on detention?"

"It seems she was talking in class yesterday a little too often, and her teacher, *Miss Wells*, put her on for being a bad seed." Jackie frowned. "She's twelve, and it's the first week of school. If she'd been using a flamethrower on Wells, okay, maybe. But talking? What *is* Wells's problem?"

Monk frowned and shook her head. "I don't know what her problem is. All I can say for sure is that she's a major bitch."

"Who's a major bitch?" a new voice asked.

Monk looked toward the front of the lab. Wells was leaning against the teacher's bench, with a careless, arrogant air that set Monk's teeth on edge.

She must've heard that. I will not bite. I will not bite. Monk pushed her unwilling features into a polite smile. She snuck a quick glance at Jackie, and saw no help from that quarter. Jackie looked stunned.

"We were discussing one of the juniors, someone we both know quite well," Monk said, instantly cringing at her reply.

"So you normally speak about your younger classmates with disrespect?" Wells asked, eyeing Monk coldly.

"I do when they assault people," Monk said with equal coldness.

"Speaking of assault," Wells said, cold, cruel smile playing about her lips, "how's the chest, Monk?"

Monk stared at her, unsure how to answer.

Catrina Walsh and Cathy Daniels strolled in, late. Monk glanced at them, irritated, thinking it unfair that there would be no repercussions from Wells for their tardiness.

Wells raised an eyebrow. "Comments about assault are interesting coming from you, Therese. I hear that you love to hit people. Isn't that right, ladies?"

Catrina Walsh and Cathy Daniels perked up.

Daniels nodded. "That's right, Miss Wells."

Walsh discretely shot Monk the finger as they sat in their assigned seats.

Monk's temper slipped a notch, and she was aware of Jackie shifting uncomfortably in her seat.

"I don't hit people," Monk said with quiet dignity. It earned her a glance from Jackie.

"Really?" Wells asked with polite disbelief. "One of these days, someone bigger and stronger than you is going to come along and give to you what you've been giving to other people all these years."

Monk tried to suppress her flinch. She said nothing and patiently continued to meet Wells's golden eyes.

They stared each other down for another minute or two, and then Wells dismissed her with a snort and a quick smile at another cluster of girls trickling in.

"Is she talking about Coopersmith a couple of years ago?" Jackie whispered to her, looking straight ahead, barely moving her lips.

"Yes," Monk said curtly.

"It's not true is it?"

"No. Never was."

"I thought so."

"Why?" Monk asked after a moment of silence.

Jackie looked directly at her. "I like you a lot. Your eyes are too kind for that rumor."

Monk smiled. "Thanks. I appreciate it."

Jackie smiled. "No, thank *you*. Most people think I don't have a mind of my own."

Monk gave her a surprised look. "Really? I think they'd be very silly to think that. It's obvious to me you do."

Jackie's smile increased.

They waited for Wells to greet the last stragglers. When they were all in, she closed the door, and then strode to the blackboard.

She drew a hydrogen gas molecule, chalk squealing. The class winced. She pointed at the diagram. "Can anyone tell me what this is?"

A few hands went up, Monk's included. Wells looked around the room. After surveying whose hand was up, she deigned to turn her cold eyes on Monk.

"Put your hand down, Therese. I don't feel particularly inclined to endure a repeat of yesterday."

The class tittered, and Monk felt humiliated. Jackie shifted in her seat, moving closer to Monk. The next few minutes were excruciatingly difficult for Monk as another girl answered, and Wells announced that she was going to do a little experiment for the class. She needed a volunteer. Jackie gave Monk a quick nudge, and Monk glanced at her.

Jackie's stare was a mix of anger at Wells and sympathy for Monk.

"Therese, I think, is the perfect candidate. Not that she's listening, anyway."

Monk's tension levels increased, and she looked at Wells. "Pardon, Miss Wells?"

"I asked for a volunteer for my demonstration, and you're the one. Come here, Therese."

Monk got out of her seat. Her knees trembled from the adrenalin flowing through her system. She made her way to the teacher's bench.

"There we go." Wells gave her a clap on the back, and her grin turned feral. "Don't worry little lab rat, I won't hurt you."

Monk raised an eyebrow and stared at her in disbelief.

"I don't think anyone would mourn you if you disappeared tomorrow, Therese," Miss Wells said softly so no one would overhear her.

"It really isn't any of your business, *Miss* Wells," Monk whispered, equally softly.

Wells gave Monk a cold smile. "Ah, that struck a nerve, didn't it, Therese? You know I'm right, don't you?" she whispered back.

Monk glared.

Wells leaned behind the bench and grabbed a half-filled balloon. "I filled this just before the start of the period." She turned to the class and gave them a knowing smile. "This is rather a dangerous experiment. Hydrogen is a gas found all around us, so one in four times the entire room explodes because of a chain reaction." She glanced at Monk and smirked. "Who knows? My little helper here might go up in a ball of flames."

Monk's guard went up, and her palms began to sweat. She could not muster any trust in Wells. She walked back to her seat, sat down, and met Wells's gaze as stoically as she could.

"Where do you think you're going, young lady?"

The class snickered.

"I'm sitting down. I'm not helping you. Go find another lab rat," Monk said evenly.

"Come back up here. I'm not going to hurt you. I was only joking." Wells looked surprised, but it did not touch her eyes.

"That was a bad joke and no, I'm not doing it. Find someone else."

"We all have to do things in life that we don't want to do. You, Miss Sharp. Come here."

Jackie twitched, and went pale. "No, thanks. I'm not that brave," she said lightly. She clenched and unclenched her hands in her lap.

"Come on, Miss Sharp. We're waiting."

Jackie's muscles tensed.

"Leave her alone, Miss Wells," Monk said. "Didn't you say yourself that you needed a volunteer? And she didn't volunteer, did she?"

"Close your mouth and stop talking, Therese," Wells said, staring at her.

Monk returned her glare.

Wells uncharacteristically seemed to take pity on Jackie. "All right then. Any other volunteers?"

This time the class chuckled, and more malice was directed Monk's way. Monk endured it with a stony expression.

Cathy Daniels put up her hand and spoke before Wells acknowledged her. "I'll help you, Miss. I'm not a scaredy cat." She looked pointedly at Monk, and Walsh snickered and shot Monk a look of loathing.

"Come on up, then."

Daniels got up out of her seat with a pretentious air. Much to Monk's disgust, she flounced to the front of the room and presented herself to Wells with a saccharine, self-absorbed smile.

Wells had tied the limp balloon to the end of a long ruler. She handed it to Daniels with a smile. "Here, hang on to this. It'll all be over in a jiffy."

🦊

Monk arrived at the auditorium for detention, exhausted and wrung out. The rest of chemistry had turned out to be every bit as horrible as the first fifteen minutes had promised.

No matter what Monk had done, it had not been the right thing. She had tried to sit quietly after the demonstration, but Wells had interpreted that as sulking and berated her for it. She had tried to protest, but that was rudeness and defiance of authority. She had tried silence, but that, apparently, was immaturity, and earned her another lecture.

"Hi, Monk."

Monk looked up and grinned. Some of the tension slipped out of her at the sight of Terri Warland who was wearing a smile and another revealing shirt.

"Hi, Terri. How's your back?"

Warland dropped onto the seat next to her, giving Monk a whiff of her intoxicating perfume. "It hurts. I think I'm going to be stiff for the rest of my life. How's the chest?"

"It hurts like hell, but at least it's not bleeding anymore." A fleeting memory of hissing in pain from the scorching heat of her cool shower shot through her mind.

"Let's get in the auditorium, and we'll talk some more. Same drill as yesterday."

"Okay, works for me."

Warland rounded up all the girls, this time only about six, including Monk.

Kilkenny, Monk noticed, joined them again. She shot Kilkenny a quick wave, and the girl grinned back at her.

Warland put them to work sweeping again. Monk looked at her as though she had gone mad.

"Well?" Warland said, settling herself on the stage next to Monk, almost too close to satisfy decorum. "It's filthy in here, don't you think? I have an idea they never clean this place, and that's just disgusting."

Monk laughed. "Yes, it is. And this is a novel idea. Did you really get Sister Constance's approval?"

Warland grinned at her. "What do you think?"

"I don't know. That's why I asked."

"I did."

Monk smirked. "Is this going to be a regular thing? Your attempt to clean up the school?"

Warland grinned, but a shadow flitted across her beautiful features. "No, I think I'm going to go back to lines for a while. Yesterday's effort was just a bit too much for me."

Monk nodded. "Yeah, I reckon. I also don't relish the idea of being tossed over a bunch of seats again."

"I know where you're coming from." Warland took a deep breath. "Can I ask you something?"

"Uh, sure, I guess."

"Are you having problems with Miss Wells?"

Monk sagged her shoulders. "I don't think it's anything I can't handle." She pushed down her panic as she contemplated ten more months of Wells.

Warland smiled sympathetically and bumped her shoulder. "Take it easy there, young friend. Can I get you to promise me one thing?"

Monk looked at her, distracted. "What?"

"If you have any problems with Wells, come and see me. I don't know if I can help, but at least I can give you a sympathetic ear." She paused and gazed at Monk. "There's one more thing to remember. I'm a science teacher, and my desk is in the science labs. If I'm not in class I'm usually right there."

Monk nodded gratefully. "Thanks. I think I'll take you up on that." She gave Warland an appraising look. "Actually. You could do something for me, but it has to be no questions asked."

Warland gave her a curious look. "Okay."

"You have Kilkenny for science, don't you? Can you keep an eye on her for me when you see her? And let me know if anything's wrong?"

"Any reason why?"

"I don't like the way she keeps ending up on detention," Monk said. "Now would be a good time to nip that in the bud. I can probably help her."

"All right," Warland said slowly. "I'll do it, no questions asked. But my offer stands firm, and now I'm going to insist you talk to me later on. Fair enough?"

Monk nodded. "Sure. I'm happy to do that."

Warland smiled.

They quietly talked for the rest of detention, mostly about Monk's university aspirations.

"Well," Warland said, glancing at her watch, "we're done for another day." She grinned at Monk. "Girls!"

The assembled group of juniors stopped sweeping.

"Good," Warland continued. "You're done."

They gave a ragged cheer and quickly piled the brooms on one side of the hall. Kilkenny shot them both a half wave. Monk grinned and waved back.

"So," Warland said, sliding off the stage. "You want a lift home?"

Monk shook her head. "Nah, I'm good. I have a lift."

"Okay, I'll see you tomorrow," Warland said, flipping off the lights as they left the auditorium. She gave Monk a half wave and made her way up the corridor in the opposite direction.

Monk headed out of the hall to Coopersmith's car. She did the five-minute walk in two flat, distracted by the hour she had just spent with Warland. She almost missed the car.

"I'm over here, Monk." Coopersmith leaned out of the window and smiled at her.

"Oh, hi, Mitch." Warm emotion washed over her at the sight of Coopersmith.

"Get in, matey." Coopersmith leaned across the car and opened the passenger side door, and Monk enjoyed the luxurious way her body stretched.

Monk climbed into the car, immediately aware of the soft fragrance of Coopersmith's perfume. She gazed at Coopersmith's clean profile as she glanced over her shoulder and pulled out into the traffic.

"Penny for your thoughts," Coopersmith said.

Thoughts of chemistry flickered through her mind, and reality came crashing back down on her. A cold ball of dread settled in her stomach. "They're not worth that much."

"What is it?" Coopersmith asked, glancing at her, concerned.

"I'm having a really hard time in chemistry."

"What happened?" Coopersmith asked.

Monk's eyes filled with tears. "I don't know. She just . . . look, it's nothing, I guess."

Coopersmith sighed. "Just tell me. Don't worry. What happened?"

Monk shook her head. "Doesn't matter. I just need to be upset for a while, that's all."

"It *does* matter. It matters to me. Tell me all the parts you've left out, and maybe I can help you."

"I can't. I just can't." Monk worked her jaw as she tried to hold back tears.

"Why can't you tell me?" Coopersmith shot her a troubled look.

"If I tell you, then you're going to get into trouble."

Coopersmith pulled up at a stop sign. She turned and looked at Monk with a raised eyebrow. "You can't be serious. What do you think she's going to do to me? Put *me* on detention?"

Monk shook her head, feeling the heat rise in her cheeks. She fidgeted in her seat.

A horn blared behind them. Coopersmith drove through the semi-deserted intersection and pulled over. She turned to Monk, took her face in gentle hands, and wiped away her tears.

"All right. I'm going to let this go for a while and trust you. But you have to level with me, and it may have to be soon. I can't just watch you go through this." She looked as though she wanted to say something else, but sighed instead.

Monk saw the troubled look in Coopersmith's eyes, and it firmed her resolve. "I promise you that I'll level with you later. I can't do it now. I need to wait for a while to see how things turn out."

"Okay," Coopersmith said, putting on her indicator and pulling out into the light traffic. "Do you want to go for a run this afternoon?"

Monk, restless and edgy, nodded. "Sure. Sounds like a good idea. I didn't bring a change of clothes, though. And what about your knee?"

"No worries," Coopersmith replied. "You can borrow some of mine. My knee feels a hell of a lot better today."

Monk nodded and grinned.

An hour later, Monk and Coopersmith were running down the bush trails of Autumn Park. That time of day found the trails deserted, and they settled into an easy rhythm.

"Your birthday is in a couple of days, isn't it?" Monk asked.

Coopersmith glanced at her. "Yeah, it is."

"Doing anything exciting for your birthday?"

"Yeah, going to work."

Monk laughed. "You're going out to dinner with your family at least, aren't you?"

Coopersmith nodded. "Yeah again, but don't worry about it. I can still get you home from school."

"That's not why I asked but that's very sweet of you, and I appreciate it," Monk said.

They came to a halt by the car. Coopersmith took a deep swig from the water bottle Monk handed to her.

"I know it's a couple of days early," Monk said. "But I wanted to give this to you now."

She reached into her pocket and pulled out a small box, carefully gift wrapped in Garfield wrapping paper.

Coopersmith smiled when she saw it. "That is so you."

"You too." Monk grinned, and then turned serious. "I know I really shouldn't have done this, but I wanted to. You're my friend." She eyed Coopersmith carefully, and her heart rate slid up a notch. She knew how Coopersmith felt about gifts and her students.

Coopersmith smiled at her. "You're my friend too. It's an honor to accept this from you."

Monk gazed into Coopersmith's emerald eyes. She saw the deep appreciation and respect in them that mirrored her own feelings. Something inside her slipped, and a strange sense of peace suffused her. She held out the gift, still holding Coopersmith's gaze.

Coopersmith unwrapped the gift and eyed the jewelry box with a slight smile. She traced the edges of it, and then opened it. Her eyes widened.

"Wow," she began. "I . . . it's beautiful . . . I . . . I don't know what to say. Thanks."

Coopersmith pulled Monk into her arms, and Monk could breathe again.

"You're welcome," Monk said. "I know you said the chain broke on your old one, and you never had the chance to get it fixed. I saw this and thought of you."

Coopersmith pulled the crucifix out of the box and gazed at it. "You didn't have to do this."

"I know," Monk said. She bit her lip, unable to vocalize how much she wanted to do it and what Coopersmith meant to her.

Coopersmith pulled the crucifix out of the box, and held it out to Monk. "You want to help me get it on? One off deal. Once it goes on it's not coming off."

Monk laughed softly, taking the chain. "Sure." She gently clasped it. "Happy birthday, Michelle," she whispered.

"Thanks, Monk," Coopersmith said softly.

That night, Monk was tired enough to go straight to bed almost as soon as dinner was over. She closed her eyes and drifted off to sleep, despite the lingering heat of the day.

"Monk?"

Monk frowned. She felt a small hand give her good shoulder a slight shake, and she opened her eyes with a sigh. She was exhausted, and obviously had not gone to sleep. She felt dry and hot sand through her thin school shirt. She became aware of the sound of breaking waves, and she realized she was on the beach. She sat up, flinching at the pain from her gouges.

"Where am I? I don't remember how I got here." She looked at the junior who hovered beside her. "You're Kilkenny Sharp."

Kilenny dropped to the sand and gave her a broad grin. "I know you. You're Monk. Thank you for saving my neck and for making my big sister's life a little bit better in chemistry."

Monk smiled and closed her eyes, feeling the hot sun beating down on her. "No worries, matey, no worries."

"Can I see your cuts?" Kilkenny asked shyly.

"Sure," Monk said, pulling her uniform back so Kilkenny could see the tears.

Kilkenny winced. "They look like they hurt."

"They do."

"Can I try something?"

"Like what?"

"Like this," Kilkenny said, putting a hand over the gouges.

Monk watched her closely.

Kilkenny closed her eyes and frowned in concentration. Monk felt a dim heat suffusing her cuts and the pain drained away. Kilkenny removed her hand, and her eyes fluttered open.

Monk looked down at her chest and did a double take when she saw the clean, unblemished skin where her cuts had been. "Well, look at that." She looked at Kilkenny. "Wow. Where did you learn to do that?"

"I don't know," Kilkenny said. "I just didn't want you to be hurt anymore."

"Thanks," Monk said.

They were comfortably silent for a moment.

"You know we're not at the beach really, don't you?" Kilkenny asked, giving her a worried look and shielding her eyes from the bright sun.

Monk smiled and glanced around. "You could have fooled me."

"I think you're dreaming."

Monk's grin broadened. "Really?"

"Yup. Listen. Do you hear any seagulls or anything like that?"

Monk looked at her curiously and tilted her head, listening for distant noise. Kilkenny was right. There were no sounds besides the seawater. The silence was suffocating and expectant, the crash of the breakers stentorian and disapproving.

"Wait," Kilkenny whispered softly, tilting her head.

Monk strained her hearing to catch any sounds.

There was a glint of silver in the distance about halfway between the poisonous ocean and unforgiving sky.

"What's that?" Kilkenny asked, peering at it.

"Who's that?" Monk asked, staring off into the distance.

They looked in the direction the other had been looking.

The now larger silver sliver in the sky glimmered in the harsh light.

"You're right," Monk said. "What *is* that? It's getting bigger."

"Who is that man running toward us waving his hands around?"

Monk gazed at a white-haired man wearing a set of laurel leaves on his head. He looked like he had a white bed sheet draped around his body. He held up the hem of his flowing robe with one hand so he could run faster. The other hand jangled from the metal bracelets around his wrist as he gesticulated wildly at the ominously large lake of water in the sky.

The soft sound of his voice penetrated the roar of the ocean.

"For pity's sake, run!" he was screaming. "Run!"

"Why?" Kilkenny asked, seemingly unable to tear her gaze away from the body of water easily thousands of feet up in the sky.

"Are you blind or just plain stupid?" he yelled as he veered off to the right toward the back of the beach. He pointed at the sky. "That's a wave getting ready to break! It's going to drown us!"

"Oh, fuck," Monk mumbled. She turned to the pale and shaking Kilkenny. "He's right."

The top of the body of water was already curling, and every splash of ocean spray from the breakers on the beach added to it. The massive, foaming cap slowly angled down toward the surface of the water lapping the shore not far away from them.

Monk grabbed Kilkenny by the hand and bolted up the beach behind what she was beginning to think of as an ancient Greek philosopher.

The breakers died down, and the ocean grew eerily flatter and shallower by the second. The brilliant blue of the water was both grizzly and troubling.

They stumbled and slipped up the long grass and onto the boardwalk, and nearly crashed into the man as he stopped and gave a quick sob of fear.

The other side of the boardwalk led to another beach and another wave building in the sky.

The man pointed to the right, at a cliff face Monk knew they could never climb in time and would not be high enough if they did.

"That way!" He hared off toward it.

Monk saw a sharp glint out of the corner of her eye just as she turned to follow him. In the distance was a roaring sound, and she knew it was the first wave they had seen breaking on the shore.

She turned to the glint, and saw Jackie Sharp uncomfortably perched in a child's chair at a small table with delicate china. In the chair opposite was Raggedy Anne, and in the other, Andy. Both had their bibs on, preparing to eat the cake and drink the tea that Jackie had apparently imagined up for them.

"Jackie, what are you doing?" Monk screamed over the top of the roaring water headed straight for them, a pitiless, brutal wall ready to kill them.

"What does it look like?" Jackie asked primly. "We're having tea and scones."

"Mate, we're about to be the coffin fodder at our own funerals! Can't you see the fucking wave coming straight toward us?"

She turned and pointed, feeling her bowels turn to water at the thousand-foot-high wall of water hurtling toward them at breakneck speed.

"Come on, Monk! Hurry!" Kilkenny yelled, racing toward Jackie as fast as her legs could carry her.

Monk bolted down the sand behind Kilkenny, and didn't question her when Kilkenny dived into a seat, put Andy on her lap, and grabbed Jackie's hand in one swift motion.

Monk, almost without realizing what had happened, found herself sitting opposite the terrified and outraged Jackie. Raggedy Anne sat on her lap, and she held Jackie's hand in a cold, firm grip.

Kilkenny grabbed Monk's cold hand and closed her eyes.

The wall of water slammed into them. Monk closed her eyes, whispering a prayer.

The water roared and roiled all around them, but they remained bone dry. Monk peeked around. They sat in a dome-shaped body of air that protected them from the unnatural fury crashing down around them.

"That won't work, Miss Sharp." Well's ice cold voice came from the doll on Monk's lap.

Monk hissed and recoiled in horror. The spots of bile yellow light on Jackie's chest were coming straight from the doll's eyes. A pinprick opened in the dome of water, and cold ocean water flowed through in a strong, thin stream. Jackie stared up at it, pale and frozen, unable to fathom what was going on.

Kilkenny ignored the doll and gripped Monk's hand in a stranglehold.

The metallic taste of fear flooded Monk's mouth, and she gaped, scalp crawling with terror.

Kilkenny's eyes shone eerie, bright, bile yellow.

The light faded out of the world as the water closed in on them. Monk's vision darkened.

"Come and see me tomorrow before school, Monk," Kilkenny whispered softly before Monk felt the ground slide away from beneath her rickety chair. "Say that Raggedy Anne sent you."

CHAPTER FOUR

Monk woke up the next morning, feeling exhausted. Other dreams had come during the night, but none as vivid—or vicious—as the dream of the beach. She thought it was stupid, but she wanted to see Kilkenny and give her the message.

She glanced down at her chest for what felt like the millionth time, and her stomach lurched. The cuts were gone. She *dreamed* Kilkenny had healed them. It could *not* be real, yet her unblemished skin said otherwise. Was it possible that Kilkenny had really healed her in a dream? Had they really shared the same dream? How else did the cuts heal overnight? If they really had been together in a dream, what did Kilkenny remember?

Her eyes went all yellow, Monk thought with a shudder.

She made her way across the junior courtyard, glancing at the groups of one or two girls scattered on the benches waiting for friends to arrive.

Monk spotted Jackie and Kilkenny and felt no surprise as she made her way toward them.

"Morning, ladies," Monk said as she settled on the bench beside Kilkenny. She gazed at Kilkenny's striking, light brown eyes that were gentle and kind.

"Hi, Monk," Kilkenny said, giving her a small smile, a question in her eyes.

They sat in silence for a while.

"I suppose you're both wondering why I'm here," Monk began.

They waited for her to continue. She watched them carefully, preparing to bolt at the slightest sign of hostility, but their calm acceptance gave her the courage to continue.

"Okay," she said in a rush, "this is going to sound awfully stupid, but I know what I'm doing is a good way to exorcise demons, so I'm going to do it. Last night I had a nightmare, and I still feel bad about it. I even have bruises on my arm that weren't there yesterday. I can't remember any way I could have gotten them during the day. I remember *dreaming* that I got them. Enough said. Exact details don't really matter, all I'm going to do is say that you, Kilkenny, told me to come and see you and to give you this message: 'Raggedy Anne sent me.'"

The sisters exchanged looks.

"Oh, boy," Jackie said.

"See," Kilkenny said triumphantly. "Those really aren't dreams. They're real."

Monk stared at them. "Is anyone going to fill me in on what's going on?" She was torn between overwhelming relief that she had not made a fool of herself and horror at the idea of a shared nightmare.

"Go ahead, Kilkenny," Jackie said, coloring and shifting in her seat.

Kilkenny nodded, firming her chin. "We're getting nightmares. Bad ones. They don't seem to be dreams. I'm lucky, I can control some of what happens in them if I concentrate hard." She tensed and watched Monk closely.

Monk frowned. "How many of these things have you had?"

"Lots. I thought I could just handle it until I realized that the people I know who appear in the dreams aren't always things from inside my head, sometimes they're real people."

"Ah," Monk said. "Like me last night. Jackie was also real, right?"

Kilkenny nodded. "On top of that, I think they're being sent to us by Miss Wells." She tensed, but Monk simply stared at her.

"Why do you think it's Miss Wells?" Monk finally asked. She felt almost light-headed with relief.

"Well, you heard Raggedy Anne last night. That was Miss Wells's voice, wasn't it? And we're all real, why wouldn't she be as well?"

Monk nodded. "That makes a certain amount of sense." She lapsed into silence as she tried to gather her furiously roiling thoughts.

Kilkenny shook her head in response to Monk's unasked question. "No, I have no idea why it would be her, or why she would be doing it."

Monk sighed. "Actually, it's more complicated than that. First, you can't be sure that Wells is actually real in the dreams until we test that theory. Second, if she is, then we need to be sure she's the one giving us the nightmares. Again, the problem lies in testing the theory."

"I think it's going to end up being a lot safer for all of us in the long run if we assume she's real in dreams," Kilkenny said. "We both have the scars to prove it. Besides, do you really want to be in a dream with a little cowboy who's got a plastic gun shooting real bullets, face him down and say, 'You're not real!' as the blood flows from your body?"

"That one sounded nasty. You're right, though," Monk said, giving her a crooked grin.

"Out of all that," Jackie said softly, "the real question is why? What is she?"

"I'm not sure," Monk said. "Let's assume for one second that it's true she's sending us dreams and trying to hurt us through them. I can see it happening if she's a Satanist, a witch doctor, a werewolf, or something else along those lines. That leaves a huge question of motive. Why on earth would she be doing this to a bunch of Catholic school girls?"

Jackie and Kilkenny exchanged looks.

"Whoa," Kilkenny said. "Do you know anything about this stuff?"

Monk gave her a crooked grin. "Not all that much. I started to do some reading because this sort of stuff is quite interesting. There are a whole bunch of religions out there that believe in a dream world and the manipulation of it."

Jackie smiled. "That's certainly true." She turned to Kilkenny. "And I don't doubt for one second we're going to have something to add to the literature."

"Best seller," Kilkenny said, nodding. All three laughed.

"Okay," Monk said, turning her attention back to Kilkenny and struggling to bring to the front at least one of the million questions that stormed through her mind. "What I find interesting is that you, Kilkenny, seem to have the same ability she does. Is there anything about you I should know about? Besides that your eyes change to yellow when you do your thing in dreams?"

Jackie looked slightly offended, but Kilkenny saw the look and waved it away. "That's actually a good question, Jackie." She turned to Monk. "Not that I know of. I feel like a regular girl to me. My eyes *do* change color, don't they?"

Jackie and Monk exchanged glances.

"Yes, your eyes change to yellow," Jackie said. "Are you sure you don't feel any different?"

Kilkenny shook her head.

They sat in silence. Monk was torn by shock and a continuing relief that she was not imagining things.

"I think," Jackie said, "that maybe it's not such a good idea to meet in person if we can avoid it."

"What end does secrecy achieve?" Monk asked.

"Safety." Jackie looked distracted. "Have you noticed the way everyone seems to go into a daze around her?"

Monk frowned. "What do you mean?"

"Nobody should look that happy when they go into a classroom with a mad woman. Cathy, Catrina, and everybody else in the class except for maybe four of us obviously think she's the best thing since sliced bread despite the fact that she's rude, arrogant, cruel, and says things that are incredibly clichéd."

Monk and Kilkenny nodded.

"That's true," Monk said. "I guess that means she can control the real world for want of a better way to put it. Either that, or she can control minds, and that's pretty nasty if I say so myself."

"If that's true, then why isn't it working on us?" Kilkenny asked.

"Either she's not trying, or it won't work on us for some reason," Monk said. "Doesn't matter, I guess, all three of us are our normal selves, and we can watch and see what she does." She wanted to point out the other obvious thing, and that was if Kilkenny could do the same things as Wells, maybe Wells saw her as competition to be disposed of.

Jackie gave her a quick look, panic lurking in her dark blue eyes, and Monk knew the same thing had just occurred to her.

"We have to get help," Jackie said.

Monk gave her a sharp look. "Who? And tell them what, exactly?"

Jackie's mouth snapped shut, and Monk nodded.

"Look," Monk said. "I've already had two offers for help, from some really good friends, but they don't know what we've just discussed. This is making my blood run cold. So in the interests of keeping them—and us—safe, I'm not going to ask them just yet. We have to work out how we're going to fight her. I'll keep her distracted and try to do some research until we know more about what's going on and how to tackle her. After that, we can get help, if we still need it."

"I'm not sure that's such a good idea," Jackie said. "I don't think we're thinking this through properly."

"Monk, you can't do that," Kilkenny said. "If Wells is really doing what we think she's doing then she's going to kill us all, and if you stick your neck out like that, she's going to kill you first, and it's going to be quick. I don't want you to die, and I won't let you do it."

Monk leaned forward, so she was sure that Kilkenny was looking straight into her eyes. "Thank you, for caring—it means a lot to me. I'm not going to get hurt. I have you backing me up, don't I? You can do the same things in dreams that she can, and with practice, I'm sure you can be more than a match for her. She has to get through me to get to you, and I won't let her do it. My—and our—best protection is her not knowing we know as much as we do, and me getting and keeping her attention on me."

Both Sharps looked set to protest.

Monk held up a hand. "If I go down—and I'm not about to let that happen—I'll find a way to tell you what happened so you can avoid my mistakes. I'll also tell you who to talk to so you have a fighting chance. I'm going to bait Wells and keep her on me until we're ready."

"Oh, Monk," Jackie said sadly. "No. That's a sure fire recipe for disaster."

Monk gave Jackie a gentle smile. "There's a lot at stake here. Potentially our lives. We don't really have time to dither about this. We have to move and move now. I'm game, are you?"

Jackie shook her head. "I'm not really comfortable about this. I think we're being too hasty. Do you not realize that you're giving yourself a death sentence?"

"You're just going to have to trust me. We really don't have a lot of options in this situation." Monk blew out a breath. "I guess this means I'll be headed to the library after detention this afternoon."

"You want some help?" Jackie asked. "I don't know if I can make it this afternoon, though. Mum needs her car back."

Monk smiled. "Sure, that's fine. I'm sure it's going to be a couple of sessions at the library. It'll go quicker if we work together."

They sat in comfortable silence.

"I'd better head back to the senior courtyard," Monk said. "Kilkenny, I don't know if you can influence who is in your dreams, so this is a good chance to find out. Come and find me tonight, and we'll talk more. I'll see you in class, Jackie."

"Okay, works for me," Kilkenny said.

Monk felt both sets of eyes on her as she stood and walked back to the senior area.

"See you later, Monk," Jackie said.

Monk gave them a quick wave and kept walking. She didn't look up to the top floor verandah. She knew she would have seen Wells staring down at them with a feral expression.

Monk made her way toward the public telephones outside the school office. A large group of junior school girls milled aimlessly, jostling one another and shoving Monk. Monk glared at a vacant-eyed girl as she rifled through her backpack and rammed Monk in the ribs with her elbow.

"Watch it," Monk said.

The girl gave her a brief, confused stare and continued as though nothing had happened. Monk shot her a sour look and lifted the pay phone's receiver.

She dialed her home phone number, not expecting anyone to be home. The telephone rang ten times, and she was just hanging up as her mother answered.

"Hello?" her mother said, sounding indistinct and tinny.

"Hi, Mum?" Monk asked.

"Yeah, what do you want?"

"I'm going to be home at around five-thirty. I have to go to the library after school. I have a project."

"Fine. We'll see you then."

Monk pulled the receiver way from her ear and frowned at it. She tensed, confused by her mother's civil words and tone.

"How come you're still at home?" Monk asked cautiously. "I'd have thought you'd have left for work by now."

"Can't get the car started. You have to find your own way home from the library this afternoon."

Monk nodded. "Yeah, sure."

"Have a good day. I think I hear the auto club outside."

There was a click and smooth hum before Monk could respond. She stared at the telephone. "Thanks, you too," she said and hung up with a sigh.

She turned, shouldered her backpack, and staggered as a junior girl bumped her and pushed her backward.

"God damn," Monk exclaimed, recovering her balance. "Watch where you're going."

The girl remained eerily silent and gave her a dazed, unfocused look.

Monk glared at the stumbling girl. She noticed that the girl had not apologized for her clumsiness.

"Are you all right?" she asked as the girl scrabbled backward, away from her.

Monk took a step toward her, and her eyebrows shot skyward.

The number of girls in the corridor had easily doubled, and they all seemed to be pushing and shoving one another. A couple of the taller girls were facing off and glaring. One of the closer ones reached out a hand and shoved the other one.

Uh oh, that was stupid. Monk watched in amazement as the second girl swung a fist in a wild, uncontrolled arc and hit the first girl a glancing blow to the tip of her jaw—hard enough to force the first one back a step. Her face twisted into a snarl of rage, and she lunged forward and grabbed a hank of the second girl's hair and tugged for all she was worth.

The second girl howled in pain, but none of the other girls paid attention. The milling crowd pushed them together in a ball of snarling, hissing girls.

Monk watched the first girl sink a punch into the second girl's stomach and decided she had seen enough. She dropped her backpack and dived into the melee.

She was unable to avoid the bodies that shoved her, the elbows that jabbed her, and the hands that pushed her toward the combatants. By the time she reached the scuffle, both girls showed signs of bruising, and the first girl had a fat lip. Both still looked dazed and uncomprehending.

Monk, thanks to a muscular physique, found it easy to grab both girls by the collars and pull them apart. She glanced around at the other juniors. They all slowly halted and stared sightlessly at her. A shiver ran up and down her spine as she recalled Jackie's words: *Have you noticed the way everyone seems to go into a daze around her?* She felt as though eyes were boring into the space between her shoulder blades and looked around. She was almost disappointed when she didn't see Wells standing behind her.

"What's going on here?" Coopersmith asked, striding through the crowd of girls and stopping beside Monk. "Monk?"

Monk shook her head. "I'm sorry, Miss Coopersmith. I didn't see the start of this. All I saw were these two girls fighting each other."

Coopersmith nodded and folded her arms, eyeing both girls mercilessly. The second girl had the decency to blush and lower her gaze. "Right. Both of you sit down on that bench. The rest of you— break it up and head back to class."

"But it's recess, Miss," one of the braver girls said.

"No, it's not," Coopersmith said, eyeing her coolly. "That finished five minutes ago. Why do you think I'm here? Get to class."

The girls quickly dispersed under Coopersmith's watchful eye. Monk glanced at her watch and stayed by Coopersmith's side.

"I have to go to the library after detention," Monk said as soon as the girls were out of earshot.

Coopersmith shot her a look. "You still want me to give you a lift home?"

Monk's heart felt heavy. "No, it's fine. I already called my mother to let her know I was going to be late." She smiled. "That's what I was doing here."

Coopersmith gazed at her and looked as though she wanted to say something. Finally, she said, "All right, no worries. If you change your mind, let me know. And if you don't feel like walking let me know. I'll come and get you."

Monk stifled the impulse to throw her arms around Coopersmith. "Thanks, Miss."

"No worries. Now you'd better go. We don't want you getting into any more trouble, do we?"

Monk shook her head and began walking to her modern history class with McCann.

Just as she rounded the corner, she spotted Wells. Her blood ran cold as Wells folded her arms and watched her, smiling. The smile did not touch her eyes.

Monk shuddered and kept walking.

That afternoon Monk emerged with a tired sigh from the auditorium after detention. She felt as though she had spent the day running on adrenalin, thanks to her poor night's sleep. She looked around the courtyard, taking in a group of girls on the far side with a small frown. They all sat on the brick wall, shoulder to shoulder, staring at the hall.

They're way too quiet. Wonder what the hell they're up to? She glanced back to see if Warland was still there, but the auditorium doors had closed behind her. She looked at the group again, and they studied her in return, faces expressionless. She suddenly became aware of the silence of the empty school, her heavy backpack, and the heat of the day. She turned toward the side passage and walked quickly down it. She heard the slap of school shoes hitting the asphalt in the courtyard, footsteps at the mouth of the passage behind her.

She glanced back at them, noticing for the first time the flash of color of a senior uniform.

Crap. Who's in with that crowd? This is probably going to get really ugly. She tensed her jaw and continued her quick pace.

The footsteps behind her sped up. She glanced back again. The girls were staring at her with grim intensity, walking quickly to close the gap between them.

Shit. Monk broke into a jog.

The group of girls behind her started running.

Monk's legs almost instantly protested as she pushed herself into an easy running rhythm. Her breath soon came in shorter gasps, thanks to the weight of her backpack.

The pounding footsteps behind her didn't falter, and she glanced back. Some of the girls had slowed down and stopped, leaning forward with their hands on their knees and gasping for breath. One or two of them kept pace with her. They were big junior girls that Monk didn't recognize, and they looked angry.

Monk forced herself to run faster. She felt as though her lungs were about to combust, and her knees protested mightily at her ill treatment of them.

I can do this! I can do this! she chanted to herself. The public library was within sight. All the parking spots in front of it were taken, and people walked in and out in dribs and drabs. She felt an instant of triumph. They couldn't do anything to her while adults were watching. All she had to do was make it through the front doors. She increased her pace and glanced over her shoulder at her pursuers.

She skidded to a halt. They stood ten meters from her, breathing hard and standing stock still. They stared at her with cold, calculating eyes.

She waited for them to threaten her but they remained silent.

Monk watched them closely for any other signs of hostility but didn't see any. Across the road, behind them, was the rest of the girls that had chased her. They slowly walked across the pedestrian crossing, faces blank.

Monk's blood ran cold. *They're probably just waiting for their mates to catch up before they beat the shit out of me.*

She quickly turned and walked as quickly as she could toward the library. She strained to hear if the girls moved, but there didn't seem to be any further signs of pursuit.

They can't wait out there forever, she thought. *They're going to have to go home sometime. They're probably going to have to leave before I do. Besides, I can always leave by the back door if I'm wrong. Hell, I could even call Mitch if I had to.*

She strode into the public library and past the circulation desk. She heard a polite cough and turned to the source—a severe-looking woman eyeing her. The woman looked as though she was expecting Monk to turn into a dangerous animal and start savaging library patrons.

Monk raised an eyebrow at her.

She nodded sagely and pointed behind Monk.

Monk turned. A large sign over a series of lockers and luggage racks by the doors said, *Schoolchildren—backpacks are not permitted in the library. Please leave here.*

Monk squeezed her eyes shut. *You're fucking kidding. I totally forgot. And I forgot what a psychopath that fucking librarian is. The others are okay but I got the bitch. Figures.*

She turned with a soft sigh and dropped her backpack at one of the bag racks. The librarian flashed a quick, superior grin, and Monk smiled back, resisting the urge to make an obscene gesture. Her eyes felt gritty with exhaustion. She reviewed a quick mental list of what she wanted to look for.

She went to the computer catalog. She scanned the menu briefly, looking for the search functionality. She quickly typed in "occult," and a series of books came back. She ran her finger down the list, memorizing the shortest catalog number and most interesting title. She headed downstairs and toward the back of the library.

The hair on the back of her neck rose. *This is stupid*, she thought, trying to dismiss it. *It's only because you're looking for books on the occult in a dark, lonely room.*

The section of the library she was in seemed empty. It was dark, and the overhead fluorescents came on one by one as she walked down the aisles, creating comforting pockets of brilliance in an otherwise ominous netherworld. She felt as though eyes were upon her, and it took all of her self-control to refrain from constantly looking over her shoulder. She finally shook herself, trying to force her building uneasiness back into the shadows.

I'm in a public library. Of course there are people around. It's a building with a whole bunch of bookshelves and lavender-scented oldies wandering around looking for bodice rippers. I just happen to be in the heretics' section. That's all. It's pretty fucking stupid to be scared.

Monk shrugged and stretched out her neck. She pulled the first book from the shelf and quickly perused it. She grinned, pulled out a couple of others, took them to a close by desk, and began reading.

She was completely engrossed in the first book when the soft squeak of a book trolley wheel disturbed the quiet. She looked up, expecting to see a librarian staring at her from over the top of bug-eyed glasses.

She frowned. No one was by her.

She peered into the darkness—that now seemed black as pitch—at distant pools of light created by the overhead fluorescents. She narrowed her eyes, trying to make out detail. *Why is it so damned dark in here?*

The lights closest to the doors seemed to be on, and she heard the soft ticking and hum from another set as they came on. The squeaking stayed at the same volume.

Monk opened her mouth to speak but quickly closed it. She had no desire to make an idiot of herself.

She watched the ceiling as the lights came on, in more or less random order. The hair on the back of her neck rose at the seemingly random pools of light. If something was coming toward her, how could one set of lights close to the stairs come on, and then another on the other side of the room?

She stood and took a cautious step back, almost deafened by the roaring in her ears and the hammering of her heart. Then, through the cacophony, she heard footsteps, unhurriedly coming toward her. She took another step back, barely aware of her feet tangling together as she collapsed backward into the chair.

She was cornered. Her only option was to hide on the floor under her desk. She stared across the room at the lights, flinched at the creaking, and tried to force her shaking body into a crouch beneath the desk.

"Monk?" a familiar voice asked.

Monk jerked and bit her lip to keep from squeaking. Her heart hammered, and she clutched at her chest. "Christ, Lightman. What the hell? You scared the fucking crap out of me."

Lightman frowned. "I'm sorry." She looked around. "What are you doing down here?"

"What am *I* doing here? What the fuck are *you* doing here?"

"I followed you," Lightman said with a grin.

"You *what*?" Monk shrank back. Her hands shook. She remembered the group of girls that had chased her and the flash of a senior uniform amongst them.

"Jesus, Monk," Lightman said, softening her tone. She frowned. "You're really afraid, aren't you? Of what?" She glanced around and sighed. "Look, this is a public library. I'm here to get my homework done. I don't want to go home yet. Probably the same as you, Sunshine."

"Down here? You could have chosen any floor, but you came down here. Why?"

"God, what *is* your fucking problem? This is the quietest part of the library." She folded her arms. "Are you going to answer me or just give me the third degree?"

Get a grip. Get a fucking grip, Monk. It doesn't matter now anyway. It's too late. If she wants to hurt me I'm done. Monk nodded. She glanced around and strained to hear.

The squeaking continued in the distance. Monk relaxed a little. If Lightman was there, squeaking and darkness could not be supernatural, no matter how unnatural it felt. There had to be a logical explanation.

"I was studying," Monk said, leaning against the desk. She shook.

"Normally studying doesn't make you shake like a leaf. Are you all right?"

Monk looked over Lightman's shoulder at the darkness oozing out from between the shelves. "I think so. I want to get out of here, though."

Lightman glanced around. "I hear you. Why the hell is it so fucking dark down here?"

"I have no idea," Monk said, staring into the gloominess. "Creepy down here, isn't it?"

Lightman nodded. "Oh, yeah." She gestured toward the ceiling. "At least there are sensors to turn on the lights. It doesn't have to be dark."

"Sure," Monk said, watching another set of lights come on about halfway down the room, opposite them.

The squeaking was louder now, and a dull, metallic thump sounded as a cart bumped the shelves and rolled slowly out of the aisle closest to them.

Lightman stiffened and shook her head.

Monk nodded. It looked ordinary but felt troubling. She didn't understand why she was trembling. She watched the lights on the ceiling flicker to life closer to them.

"Wait," Lightman said in hushed tones. "Did you hear that?"

"What?" Monk whispered.

Lightman clutched Monk's arm and stared into the darkness. "There. Did you hear that?"

Monk shook her head. She strained to hear. Just as she opened her mouth to ask Lightman what she had heard, she heard it herself. She narrowed her eyes at the gentle patter of feet somewhere in the stacks.

The lights in the aisle furthest from them came on, flooding the mouth of the aisle with unexpected brilliance, and Lightman took a step back beside Monk. Monk almost hummed with tension, and her heart rate picked up. A low, basso growling sent shivers up and down her spine.

"Monk?" Lightman croaked.

Monk nodded. "Yeah."

She grabbed Lightman's wrist, and they headed into the closest aisle. The lights flickered to life above them. The footsteps became the sound of pounding feet as they tried to escape them.

Monk cursed virulently at the lights and the rapidly gaining footsteps.

"Separate," Lightman said, peeling off to the right as Monk peeled off to the left. She bolted down the aisles, which now seemed to have grown miles long, trying to head toward the stairs. The footsteps chased her, and the growling increased in volume. Books clattered and thudded to the floor behind her.

Lightman screamed in pain in the distance, and Monk heard her footsteps falter.

"Lightman?" she yelled. "Lightman!"

"Run, goddammit!" Lightman screamed from the aisles behind her.

Monk almost sobbed with relief as she found the stairs. She tripped up them and crashed to her knees with a startled yelp of pain. She lost precious seconds as she levered herself to her feet and tried to keep running up the stairs. Her feet tangled again, and she jarred her wrist as she grabbed the banister to keep from falling on her face.

She yelped as a hand grabbed the collar of her shirt. She began to struggle.

"It's me, dummy," Lightman said. "Fucking move." She held Monk's shirt in an iron grip and dragged her up the stairs.

The footsteps reached the lower landing as they exploded out onto the main floor of the library. Monk's chest heaved as she fought for breath. She leaned forward with her hands on her knees as Lightman sagged against the wall behind her.

The librarian behind the circulation desk looked at them sharply, her mouth tightening into a thin line of displeasure. She pointed to a sign hanging on the wall behind the desk. *Silence is golden*, it said.

Monk exchanged an incredulous look with Lightman, and they giggled. Soon they were clutching each other convulsively, gasping from hysterical laughter.

"Please leave, girls," the glaring librarian said.

Monk made the okay sign at her and exchanged a glance with Lightman. They quickly scooped up their backpacks, and Lightman giggled again. Monk grabbed her and dragged her toward the doors before the librarian could call for reinforcements.

Once they were outside, they jogged down the stairs and leaned against the sandstone wall. Both tried to catch their breath. Monk scanned up and down the road for the girls that had followed her to the library. They seemed to be gone.

Monk gave Lightman a grin that fell away as she took in the blood and tears on Lightman's shirt. "What happened to you?" She reached out a shaking hand.

"Whatever it was—and you'd better start talking—took a swipe at me."

Monk moaned and began to pull back Lightman's shirt but Lightman grabbed her wrist.

"Not here," Lightman said softly. "Not here. Come with me."

Monk nodded and almost robotically followed Lightman to a white BMW. Lightman grabbed Monk's backpack, threw it on the back seat, pushed the stunned Monk into the front passenger seat, and got into the driver's side.

Monk did not move. She felt numb.

Lightman turned to her.

Monk's paralysis finally broke. She pulled aside the tattered flaps of Lightman's shirt, shaking more than she had before. Her eyes widened as she took in the claw marks scraped across Lightman's stomach. They were full of half-dried blood smeared across her smooth skin.

"Oh," she said. Up until now, nothing had seemed genuine. The nightmare she had seemed just a bad dream. Wells seemed a complete bitch. Her blood and mortality meant nothing to her. Even the episode in the library, despite her terror, had not felt like fact until she saw Lightman's blood. Now she saw and smelt blood everywhere and shivered at remembered growling. Terror flooded through her system, her heart thudded, and she tasted metal. She gasped.

"Monk?" Lightman asked calmly. "Are you all right?"

"You're hurt," Monk said, sagging back in her seat.

"I noticed."

"What did this to you?"

"Huh? I have no idea."

"Oh, crap." Monk sighed. She realized her promise to Jackie and Kilkenny meant actual violence. It meant people getting hurt. An image of Coopersmith's beautiful face swam into her mind, and she shuddered. *Oh my God, what have I done?*

"Monk?" Lightman said. "Don't make me slap you."

Monk looked at Lightman, trying to focus on her. "Lightman?"

"We have so established this, that I'm ready to thump you on general principles," Lightman said. "Now let's try this again. What the blue bloody fuck is going on around here?"

"I'm sorry," Monk said. "I never meant for you to get hurt."

Lightman rolled her eyes. "Christ. All right, I give up. If you feel like talking then speak. Until then, shut the fuck up, all right?"

Lightman drove them to the McDonalds drive through, and after a quick glance at the silent Monk, ordered for both of them. She parked on the far side of the parking lot and handed Monk a bag of hot food.

Monk mechanically ate her fries. All she could think about was Lightman getting hurt. Every glance at Lightman was another stab of guilt.

"Look," Lightman said in gentler tones. "Tell me what's going on. You owe me that at least."

"I can't," Monk said. "It's going to sound crazy if I do."

Lightman's eyes widened, and she snorted a laugh. "You've got to be kidding me. Look at me. Do you comprehend what happened to us back there? It sounded for all the world like a big dog was stalking us. In a *public library* of all places. How much more nutty can you get than that?"

Monk flushed and dropped her fry, appetite done. "Controlling dreams."

Lightman raised an eyebrow. "Speak. I'm listening."

Monk sighed. She wondered if she should mention names. Why not tell Lightman? She realized. Lightman and Wells had already clashed in class, and it was clear they hated each other. She and Lightman had both been physically hurt and Jackie and Kilkenny were next.

She told Lightman everything, but left out all mention of Coopersmith. When she finished, Lightman stared at her and thoughtfully chewed her bottom lip.

"You're sure about all this?" she asked.

Monk nodded. "I've seen it with my own eyes."

"And you think Wells is behind all of this?"

Monk nodded. "Yeah."

Lightman nodded. "All right. Now all we have to do is prove it."

"We?" Monk asked.

"Yes, we," Lightman said with a slight smile. "I'm involved in this now, remember?"

"No," Monk said. "I don't think so. You just had a minor brush with her, that's all. You're still in the clear. As far as she's concerned you were just in the wrong place at the wrong time."

"Christ, you've got to be kidding me," Lightman said, shaking her head. Her jaw tensed, and she leaned forward, glaring at Monk. "In case you haven't noticed, Sunshine, now I'm right smack in the middle of all this, whether I want to be or not."

"I'm not wearing your safety as well, Lightman," Monk said, temper sparking. "Back off. It's not negotiable."

"Stiff shit," Lightman said. "I'm in it now, and you can't cut me out. I'm not a chicken like Jackie, or a kid like Kilkenny. I'm a grown up. I can make my own choices and live with the consequences." Her eyes glittered. "I'm thinking you can't, can you?"

"What the fuck is that supposed to mean?" Monk asked. "Just because I don't want a tagalong doesn't mean I'm doing it because I want to protect you."

"Whatever." Lightman waved a negligent hand and took a sip of her coke. "The fact remains, you've told me all of this. A woman dog beast—and I must say the term bitch suits her admirably—took a chunk out of me. I'm going to do my own research and have some fun with her. We work either together or separately. You choose."

Monk thought about it for a moment. She didn't want to work with Lightman, but she also didn't want to be alone. She cursed herself for her fear and her weakness.

She nodded slowly. "All right. Have it your way." She held out her hand, and Lightman solemnly took it.

"Equal partners?" Lightman asked.

Monk nodded. "Equal partners."

"All right," Lightman said. "We're going to eat up, and I'm going to take you home. I'm a bit busy tonight, and now I'm running a little late."

Monk felt a blast of unreality wash over her. "Oh? Where are you off to?"

Lightman smiled and bit into her burger. "My girl is in town, and I have a hot date."

"Doesn't your mother have a problem with it being a school night?" Monk asked. *And it's pretty weird you care about getting fucked after you nearly got your guts unzipped at the library. Shouldn't that bother you a bit?*

"No," Lightman said. "I barely register on her radar anymore."

Monk wondered what that felt like.

"Are you going to go to sleep tonight?" Lightman asked.

Monk nodded. "I don't have a choice, really. I can't leave Kilkenny or Jackie by themselves in there. I just hope the dreams aren't too nasty."

Lightman nodded. "I hear you."

They lapsed into silence, wolfing their food down, and Lightman drove Monk home.

Monk watched Lightman's BMW pull away from the curb and

pondered the latest twist of fate. She still had the foul taste of the aftermath of fear in her mouth, and she grimaced. Lightman was tangled in the events that had happened in the library. Who would be next? Would it be Coopersmith? Warland? Or would it be Kilkenny? Would she be strong enough to stand fast, or would she run while she watched one of her friends get hurt?

Monk turned to go into the house. She thought about telling Coopersmith everything and begging her for help. The thought collapsed almost as soon as it went through her mind. *Right. Mitch, my chemistry teacher is some kind of supernatural creature. We're not really sure what kind. We're sure, though, that she wants to kill Jackie, Kilkenny, Lightman, and I. She just finished stalking me in the library.* Monk rolled her eyes and shook her head. *That's just not going to work. She won't believe me. Who would? This is insane. On top of that, I've already gotten hurt in all this, and I'm sure that if I told anyone, Wells would go after them as well. I couldn't stand it if Mitch got hurt because of me. I think I'm really on my own for this one.*

CHAPTER FIVE

The next morning at school, Monk found Lightman in her accustomed spot against the wall, legs up on the seat, snoring.

Monk grinned, despite herself. She dropped her bag lightly on the asphalt and then bent over Lightman. "Hello, mate, what are you doing here at this hour?"

Lightman awoke with a start. She stiffened, blinking, and eyed Monk owlishly. After a few seconds, she stretched and yawned. "Morning, Monk. Do you normally get here now?"

Monk smiled. "When my mother gives me a lift, more often than not, yes I do. She doesn't really like having me around."

"Really?" Lightman gave her a curious look. "Neither does mine."

Monk snorted a laugh despite herself. "It works well for me. I don't think she's really going to notice I'm home late this evening. I want to try and find out more about Wells."

Lightman nodded. "What are our plans for today?"

"We can do another research trip to the library, or . . ."

"Or?" Lightman asked, gazing at her expectantly.

"We can follow her and keep a close eye on her to see what's the what."

"I'm there."

"Good," Monk said. "Works for me. I'll catch you after school."

Lightman nodded.

Monk took in the tense set to her shoulders and her pale complexion. "Are you all right? How was the hot date last night?"

"It didn't happen."

"What?" Monk asked.

"My mother got back from one of her boring fucking business trips two days early, just in time for my date last night. She managed to ruin it for me."

Monk nodded in understanding, dimly amazed at how Lightman

seemed more interested in her aborted date than her inhuman teacher. "I know where you're coming from."

"Y'know," Lightman began thoughtfully, "I don't get it. She keeps telling me I'm an embarrassment to her good name, and that she should never have had me, but she still insists on interacting with me. It's like she gets in a bad mood and comes looking for me so she can kick the shit out of me."

Monk nodded. "So does mine. All that ever comes out of her mouth is 'why can't you be more like your older sister? She's fine and you're not. You're a jerk, Therese. I don't like you at all. You may be my child, and there may be a maternal bond, but I can't stand the sight of you.'"

Lightman nodded. "The thing my mother likes to add to that is, 'Are you enjoying being young and single?'" Hectic red spots appeared on Lightman's cheeks, and she studied the discolored asphalt with interest.

Monk winced. "Are you okay?"

Lightman's eyes shone with unshed tears as she looked at Monk. "Should I be? I lost the one person I ever really loved, and now my mother is taking it as a good excuse to gloat. I want to kill her."

Monk was not sure how to respond, even though she understood the sentiments. She took Lightman's cold hands into hers. "Easy, Lightman."

"Why the fuck should I take it easy?" Lightman said. "I'm so alone now. It's just not going to get any better with my mother."

"You're not alone," Monk said almost unwillingly. "You have me."

Lightman looked at her sharply. She sniffled. She collapsed into Monk's arms, and Monk held her close, tears raining down on her uniform blouse.

Lightman finally quieted a bit, drew back, and wiped her eyes with the heels of her hands. She sniffed, and her breathing sounded heavy and watery.

Monk gently patted her shoulder. "Better?"

Lightman nodded. "I'm sorry. I didn't really mean to fall apart like that."

"Every now and again it really gets to you, doesn't it?"

Lightman smiled. "Yes, it does. I guess my nose is so out of joint because I finally found her. I called her, and we were meant to get together on the weekend, but of course that didn't happen."

Monk stared at her, trying to absorb the news. "Are you going to get together with her again?"

"Yup. She still wants me. We're going to have to sneak around my mother for a while, if we can. I think my mother's not going to notice because she's not around all that much, thank God."

Monk nodded, trying not to think of her own mother.

"What about your lady?" Lightman asked. "Want to tell me about her? I can probably help you, you know. I can tell you mistakes to avoid."

Monk thought about it for a minute. "I . . . there's nothing going on. I can't." She stopped and felt the color rising in her cheeks. "I . . . We're not . . . I . . ." She felt dimly relieved she could not talk about Coopersmith. Deep down, she really didn't want to.

"Does she have a name?"

"Yes." She looked up apologetically.

Lightman smiled, brown eyes gentle. "It's okay, you don't need to say anything. Just remember you have me to talk to if you need to."

"Thanks. The same goes for you."

Monk sat with her eyes closed in her accustomed position on the hard concrete outside her roll call room.

"Monk?" a cheerful voice asked. "What on earth are you doing? Why are you always sitting out here?"

"I'm being punished for being late for roll call," Monk said, returning McCann's happy grin.

McCann's golden eyebrows contracted. She pushed her short, thick, honey blonde hair out of her blue eyes. "You're kidding me, right?"

Monk shook her head. "I'm afraid not, Miss McCann."

"Are you sick of living in blissful oblivion yet?" McCann asked, customary grin creeping back.

Monk nodded. "Oh, yeah. Sick to death of it. I love listening to Sister Constance's voice over the speakers, and I miss her dreadfully, Miss."

McCann mock frowned. "Bad seed. Blasphemy. Come with me. As your punishment, I sentence you to roll call with a bunch of unruly seventeen-year-old girls."

"That's my punishment? To be in your roll call class?"

"No, your punishment is to put up with me for fifteen more minutes a day. No rolling your eyes at me. It's not going to work. All the begging in the world isn't going to save your neck this time."

Monk burst out laughing and allowed the grinning McCann help her up off the cold concrete.

McCann smiled at her, and they walked down another couple of classrooms to hers.

"Miss McCann, on a more serious note, do you mind too much if I do show up late? I have to get officially kicked out every day otherwise I'm going to get crucified for not showing up to school."

McCann smiled at her. "That's fine. Do what you need to do. Just come on down and join us when you're ready, all right?"

"Okay."

McCann pushed open the door to her roll call room. Girls sat around on the desks, quietly talking. As soon as McCann walked in, Monk trailing behind her, they all stopped talking and took their seats. Connie Kirkland, a plump and homely girl in Monk's maths and chemistry classes, smiled and waved her over.

"Thanks, Connie," McCann said. "Girls, we have a visitor. Probably a permanent one. Make her feel welcome." She shielded her mouth so Monk could not see her lips move. "We'll pull her fingernails out later when she's more comfortable, okay?" she said in a stage whisper. She looked up and gave Monk a large, fake smile.

Monk laughed, along with the rest of the girls in the class.

She slid into the seat beside Connie, giving her a cheerful grin, and settled back to sleep comfortably for fifteen minutes.

Monk glanced at her watch as she walked past the science area on her way to the library for her study period. It was nearly eleven. *Hells bells, I'm late. I can't believe I missed a quarter of my study period already. Bugger. To hell with it. If I'm lucky I can sneak into the library, and no one's going to notice.*

She almost bumped into the woman who came out of the prep room.

"Sorry," she mumbled and tried to move aside. She found her path blocked again and looked up.

Fuck, she thought, gazing at Wells's smug features.

Wells crossed her arms. "So, Therese, shouldn't you be in class or somewhere other than outdoors?"

"I'm on my way to the library for my study period," Monk said, returning her stare.

"Then technically you have a class, don't you? Would be safer to put you on detention with me for lateness, wouldn't it?" Wells crossed her arms, smiling in a way that Monk did not like.

Monk met her smile with a stony glare and said nothing.

"What? Not going to answer me, Therese?"

Monk stared at her. "Why should I? All you really seem to care about is putting people—most notably me—on detention, for little or no excuse."

"You got your detention," Wells said with satisfaction.

Monk was desperate to throw a punch at Wells's self-satisfied face, but restrained herself.

Just at that moment, Coopersmith came down the stairs, followed by Jackie Sharp. Coopersmith faltered and stopped when she saw them.

Monk glanced at them, heart sinking.

Warland came out of the prep room, stopped, and looked at them curiously.

Wells's smile increased. She leaned forward and whispered in Monk's ear, "Well, Therese. This is interesting, isn't it? You have friends. Should I hurt them? I think you know how good I am at playing hide and seek, don't you?"

"I noticed, Wells. And I suppose *you've* noticed I'm not frightened of you," Monk said with as much dignity as she could muster. "What do you really want?"

"I want the red-headed whelp," Wells said. "Stand aside, or I'll kill you, too."

Monk went cold. "Stiff shit, Wells. We don't always get what we want." Her heart hammered. "You're going to have to kill me to get to Kilkenny. As I live and breathe, you *will not* touch one hair on that girl's head."

"Really? As you live and breathe? Not for long, Therese," Wells said with grotesque easiness. "I can handle this a couple of ways. I could tell you I'll kill your friends unless you stand aside, or I can kill you and enjoy doing it, despite the fact you're no match for me. I like the second option. It's a refreshing diversion for me. Besides, you have courage, and I like that."

Monk leaned forward, despite her fear, her gaze boring into Wells. She allowed her temper to take over. "Well, your answer for both options is I don't take kindly to being bullied. You leave Kilkenny and my friends alone. You will not harm any one of them. If you do, it'll be over my—and your—dead bodies. I will fight you to the death no matter who you decide to go after, because now you just pissed me off. If you think I won't or can't kill you, think again."

Monk glanced at Coopersmith, and the surge of emotion that went through her was so strong she shook in its wake. Her courage came out in full force, and she straightened.

"Still like my courage? You fucking useless cow." She smiled. "What makes you think the prospect of beating the living shit out of you isn't fun for me, fuckhead?"

Wells's eyes flared yellow. "You sure that's the way you want it? Killing you will be a pleasure."

"Right back atcha," Monk said. "Just you and me. To the death. Go ahead, I dare you. I double dare you. If—and it's a big if—you kill me, you have your chance with them. But I'm sure it's not going to take a lot to hold off a dildo like you."

"You're on," Wells said. Her self-satisfied smirk came back in full force. "Detention, Miss Monkhouse. After the one you're on this afternoon finishes."

Coopersmith and Warland both took a step toward her.

Monk let instinct take over. She dropped her backpack and jumped, punching the air. "Yippee! I'm on detention. That is sooooo cool." She gave Wells a quick squeeze around the shoulders. "Ain't this lady just to die for?"

She picked up her bag and jogged toward Warland.

"Did you hear that?" she asked the surprised Warland. "I got detention."

Warland stepped back into the prep room.

Monk jogged toward Coopersmith and Jackie and leapt around with enthusiasm. Coopersmith's eyes flashed and narrowed. Jackie, deathly pale, nibbled her lip.

Monk could feel Wells's hostile eyes on her. "Did you hear that? I'm on detention with her after this one finishes. Yay."

Coopersmith's eyes flickered. Monk felt Wells moving toward them.

Coopersmith folded her arms and stared at Monk. "That's not the only one you have. Downstairs in one oh one for lunchtime with me. I don't know what you're doing, but you're behaving like a junior."

Wells moved closer to them. "Let me handle this, Miss Coopersmith." She glared at Monk. "Come here, Therese. Now!"

Monk glared at her. Her mouth opened, and words shot out before she could stop them. "You can't handle anything, least of all me."

"Come with me, Monk," Coopersmith cut in.

Monk shot her gaze between Coopersmith and Wells.

Monk looked at Coopersmith, silently apologizing to her. "No," she said softly and vehemently. She raised her voice. "I can't go with you now. Miss Wells and I were just bonding, weren't we, cupcake?"

"You like detention, don't you, Therese?" Wells asked. "How about I give you another one?"

"You can give me as many as you like, it doesn't mean I'm going to turn up to any of them," Monk shot back. "In fact, you can take your detentions and stick them up your—"

"Monk," Coopersmith exclaimed.

Monk glanced at her, clenching and unclenching her hands.

Jackie took a step back. Wells continued to move slowly toward them. Monk turned back to Coopersmith and felt her heart twist. A glint entered Coopersmith's eye.

"You're going to be on detention with me for the rest of your life, Monk," Coopersmith said coolly. "If you're late to one oh one I'll put you on afternoon detention with me, understood?"

"Yes, ma'am," Monk said.

Coopersmith nodded and continued down the stairs, Jackie in tow.

Wells came to stand beside her. "Well, Therese," she said when Coopersmith and Jackie were out of earshot. "That was impressive, but it won't work forever. You're done." She grabbed Monk's arm. "That's enough out of you, Miss Monkhouse. Let's go and see Sister Constance."

Monk saw Jackie and Coopersmith falter on the stairs and willed them to keep going. After a second they did.

Wells dragged Monk up the stairs and pulled her toward the office. She strode inside, jerking Monk behind her. She paused to knock before barging into Sister Constance's office.

Wells threw Monk forward. "I have a problem for you, Sister Constance." She leaned on her knuckles on the edge of the principal's desk.

"Oh?" Sister Constance said, looking up from the papers on her desk and dropping her pen. "What seems to be the problem, Miss Wells?"

Monk watched in amazement as the old nun leaned forward with grotesque eagerness, eyes glittering, completely unlike her normal, reserved self.

"Miss Monkhouse here displayed a great deal of defiance. I think it's a caning offense." Wells's eyes, bright, bile yellow, flashed between them, and Monk's stomach did a slow roll as terror washed over her.

"All right," Sister Constance said. Her eyes widened, and she gazed at Monk in a way she didn't like.

Sister Constance stood and grabbed Monk in an iron grip. She threw her across the desk before she could react.

Wells's strong hand held her forward and down, as the rasp of a filing cabinet sounded behind her. She heard a brief rustling and the whoosh of air from a cane hefted experimentally in the air. Wells held Monk's arms out and tugged her around like a rag doll. Sister Constance pulled off Monk's shirt and tore her underwear. Monk was half naked from the waist up.

You've got to be fucking kidding me. This is not *happening to me.*

She barely had time to prepare herself before the first blow landed square across her bare back. She gasped and flinched.

Pain roared through her body, and she was only dimly aware of Well's soft laughter as the cane continued to descend.

Monk staggered out of the office about ten minutes later, squeezing her eyes shut against the tears that threatened to escape. She had lost count of the blows to her back and her behind. She was grateful she had survived the experience without screaming, although she had come close.

She tried to will the pain in her back out of existence. She walked, not paying attention to where she was going, and almost collided with a tall figure.

"Monk?" Warland said.

"Hi." Monk hung her head, humiliated.

"What happened? I followed you up from the prep room, and saw you dragged into the office."

"I got the cane," Monk said, blinking back tears.

Warland's eyes darkened with anger. "The cane, huh? Okay, follow me."

Monk obediently followed Warland down to the science labs and into the sick room.

"Let me see your back." Warland helped her pull the shirt away from her back so she could see the marks left by the cane. "Oh." She gasped. "Wow. You're bleeding."

"Fuck," Monk muttered. "Another busted shirt. Mum's going to kill me."

"I'll get you another shirt," Warland said. "Expect it this afternoon." She hissed.

"What?" Monk asked.

"Your skin's split open and you have horrible bruising," Warland replied. "You look like you went a couple of rounds with a can opener."

Monk snickered, despite herself. "That's a hell of an image."

"Maybe so, but the fact remains, those tears are deep, and you're bleeding like a stuck pig." She gazed at Monk, gray eyes aching. "You're going to have to take your shirt off. I've got to put something on those."

"I can't," Monk said in an agonized voice. "I have a lunchtime detention with Miss Coopersmith in about ten minutes and she'll kill me if I'm late." Her knees went weak, and her back was a blaze of pain. She gingerly leant against the desk by one wall of the dark room, hissing in pain as her backside touched the hard wood.

"I promise I'll make it quick. You'll be there on time. If you're not, I'll even go down with you and explain if you like—so the right person gets the blame," Warland said, gently wiping away Monk's tears.

Monk tried for a smile and found half of one. "No. I brought all of this on myself. I fully deserve everything I just got."

"The caning you just got was unreasonable," Warland said.

"I deserved it," Monk said. "I guess you now know why I have the reputation I do."

Warland gave her a brief grin, gray eyes piercing and intense. "Why did you do what you did?"

"No impulse control?"

"Don't bullshit me," Warland said, leaning forward conspiratorially. "I'm going to be completely honest with you, all right?"

Monk nodded, drained. "Please."

"Ever been around one of those kinds of people you instantly click with? You know, you feel as though you're friends right from the moment you say hi to each other?"

Monk understood. She nodded. "Yep."

"Good. That's what I think happened between the two of us. Do you agree?"

Monk nodded and smiled. "I totally agree."

"Good." Warland smiled. "I can read you quite well because of it. If you think I think you're a monster because of what happened today, you'd be wrong. I saw something happen to you when you were standing there with Miss Wells. I saw you go pale, and then you began your happy dance. I saw the look in your eyes, Monk. You pushed me back into the prep room. Why?"

Monk flushed. "I had my reasons."

"And you're not going to share them?"

Monk stayed silent, and Warland shifted and gazed into her eyes.

"All right," Warland said. "Let me try this from a different angle. I can see you have a problem with Miss Wells, and I can help you, thanks to the fact that I'm a teacher, remember?"

"Terri," Monk began. "I'm fully aware that you're an adult, but remember that I'm one as well. I had my reasons for doing what I did. You're absolutely right, I don't get on with Miss Wells at all. I'm not comfortable going into details about it, so do you mind if we let that part of it go for the moment?"

Warland looked at her, respect in her eyes. "Nicely said, and yes, I'll honor what you've just asked of me, and I won't ask details of all your interactions with Miss Wells. However, I do want to know what she could possibly have said to you to make you turn as white as a sheet. I also want to know what you said to make that girl behind Miss Coopersmith turn an uglier shade of white than you." She gave Monk a genuine smile. "It doesn't take a degree in astrophysics to work out something is horribly wrong. Maybe it's not such a good idea to wait until it's too late to ask for help."

"Are you offering to help me if I get into trouble?"

Warland folded her arms. "Yes."

"How far are you prepared to go?"

"Meaning?"

"Exactly that. How far are you prepared to go?" Monk asked.

"How far do you need me to go?"

"All the way."

"What does that mean?"

Monk shook her head. "Look, what's the worst thing she can do to me? Put me on detention for the rest of the year? Send me in for the cane? I'm just rattled because I'm not looking forward to either of those things happening to me. Forgive me, I'm not in the best of moods, is all."

Warland stared at Monk. Monk calmly gazed back at her and gave her a charming, crooked grin. She bled inside. *I can't tell her anything. Now or ever. It's safer for her if I don't.*

"You want to let this go for the moment?" Warland asked. "I know you're not telling me the truth, and that's all right as long as we both know that's what's happening."

Monk nodded, looking away so Warland would not see the desperation in her eyes.

"Hey," Warland said, and tilted Monk's face back so they could look into each other's eyes. "Better. Listen to me and never forget what I'm about to tell you. You saved my life. Everyone else was prepared to stand around and watch me get beaten to death, but not you. You jumped in without even thinking about what it could cost you, and you saved my neck. I'll do what you ask because I *know* you're my friend. I'll make my offer again, and I'll leave it on the table—if you need my help, I'll give it to you. All you have to do is tell me when."

Tears stung Monk's eyes. "Thanks. I appreciate it."

"You're welcome, my friend," Warland said, smiling.

Monk slowly and painfully encircled her arms around Warland. For a split second, she wanted to tell Warland everything. *She's just going to think I'm nuts if I start spouting about horror movie creatures.*

Warland slipped her arms around Monk, pulling her in close, mindful of her damaged back.

Monk arrived at one oh one downstairs just before the bell signaling lunch rang. She leaned against the wall, trying not to tremble. She had no idea of what she was going to tell Coopersmith. The door opened when the bell rang, and a Year Eleven maths class spilled out into the hallway.

Coopersmith sat on one of the desks in the front row, feet propped up on chair, watching Monk balefully as she walked in. Some girls still loitered in the corridor.

"Close the door behind you, Therese," Coopersmith said coldly. She stared at the girls outside, catching the eye of a few of them. "Can I help you, girls?"

The girls shook their heads and fled.

Monk closed the door behind her. Her knees shook.

Coopersmith sighed, her eyes gentle, as they always were when she really looked at Monk. She gestured at the desk in front of her.

"Take a seat," she said.

Monk dropped her backpack and slowly sat down, watching Coopersmith carefully.

"That was an interesting display you put on," Coopersmith said. "You want to tell me what happened?"

Monk shook her head. "It wasn't much. She just bailed me up because I was late to my study period. She put me on detention for it."

"That's it?" Coopersmith's eyebrows contracted. "You're kidding me, right? Is that what made you go so pale?"

Monk knew she was pale again, ashamed of her behavior toward Coopersmith. "I'm sorry, I didn't mean to be rude to you like that."

"You just wanted me out of there, didn't you?" Coopersmith asked. "Why? What did she say to you to upset you so much? You know your follow up comment to her was deliberately antagonistic, don't you?"

"I got what I deserved for it. I got the cane." Monk sighed. "She just doesn't like me, and it stresses me out." She gazed at Coopersmith, taking in her beautiful features, her willowy form, her gentle, comforting presence.

"You got the cane?" Coopersmith's voice was raw.

"Yeah," Monk said, unwilling to say any more than that.

"Where did she hit you?"

"Back and behind."

"Let me see." Coopersmith stood and lifted Monk's shirt with gentle hands. She took a sharp intake of breath. "Your back is a mess. How many hits?"

"A couple."

"Oh God." Coopersmith moaned, and Monk shivered as her hand brushed her aching and bruised back.

"Don't worry about it," Monk whispered. "I'll heal."

Coopersmith was silent for a while. "There's more to all this stuff with Wells, isn't there? If you know she holds the power of life and death around you, why are you deliberately poking her? Isn't that self destructive? You're no coward. It takes a lot to scare you, and Wells has done it. I'm not convinced this is just about academia and normal nastiness. Let me help you."

Monk thought about Wells's open threats. "I just can't tell you."

She saw the flicker of pain in Coopersmith's eyes.

She stood up and got so close to Coopersmith their bodies almost touched. "I'm not shutting you out. I just can't tell you—*yet*—what's going on. And I'm sorry I pushed you back. I don't like hurting you."

Coopersmith smiled ruefully, but her eyes were gentle, accepting and forgiving. "You're forgiven. I want to help you, though. I'm not sure what it is with Wells, but I think she's bad news, and you need to stay on guard around her." She paused, jaw working. "I don't like it when you get hurt. I don't like you getting the cane. I certainly don't think you deserved it for any of this."

Monk encircled Coopersmith in her arms and pulled her in until Coopersmith's head rested against her chest. "I know you want to help me, but it's not time. Please, just for me, please be careful around Wells. You're right—that woman is a whole mess of trouble."

Coopersmith nodded. "I'll wait for you this afternoon. I'll give you a lift home."

Monk nodded. "Thanks, Mitch."

She felt Coopersmith melt in her arms, felt her arms tighten around her, felt her sigh. Monk bit her lip to swallow a yelp of pain.

Her resolve to beat Wells increased, as did her sinking heart. She could hear a clock ticking inside her head, a countdown to her own death.

"Monk?" Jackie asked, raising her voice to over the lunchtime crowd of juniors playing with a tennis ball.

Monk stopped walking. "Hi, Jackie."

Jackie jogged up to her, neatly avoiding a girl running down the hallway toward the staff room.

"What's the matter?" she asked without preamble. "You're wearing your jumper, and it's too hot for that." She eyed Monk. "What did Wells do to you?"

Monk sighed. "I got the cane."

"What?" Jackie pulled Monk's shirt away from her back before she could protest. "Jesus. You're hurt."

"So everyone keeps telling me." Monk gently pulled the shirt out of Jackie's grasp. "I'm okay. I'm just tired."

Jackie grabbed her by the wrist. "No. This is more than I can handle."

Monk nodded, feeling drained. She couldn't look Jackie in the eye. "Well, our trip to the library is off for this afternoon, anyway. I guess we can go tomorrow."

"That's not what I meant."

"It's all right," Monk said, gently squeezing her arm and smiling at her. "Don't worry about it. I can handle this stuff pretty well."

"I can't let you do that."

"You have to," Monk said. "Please. You have to stay with Kilkenny and you have to stay out where people can see you. It's safest there."

Jackie looked at her curiously. "Why? Something happened to you, didn't it? What? What did Wells say to you?"

"Nothing," Monk said, trying not to fidget under Jackie's gaze. "Nothing happened. Don't worry about me. Worry about Kilkenny." She was quiet for a moment. "Last night. Did you dream?"

"Yeah," Kilkenny said, coming up behind them. "We both did." She met Monk's eyes. "Where were you? I tried to call you like I did for the beach dream but I couldn't get you."

"I don't know," Monk said. "I don't have control over my dreams like you do. I wasn't even aware you called me at all the other night."

Kilkenny nodded. "Well, I tried last night. I couldn't find you."

"Okay," Monk said. "Maybe you made a mistake when you called for me?"

Kilkenny shook her head. "No. I can feel how to do it."

"All right," Monk said. "Can you keep everyone safe in your dreams?"

Kilkenny nodded. "Uh, huh."

"Can you keep doing that for me?" Monk asked. "And make sure . . ." She trailed off as she bit her tongue. She felt a cold sweat. She wanted to talk about Coopersmith and Warland.

"Make sure what?" Kilkenny asked.

The memory of Lightman's scratched stomach surfaced, and Monk flinched. "Coopersmith. Warland. Kilkenny, please."

Kilkenny nodded. "I will."

"Thanks," Monk said. A wave of panic started to overwhelm her, and she pushed it back. *This is what I chose. I can do this. I can do this*, her mind chanted, driving away the nagging voices in the back of her head.

"Kilkenny?" Jackie asked, dragging Monk back to earth.

"Yeah?"

"Monk's back. It's hurt. Can you—?"

Kilkenny watched them both for a moment and then nodded. "I think so." She stepped toward Monk. "Hold still." She held out her arms and slipped into an embrace before Monk could react. She closed her eyes and buried her face against Monk's chest. Monk felt heat under Kilkenny's hands and warm tingling in her back. The ache slowed and stopped.

"Did you just do what I think you did?" Monk asked, pulling back and eyeing Kilkenny.

Kilkenny watched her warily for a moment, and then nodded.

"Thank you," Monk said. "From the bottom of my heart."

"You're welcome, Monk."

CHAPTER SIX

The day passed at its normal pace, which seemed far too quickly for Monk's comfort. Last period ended, and it was finally time for her detention with Wells. She hadn't seen Lightman since the morning, so hadn't been able to tell her about her after school detention with Wells, effectively canceling their trip to the library.

She quickly made her way down to the science labs. Thick, fluffy, dark gray clouds joined in a huge blanket of threatening gloom that covered the already darkening sky, the sign of an impending thunderstorm.

She stood in the doorway to the empty science lab, blinking uncertainly. She turned and crashed into Wells, who shoved her back with breathtaking speed.

"As usual, Therese, you're late."

Monk bit back her denial.

"Go inside." Wells pointed into the lab, and Monk walked in. She could feel Wells's odd, yellow eyes boring into her back.

She went to her accustomed seat and sat down. Her hands trembled, and she clasped them together on the bench top to hide it. She expected Wells to tense and spring on her.

Wells strode into to the room instead and dropped her books onto the front bench. She gazed at Monk.

"You would think," she began, almost reflectively, "that you've been on enough of these things to know what the drill is. Get out some paper and start doing lines."

A wave of unreality washed over Monk. *Why the bloody fuck are we talking about lines when the last time she came near me she told me she was going to kill me? And why the hell am I about to pander to her?* "Why don't you just let me do my homework? I'm not twelve."

"You may as well be. No, I'm not going to let you do your homework. That would hardly be punishment, would it?"

Monk opened her mouth, despite her brain screaming warnings at her to stop. "Why the hell are we even doing this? It's already punishment enough being stuck in this room with you. Okay, so what do you want me to write?"

Wells glared at her. She ignored Monk's comment and gave her an appraising look. She turned to the black board and grabbed a piece of chalk.

I will not be rude to my elders and betters, she wrote with a flourish.

Monk dropped her pen onto her open folder.

"This is ridiculous. I'm not writing that." Monk shook her head. The unreality of the situation washed over her in cold waves, and she couldn't stand it anymore. "You know, Wells, I'm starting to get a little fed up with this. You've already told me you're going to kill me. This is fucking crazy. Why the fuck are we doing this?"

"Stop cursing. We have to observe the forms of school life, Therese."

Monk folded her arms and leaned forward on the bench. Her temper flared almost beyond her control. She wanted to launch herself and pummel Wells.

"I'm not really sure why we're observing the forms of school life, not that I even know what the hell that actually means. Why can't we just have it out now? What are you hoping to achieve? You can walk out of here, me bleeding and broken, and just be done with it. Although, I'm not sure it'd be me that was bleeding and broken."

"You really are a complete moron, aren't you? No matter what, Monkhouse, I'm a teacher, and I'm giving you a lesson you'll never forget." Wells smirked and pursed her lips. "It'll be you bleeding and broken." Her eyes flared an unsettling yellow. "Or should I go after Coopersmith first? You're in love with her, aren't you?"

"You're no teacher. Of anything." Monk clenched her fists and forcibly relaxed them. "Drop it. *All* of it. You already told me my neck is on the chopping block first."

"So you *are* in love with Coopersmith."

Monk clamped her jaw shut. *Fuck.*

"Well, she is *very* lovely to look at," Wells mused. "Wonder if she tastes as good as she looks?"

Monk felt sick and struggled to hide it.

There was a low rumble of thunder from outside.

Monk stood up. "How about we end this right now?" She took a step toward Wells.

Wells's eyes flared bright, bile yellow, and Monk felt her blood turn to ice.

"Sure. Now is good." Wells took a step forward, one foot on the teacher's bench, her step up unnatural and stomach turning.

"Grow a brain, bitch," Monk said, amazed she sounded as angry as she did, when on the inside she was really weeping. "Not right at this second in time. I mean, stop fucking around and just get it over with."

"All right, Therese. Time?"

"At a time of your choosing."

They heard the sound of footsteps in the prep room, heading toward the lab. The door opened. Monk glanced at the door and started when Wells, not an inch from her, watched her with baleful eyes.

Mrs. Wright, the science coordinator, stuck her graying head in the doorway.

"Ah! Miss Wells," she said. "I didn't realize you were still here. I thought the lab was empty."

"Miss Monkhouse and I were just leaving." Wells took a step back and gave Monk a smile that did not touch her eyes. "I'll see you tomorrow in class, Miss Monkhouse."

Monk inclined her head, eyes hot and angry. "Certainly, Miss Wells. Have a good evening, now." She turned to the science coordinator. "'Bye, Mrs. Wright."

"Oh, I will," Wells said. "You too, Monkhouse. Pleasant dreams."

"See you tomorrow, Monk," the science coordinator said cheerfully, seemingly oblivious of the tension pervading the lab.

Monk nodded and left as the first drops of rain hurtled down from the clouds.

Monk walked through the driving rain to where Coopersmith normally parked her car. She couldn't see it. She frowned. It was completely unlike Coopersmith to leave her without telling her something had come up. A surge of panic bubbled up, and she fought it down. Her mind helpfully supplied her with images of Coopersmith and Wells, and her insides twisted.

Coopersmith would *never* have voluntarily left her standing there.

Something had to be wrong. It would certainly explain Wells's gloating. Her question to Monk of whether or not she was in love with

Coopersmith rang in her ears. No one needed to know the answer to that question, least of all Coopersmith.

Monk knew it would be too late, but she decided to walk past Coopersmith's home. She had to check. She had to *know*.

She started the thirty minute walk toward Coopersmith's flat. She wanted to think about what she had read in her aborted attempt at the library. She did not want to think about what Coopersmith not waiting for her possibly meant.

She tried to concentrate, but the only thing she could focus on was the feel of Coopersmith in her arms at lunch, and Jackie's pale and grim face. She wondered what had happened to Lightman. Had Wells gotten her?

She found herself at the end of Coopersmith's street and wondered what she'd find. Would she see the lights on in Coopersmith's corner unit? Or would she not be home?

Monk felt chilled to the bone, and not just from the cold rain soaking through her clothing.

She walked up the street, each step a millstone. She came to a halt in front of Coopersmith's building, feeling like a troublesome, unwanted interloper.

She stood in the shadows, scanning the corner of the building. Her shoulders sagged with relief. Coopersmith's living room light was on, her balcony door partially open.

The front doors of the building opened, and she almost dismissed the indistinct voices drifting toward her on the cold night air.

She looked at the square of light in the entrance and blinked.

Coopersmith stood in the entrance with Warland. They were laughing over something, standing too close for Monk's comfort. She felt as though her heart shattered into a million pieces when Coopersmith slid into Warland's arms and received a kiss for her troubles.

Monk tried to shove aside the pain. Coopersmith was her friend. That was as far as it went for her. Coopersmith would *never* look at her that way, and the sooner she faced the fact that her fantasy *was* a fantasy the better off she—*everyone*—would be.

Monk shivered and slipped back into the darkness, clutching her soaked jumper closer to her body.

Monk finally walked through the front door of her parents' house at around ten-thirty that night. The hair on the back of her neck stood on end, and her muscles tensed up.

The house was in darkness. There was no sign of her father or Jean. A lone figure sat in the living room, and the television was off. One light pooled on the ceiling, and in it, Monk saw the thick, cloying shadow of her mother.

Slowly, with effort, her mother got to her feet. She was a good six inches shorter than Monk, middle aged, with a stern, harsh face creased in hard lines. One hand held the sheet of crumpled paper, the other hand clenched into a fist, and then unclenched. Her faded, greenish-gray eyes blazed with rage, and a baseball bat lay close by.

At that moment, her mother seemed seven feet tall, and it took all of Monk's courage to stay put and not run from the house. She had a fleeting image of Coopersmith, but pushed it to one side. Her beloved friend couldn't help her now.

Her mother's eyes burned with rage. "You know what this is, don't you?" She held up the paper. "Therese, you are an arsehole."

Monk saw the letterhead, the neat, horribly familiar signature, and knew exactly what it was. Sister Constance had sent home notification of the detention.

Monk nodded. She tensed, so close to tears she could taste them in the back of her aching throat. She hated herself for her inability to stand up to her mother.

Her mother stared at Monk with contempt. "I would ask you what happened, but I know you'd lie to me. You always do. You couldn't admit the truth if your life depended on it. All you care about is how you can blame your own actions on other people."

"No I don't. I don't lie."

"Shut up. I'm not interested in anything you have to say." Her mother took a step closer, knuckles going white.

Monk stepped back.

"Don't you walk away from me, you stupid bitch. Stay put," her mother said.

Monk froze.

"I'm your mother so I have a mother's love for you, but I don't like you. I hate you. You're a major embarrassment and disappointment to your father and I. Why couldn't you have come out more like your older sister? She has the best qualities of your father and I. She's everything, and you're nothing. This proves it." She waved the paper, and Monk took another step closer. "You can't even make it through your last year of school without throwing a temper tantrum. You can't even be nice to something as harmless as an old nun, you stupid, fucking coward!" She swung her fist at Monk.

Monk leapt back, but the blow connected solidly with her stomach. The air left her lungs with a whoosh. "I didn't—"

Her mother slapped Monk's face. Monk put her hand to her cheek.

Her mother's fist connected with Monk's other side. Monk yelped and doubled over. Her mother shoved her back with surprising strength.

"Shut your stupid, fucking trap. I don't want to hear another word out of you. You will go to detention and you will come straight home afterwards. I want you in this house where I can see you." She punctuated this with another swing of her fist.

Monk yelped as it hit her dead center. She stumbled.

"You really thought no one would tell me about this?" her mother asked. "You have no friends. I have lots. No one likes you. Everyone likes me. That means you can't hide anything from me. Even if that weren't true, you're too transparent and shallow. You're too dumb to hide anything from anyone." She ground out between blows.

Monk tried to dodge as many of the hits as she could, but the pain finally brought her to her knees. The fight went out of her, and she curled up on the dusty, threadbare carpet.

All she could think about was Coopersmith, her long, warm, loving arms and sweet nature. She wanted her beloved Mitch to hold her and tell her it would be all right. She waited until her mother tired of her and left her lying on the living room floor.

Monk slowly and painfully climbed to her feet, swaying back and forth, as black flowers mushroomed before her vision.

She couldn't stay there.

She didn't want to think about the truth behind any of her mother's words.

She scooped up her backpack, unsure she was ever going to return. She snuck out of the house as quietly as possible. She half expected to feel her mother's hard hand land on her shoulder squeezing mercilessly and pulling her back. She clumsily ran down the front path and out onto the road.

She stood in the center of it, on the lane markings, her head bowed as she tried to think of what to do next.

She didn't know Jackie's or Lightman's addresses. Fletch and her other school acquaintances were not good enough friends to put her up for the night.

Her only option was Coopersmith.

One night. She could last for one night.

She walked toward Coopersmith's unit, cursing herself for her weakness.

Her mother's voice echoed in her mind, *You have no friends. No one likes you. You're too transparent and shallow. You're too dumb to hide anything from anyone.*

Christ. Why did Mum have to say that? Now I can't stop wondering how true it is. I don't know what to think. I hate the way she makes me feel. I hate the way she talks to me. I hate the way she calls me names all the time. I'm afraid of her, and I don't know how not to be! Shit!

An hour later she sagged against the front intercom and pushed the button for Coopersmith's unit.

"Hello?" came Coopersmith's cool, disembodied voice a moment later.

Monk felt relief flood her system, despite herself, and forced back tears.

"Hi, Mitch?" she said softly.

"Monk?" Coopersmith asked, sounding concerned. "What are you—? Look, come on up."

The front door buzzed, and Monk let herself in. She left the elevator and saw Coopersmith down the hall waiting for her. Monk walked toward her, trying not to flinch.

"Monk?" Coopersmith asked.

Monk stopped in front of her. Her chest hurt, her back hurt, and her heart hurt.

"Mitch," she said.

"Come in." Coopersmith quickly pulled Monk into her unit. "Are you all right?"

Monk shook her head. "I'm tired. Can I crash here tonight?"

Coopersmith studied her, concern lurking in her green eyes. "You know you can." She hesitantly reached out to touch Monk's cheek.

Monk flinched, and a bitter tear crawled down her face.

Coopersmith faltered and pulled Monk into her arms.

Monk struggled against her briefly, and then her reserve broke as

Coopersmith tightened her arms. She cried silent tears, soaking the front of Coopersmith's tee shirt.

"What happened to you?" Coopersmith asked when Monk quieted.

"My mother," Monk said. "Sister Constance sent a note home."

"No, Monk," Coopersmith moaned. "She didn't, did she?"

Monk nibbled her lip and remained silent. She felt Coopersmith pull up her shirt, heard her hissing intake of breath.

"No," Coopersmith said. "God, no."

"Mitch," Monk said. "Please. I don't want to be alone. I'm afraid."

Coopersmith nodded. She took Monk's hand and led her into the master bedroom. She lay on the bed, pulled Monk into her arms, and gently stroked her hair as the tears came again.

Coopersmith's breathing eventually deepened and evened out as she fell asleep. She held Monk in her arms, but Monk could not sleep, despite her exhaustion. She felt empty, and although she was in the one place she had always dreamed of being in, she felt alone and isolated.

Monk arose just past dawn and gently disentangled herself from Coopersmith's arms. Her eyes felt gritty and burned. Her head and chest hurt and the bruising on her battered body ached abominably.

She leaned over and smoothed Coopersmith's hair off her forehead, leant over and gently kissed her cheek.

She pulled on her shoes and slipped out of Coopersmith's unit. She wanted to go back to her parents' house so she could shower and change. She would go to school and check on Kilkenny.

After that, she would hunt Wells.

She walked down the road, exhausted and hungry, barely aware of the car that pulled up beside her. The window went down and a puzzled face appeared.

"Monk? My God, Monk? Is that you? Where the hell you been, mate?"

Monk looked at Lightman. "I could ask you the same question."

Lightman pursed her lips and put the car in neutral. "Get in. We're skipping it today while you tell me what's wrong."

Monk mechanically walked to Lightman's car, opened the door, and got in.

Lightman took off in a spray of gravel in the quiet street. She kept driving, heading, it seemed, toward nowhere at all.

Monk tried to collect her scattered thoughts and shattered heart.

Lightman glanced at her. "C'mon. Spill. What's the problem?"

"I'm having an amazingly horrible morning." Monk shielded her face with her hands as she sobbed. She felt the car veer off to the left, slow down, and stop. Lightman shifted in the driver's seat and pulled Monk into her arms.

"What's the matter? Just tell me. What happened to make this morning so bad?"

"You know I told you about the most wonderful woman on the face of the planet? Well, it seems she's not so wonderful after all."

Lightman nodded. "Okay, let me see if I can get this. She's an older woman, isn't she? You told her you loved her, and she brushed you aside, telling you that you have a crush on her?"

"No. It's not that. I just ignored something, and it came back to bite me, that's all."

"She loves you or she doesn't? And she's older or not?"

"She's not in love with me. Yes, she's older."

"It's Coopersmith, isn't it? I've seen you with her."

Monk said nothing. No matter what had happened, she would not betray Coopersmith.

Lightman looked at her carefully. "It *is* her, isn't it?"

Monk remained expressionless for as long as she was able, hoping that Lightman would not see her trembling. After another moment or so of scrutiny, Lightman leaned back apparently satisfied with whatever it was she thought she had seen.

"I won't tell. You don't need to worry about that."

Monk tried to relax a little, but couldn't.

Lightman sighed. "Don't worry about your lady love. You probably just misread how deep your friendship is with her, and if it could develop into something more. It's not a big deal. You just have to gain some independence and learn not to lean on her so hard."

Monk thought of a life without Coopersmith and felt empty. It seemed she craved Coopersmith's attention so much that she had no life outside of her. It was a horrible feeling.

Lightman nodded. "Yes, that's right. You hang around with people your own age for a while. Take advantage of the friendship I'm offering you. Stay with me for a few days to get away from it all. You're in other trouble, aren't you?"

"How did you know?"

"I'm not blind. I can see the bruising on your body. What happened to you?"

"My mother beat the crap out of me."

Lightman shot Monk an enraged look. "Now that was pretty un-fucking-called for, wasn't it? You wanted to go with your beloved for a while, didn't you? You were hoping something more would happen, didn't you?"

"No," Monk moaned. "That's not it. I just saw something I wasn't ready to see, that's all."

Lightman grimaced. "That's a bitch, isn't it?"

Monk nodded. "It is." She glanced at Lightman. "What happened to you yesterday? We were supposed to go after Wells."

"I'm sorry. My mother happened. She dragged me home."

"Fuck," Monk muttered. "Don't you realize that there are lives at stake here? Wells is zeroing in on me. I have to know what she is so I can fight her. This is all totally screwed up."

"Look," Lightman said. "How about we do that today? Not this evening—today. We'll go back to my place, you can grab a shower, and we can plan out how we're going to go after her. All right?"

Monk nodded. "All right."

"Good," Lightman said as she pulled out into the traffic again.

Monk was amazed by Lightman's house. It looked as though it had been finished yesterday, and was still waiting for someone to move into it. The brickwork was white, neat, and clean, with impeccable, dark cement holding each brick perfectly in place; the front path was perfectly smooth and the windows sparkled. Even the gardens looked as though they were out of the centerfold of a landscaping magazine. A spray of immaculate white gravel sheltered neatly weeded, flourishing garden beds out the front, all of it nestled in freshly mowed, rich, green lawn.

Lightman pulled up into the white-painted garage. The concrete floor was scrupulously clean, and she shut off the engine with a flourish.

Next to them was a snowy white car gleaming under a new coat of thick polish.

Lightman groaned. "Gawd help us. My mother is home."

Monk looked down at her school uniform and sighed. There was no hiding that they were cutting class.

Lightman grinned, as though reading her thoughts. "Relax, will you? I can handle my own mother. She's not going to give you any kind of shit, and she won't tell anyone you're here."

"Really?" Monk asked sarcastically.

Lightman laughed. "Yeah, really."

She led the reluctant Monk into the house by the garage door and into the living room. A figure sat in a pristine, white leather lounge in the middle of the white carpeted, sunken room.

"Hi, Mum," Lightman said cheerfully, bounding down the stairs, two at a time. "I've brought a friend with me."

Monk had honestly thought her day couldn't get any worse, but in one swift, clawing stroke, she realized she was wrong.

More importantly, she realized she was trapped.

Wells got up off the sofa and stared coldly at Monk. Her eyes faded away from light brown to a definite shade of yellow, the color of bile.

Monk stared at the smirking Lightman, who stood watching her, arms crossed.

"Please don't tell me this is your mother." A slow moving sense of horror began to crash over her, an unstoppable wave.

Lightman stared at her, eyes flaring red. "Not exactly my mum, are you, you fucking bitch?"

"Watch your mouth, Vanessa." Wells flashed her horrible yellow eyes at Lightman.

Monk felt the strength go out of her knees, and she fell, staring intently at them.

"Watch yours, hag."

Wells casually reached out and hurled Lightman across the room with shocking strength. Lightman crashed into the far wall with a bone-shattering crunch and fell in a wretched heap onto the carpet. She lay still.

Wells folded her arms and stood over Monk.

"Ah, Monk. We have a lot to talk about. I think you know what about. How's unfaithful, tasty, sexy little Mitch and her big, bad, fuck toy Warland? Does it bother you that she cheated on you? She did, didn't she?"

Monk gasped and flinched. Wells grinned.

"How's it feel to know they're fucking each other's brains out? And that Coopersmith's never going to fuck yours out?"

"Miss Coopersmith is *not* my lover or my girlfriend. Leave both of them out of this," Monk said in cold, clipped tones.

"At a time and place of my choosing, remember? I choose here and now."

Wells leaned toward her, and Monk, despite herself, shrank back from her blazing, yellow eyes.

She grabbed the lapels of Monk's blouse and pulled her forward.

Lightman staggered up behind Wells, holding a large, blunt, silver candlestick. She brought it down on the back of Wells's head with all her might. Wells went limp and released Monk, who scrambled out of the way of her falling body.

"What the fuck?" Monk asked, staring suspiciously at Lightman.

"Come with me. She's going to kill you as soon as she wakes up if you don't." Lightman held out her hand, eyes flaring red for a moment as she swayed. "Hurry. She won't be out for long."

"Why the hell should I trust you? Got some alligators in the basement that need my body for food?"

"No, no basement. Yes, I'm her familiar. Yes, I'm bound to do as she tells me to, we're bonded. No, I don't like her. Yes, I want to get rid her. Yes, I want you to stay alive. I need you to help me."

"You still haven't answered my question, even though I rather like the killing her bit."

"I'm more human than she is, but not really anymore. I still feel. I do actually care about you, Monk. I want you to live. You shouldn't be a snack for a scum sucking bottom dweller like *that* fucking bitch. I'm your only chance to get out of this alive."

"Why do you want me to live? I thought you wanted her to feed off me?"

Lightman shook her head, eyes flaring a brighter red. "No, my dear. I want her gone. I hate her. I loathe her. I despise her," she said with a hint of impatience. "I need help. Yours. It's a two person job, and we both seem to be headed in the same direction. Now, time's running out. Make your choice. Life with me or death with her. Which will it be?"

Monk didn't have time to think it through. She took Lightman's hand and allowed her to drag her to her feet. Before she could move out of the way, Wells stirred. Her eyes barely opened, and she exploded into motion. She grabbed Monk and tossed her across the room. She crashed into the wall with a bone-jarring thump and slid to the white carpet, out cold.

CHAPTER SEVEN

Monk opened her eyes and was aware of two things: her wrists were bound, and she was lying on a soft surface she idly identified as a bed. She could feel someone watching her.

She jerked and tried to sit up, straining against the overly tight ropes around her wrists.

The figure was instantly by her side and pushed her back down and roughly rolled her over. "Easy, Monk. I'm going to untie you."

Monk groaned as she felt her ribs grind together. "Why?" she grunted. "Why did you go to the trouble of tying me up if you're just going to untie me again?"

"I was told to tie you up." Lightman grunted, and Monk felt more tugging on her wrists as Lightman loosened the knots.

Monk gave the ghost of a grin. "Do you always do what you're told?"

The tugging faltered, and Lightman let out a deep, inhuman growl. Monk found herself held up by the lapels of her shirt. Lightman's eyes flared red, unnerving Monk, her jaw tense as she ground her teeth.

"Don't mock me, or I will kill you myself."

Monk growled back at her, sounding much weaker than Lightman. "How is that any different to what's happening to me with Wells?"

"I don't want to kill you, but I will if you annoy me enough." Lightman's eyes flared a brighter red, and she threw Monk back down onto the bed.

Monk slowly sat up, heart hammering, rubbing her raw wrists. "Tell me more. What's the deal with you and Wells? What the hell are you both?"

Lightman sat down on the bed opposite Monk and closed her eyes. Monk watched her with curiosity, trying to regain her sense of control.

After a moment, Lightman's eyes opened, and they were a blessed, wild brown again. "Wells is a shape-shifter, more commonly referred to as a werewolf. I'm her helper. We are normally called familiars, but that's not really right. Familiars belong to vampires, and Wells isn't a vampire. A familiar, for a werewolf, is someone who has an empathic bond to a werewolf. The bond is not something that just happens, it's something that both parties must agree to. I am virtually her slave because of it."

Monk shook her head. "That doesn't fully answer my question. First, Wells is a werewolf, so she's obviously not human. What about you? Are you human or are you something else as well?"

"I'm something else. I'm not alive by human standards, nor am I a shape-shifter. Plus, I'm not insane. Wells is."

"You mentioned something before about killing Wells? What's that all about? How? And the most important question of all, what the hell are you both doing here? Surely you should be in some forest in Transylvania feasting on unsuspecting travelers who've guzzled too much Paprika-laced gruel at the local inn?"

"We move around, and Wells just wanted to stop here for a while," Lightman replied. "She wasn't expecting to find another werewolf here, but now that she has she wants some fun."

"You're talking about Kilkenny Sharp, aren't you?" She sighed. "Wells can control other people. Is she telepathic?"

Lightman gave her a rueful grin. "What she uses to control humans is not really telepathy, it's a bond. She can control humans through a kind of shapeshifter bond."

"What's that?" Monk asked.

"I don't fully understand it. All I know is that she and I have one to each other. I can feel I'm on the receiving end of an empathic link. I am compelled to do what Wells tells me to do. If I don't, I get . . . punished." Lightman's eyes flickered. She looked carefully at Monk. "Wells can also control dreams. She uses them to break people down so they're easier to manipulate."

Monk shuddered, vaguely recalling some shocking nightmares involving Coopersmith and a lot of blood. "Why bother with the dreams thing? If she's as powerful as she likes people to think, why doesn't she just go rushing in with fangs bared?"

Lightman snorted. "She's not the same species as you. Shape-shifters are not necessarily cruel and vicious except with each other, and murder is not a biological imperative. Wells kills humans, slowly and viciously, because she's insane. You drew her attention because you're standing in the way of her reaching Kilkenny. You see through her, and she doesn't like that."

Monk felt revolted. "She hated me from the get go. I don't particularly want her to kill either of us."

Lightman grinned outright, and her eyes flared a faint red again. "You're a walking corpse, Monk, and you have been since she first laid eyes on you. That is, unless you want to help me and get rid of her."

Monk shrank back, palms sweating, metallic taste of fear in her mouth. "Given that's the only way I'm going to get out of this alive, yes, I'll help you. I also don't like the idea of that obnoxious bitch snacking on human beings."

"Wells is seriously insane. I had hoped that I was wrong, but she's killing because she can, not for self defense." Lightman sighed, eyes misted with memory. "She was a gentle, wonderful lover when we first met. I want to do this to honor the woman I once loved more than anyone else in the world."

"She's seriously insane?"

Lightman nodded and leaned forward, beseeching. "I can't do this. It's driving me mad, slowly, just as mad as she is."

Monk remained poker faced, despite her loathing. "Let's go back to something else. Why don't you do this yourself? Why do you need me to help you?"

"Wells and I are tangled together. If I die, she dies. If she dies, I die. She's insane so I'm not sure that she isn't just going to kill me, regardless of the consequences to herself. I need someone to help me to make sure that if I go she goes quickly and doesn't take anyone with her."

Monk started, palms sweating, and turned her horrified groan into a cough. Lightman looked at her curiously, and Monk slapped her chest, looking apologetic. "Okay. So far, so good. I have another question for you. What's the deal with Sister Constance and Angela Michaels? They're a pair of psychos. They're more nasty and annoying than they ever were."

"They're one of those side effects that you get in these situations."

Monk felt sick. "Side effect?" Her temper slipped. "What the fuck do you mean by side effect?" she asked, gritting her teeth.

"Wells causes nightmares, you know that. Well, Sister Constance is a twisted fuck who's gotten them worse than other people. Michaels isn't that much different. She's been playing with them both since they respond so well to the images she sends them. The more control she has over Sister Constance, the more she can play with the other humans in the school without interference."

"Goddamn fucking hell," Monk muttered. She gave Lightman a cold look, her decision made. "How the fuck are we going to get rid of her?"

Lightman smiled approvingly. "Now that's what I like to hear. We're going to stick with the traditional method of silver."

"Ah. Now we come to another, considerably more interesting question. How do I know you're not Wells?"

Lightman gave her an admonishing look. "I'm a red eyes. You've seen that. Wells is a golden eyes." Her eyes flared red to underscore the point.

"So she can't change the color of her eyes?"

"Nope. When her eyes go they're always golden, never red."

"Why the color change anyway?"

"I don't know. It's just in our nature."

Monk nodded. "When do you want to do this?"

"We're going to have to move quickly. Wells is going to kill you in the next day or so. The length of your remaining life will be measured by how much entertainment you provide her with."

Monk felt sick, and swallowed bile. She closed her eyes to hide her swift bolt of terror from Lightman.

Lightman tensed as heavy footsteps sounded on the stairs. "Trust me. Are you in or out?"

Monk opened her eyes. "I'm in."

"Trust me. Just trust me." Lightman leaned forward.

Monk's eyes widened as she saw Lightman's fist coming at her, and she tried to shrink back, but the blow hit her jaw, and she sagged back on the bed.

Monk opened her eyes, disorientated and in almost total darkness.

"It awakes," Wells said coldly.

Monk zeroed in on the deeply shadowed corner of the room and felt her heart sink. "Why can't you just fucking kill me and be done with it?"

"No, I don't think so," Wells said. "If I kill you now, you've learnt nothing." Her eyes glowed yellow as she emerged from the darkness.

She sat down on the bed beside Monk. "In the final analysis, this little sacrifice you're making for Kilkenny means exactly nothing. Kilkenny will die, and that fact people will remember, not your sacrifice to save her. Your life means nothing, and you don't matter."

Monk tensed her jaw.

"You disagree?" Wells asked conversationally. "Well, Therese, the thing about you and idiots like you, is that you think everyone thinks like you do. You're wrong. It's all about deceit. Most humans aren't noble beings. They're mindless animals who really only look out for themselves, despite grand words to the contrary. You've painted yourself into a corner with me, and I can guarantee you, you're doing it for no good reason."

"You're a lying bitch, Wells."

"Really?" Wells asked. "You want to put that to the test?" She snorted. "You're in love with Coopersmith. You think she feels the same toward you, but you'd be wrong. Very wrong. She doesn't. She doesn't love you, Monkhouse. Nobody could. She'd probably be amused by your feelings for her. If I'm right, though, she'll lie to you and say yes she loves you so your love can die a romantic death, and she can spend her life pining for you. If I'm wrong, she'll tell you the unvarnished truth—you are as unlovable as they come."

A small spark of fear ignited inside Monk. She already knew the answer to the question. "Fuck up and die, Wells," she said, but without her normal heat.

"You want to put it to the test, hmm? You want to find out how much your friends think like you?" Wells asked. "How about a small wager between predator and prey?"

No matter what happens here, I've lost. I'm finished. Monk nodded. "We'll see who's right."

"All right," Wells said. She gave a cold smile. "How about this? I'll drive you to your friends myself. Let's find out if I'm right or wrong. If I'm right, they'll lie to you. Your friends are all like you, and live in castles in the air. I'll kill you so your fantasy world stays intact, and you get to be a martyr for them. I'll kill them all so they can go down in romantic flames. If I'm wrong, they'll tell you the truth. They won't hold back to spare you. I'll kill you and let your friends go. It doesn't matter whether they live or die. They're not really your friends so it shouldn't matter to you anymore."

"I die either way? What kind of bet is that?"

"Moron. The point isn't your miserable life, it's whether or not you die a death no one will remember with your secrets intact—you win—or you die exposed and humiliated—I win."

Monk nodded. She had already won and felt at peace. "Bring it on, Wells." She knew exactly what she would say to Coopersmith and what the answer would be. She would be humiliated but it didn't matter. Only Coopersmith, Warland, Jackie, and Kilkenny mattered, and they would be safe.

Wells nodded and gestured toward Lightman. "Let's go."

Wells pulled up in front of the school and leaned toward Monk, eyes bright, bile yellow. "Don't try to run."

"Why? You going to kill me if I do?" Monk asked, trying to muster a spark of defiance.

Wells smiled. "No. Not you. Your friends. Run, and I'll go after them first."

"You're a fucking bitch."

Wells laughed. "Whatever you say, Therese." She got out of the car and gestured for Monk to walk ahead of her.

Monk made her way into the school and stopped as she felt Well's strong hand on her bicep, pulling her to a halt. She turned to her. "Why are we stopping?"

Wells pointed over her shoulder.

Lightman strode toward them, Warland in tow. Kilkenny walked directly behind her, face pale. Warland stopped close to Monk.

"Problem, Monk?" Warland asked, pointedly glancing at Wells.

Monk tried to swallow the lump in her throat. She shook her head and blinked away tears.

Warland studied her closely, but Monk was looking at Kilkenny. The girl looked terrified and clutched the back of Warland's shirt. She raised her eyebrows in question. Monk tightened her mouth, and she fought to remain expressionless.

"Sit down, Warland," Wells said coldly.

"Pardon?" Warland asked, crossing her arms and glaring at Wells.

"Go away," Wells said, clearly and distinctly. Her eyes began to lighten.

Kilkenny eyes widened. She grabbed the back of Warland's shirt and tugged for all she was worth.

Warland glanced at her, annoyed, and turned back to Monk and

Wells. Her eyebrows shot skyward, and she took an involuntary step back at Wells's now bile yellow eyes.

Monk crossed her arms and jerked her chin toward the seats.

Just at that moment, Lightman jogged down the stairs toward the science area. Coopersmith strode behind her, looking annoyed. She faltered when she saw Monk standing by Wells. She glanced at Warland heading toward her, and Monk felt her heart twist.

Monk took a step toward them and glared at Wells. "A bit of privacy, please."

"Oh, no," Wells said. "I don't want to miss this. Besides, how am I going to tell who's won?"

Monk gasped as she felt an icy hand invade her mind, and a cold ball of hatred settled inside her. It was Wells.

She cringed and braced herself. Humiliation was a small price to pay for everyone's continuing life, she reminded herself. "Have it your way, you sadistic fuck."

Wells laughed.

Monk took a step forward out of Wells's earshot and gestured for Coopersmith.

Coopersmith stared at them warily. "Monk?" she asked, casting baleful glances at the smirking Wells.

Monk coughed, clutching her aching chest.

"I have something to say to you, Mitch," she said softly. "Look at me, only me, and this will go easier."

Coopersmith frowned. "All right."

"What happened to you yesterday? You said you were going to pick me up but when I walked past your house I saw you with Terri? I don't blame you for being interested in her. She's absolutely beautiful."

Coopersmith's mouth tightened. "This isn't a conversation we should be having right here and now." She stared pointedly at Wells.

"We have to," she said. "There's never a better time than right now." She met Coopersmith's eyes, feeling as though glass shards were shredding her insides. "I have some things I need to say to you and I need you to let me say them. Can you do that?"

Coopersmith stared at her expressionless for a moment, and then nodded warily.

"I saw Terri at your place last night, and I got jealous. I always thought there was something between us, something more than friendship, and that you felt it too. I now know that was wrong. But I still love you, Michelle, with all my heart and soul. I can't stop it. You're the first thing I think of in the morning and the last thing at night. I love the way you think, the way you feel, and the way you make me feel." She nibbled her lip and forced herself to continue. "I need to know if you feel the same way about me? Do you have feelings for me?" She held Coopersmith's gaze, but Coopersmith remained expressionless and silent.

Monk could not draw strength from her presence no matter how much she wanted to do it. She felt empty. The pain of actually seeing Coopersmith's lack of reaction was worse than she had expected, and it took all of her self-control to stop her tears from falling.

Coopersmith's shoulders sagged, and she shook her head. "Why are you telling me this now?" Her eyes showed deep pain. "I can't do this. *We* can't do this. I'm your maths teacher, and you're my student." Her eyes began to tear. "God, why couldn't you at least have waited until we were alone? And above all, why did you do it in front of Wells?"

Monk reached out, wanting to touch her, but pulled her hand back and let it fall. "I just wanted you to know. I love you. I always will."

She turned back to Wells, before Coopersmith could respond. She felt as though her heart was in a million pieces. She wanted to cry but was too hurt for it. "You got your answer, you twisted fuck," she said, glaring at Wells. "Now let them go."

"Monk?" Coopersmith asked with a voice thick with tears. "What do you mean?"

Monk glanced at her. The sight of Coopersmith's tears tore something deep inside her. "Nothing, Mitch. Just go. Please." She turned back to the smirking Wells. "I'm going to go peacefully with you, Wells. You won."

Wells laughed. "Splendid."

"Monk," Coopersmith said sharply.

"Come with us," Kilkenny exclaimed.

"I can't, and you know it," Monk said. "Tell them." She glanced at the shell-shocked Jackie. "Tell them everything." She quickly turned away from them and wiped the tears from her eyes. She stopped in front of Wells. "I guess I'm yours."

Wells nodded. "Come with me."

Monk felt the ball of hatred in the corner of her mind slowly fade away as Wells withdrew.

They headed back toward the car, Wells on one side of Monk, Lightman on the other.

When they got back to Lightman's house, Wells slung Monk over a broad shoulder and brought her back to Lightman's room. She tossed Monk onto the bed and turned toward the silent Lightman.

"Tie her up again."

Lightman did as she was told, but did not tie the ropes as tightly as she had done the last time.

"So, Monkhouse. Satisfied?" Wells asked, folding her arms.

"Knock it off, I got the picture," Monk said coldly. She felt burnt out, and the place deep inside her that belonged to Coopersmith screamed in exquisite pain.

"She doesn't love you. She and Warland just feel sorry for you. You're nothing to them. Hell, you don't even rate high enough for you to call them friends."

Monk felt a surge of misery, but remained outwardly calm.

"I'll let you think about that," Wells said. "Me? I'm going to send all of you to sleep so we can have some fun."

"Let them go. If you do manage to kill me then you can go after them."

"No, I don't think so," Wells said. "I like this way better. It salts the meat."

Monk felt sick. She coughed to cover her moan and a bolt of pain ripped through her chest. She felt as though she were breathing underwater.

"Are you ready to do things my way and be a good little snack?" Wells asked.

"Are you going to let them all go?"

"Our agreement. Yes."

"Let them all go."

Wells stared at her for a long moment. "How are you going to know I held up my end of the bargain if I kill you first?"

Monk glared at her. "I have no idea if you're going to hold up your end of the bargain at all."

Wells smiled. "Your lives are all in my hands."

"You fucking bitch," Monk snarled. "I won the bet. If you claim moral superiority, why don't you just hold up your end of the bargain?"

"I don't claim moral superiority, prey. Just basic hunger." Wells leaned forward, eyes glittering. "To answer your question, no, I'm not going to let them live. I'm going to kill them. Nothing would give me more pleasure than to hold onto Coopersmith's beating heart after I ripped it out of her chest." She stared coldly at Monk. "I want you to be watching when I do it. I want to hear you scream in pain. I want you to see me do it over and over again in your mind, knowing you were too weak to stop me."

"Fuck you. I will kill you if it's the last thing I do."

"You don't have it in you to kill me," Wells said. "You're too much of a coward. You swagger too much. All talk and no action. You only do things to those weaker than you, the ones who can't fight back. You just don't have what it takes to hurt me. You want to try it? Come and take swing at me. Go on, I dare you." She held her arms out by her sides. "I *double* dare you."

Monk froze, staring at her. She could feel herself hesitate, felt the self-loathing when Wells laughed at her.

"See?" Wells said. "What did I tell you? You don't have a chance. I'm willing to bet I could disembowel all of your friends right in front of your face, and you'd find some way to rationalize it."

Monk shook her head and thought of Coopersmith. The blast of pain and misery that tore through her left her teary-eyed and shaking.

"Let's test the theory then, shall we?" Wells leaned forward, grabbed Monk's wrist, and pulled her across the bed with a casual strength that made Monk gasp.

Lightman leaned forward and held Monk down by the shoulders. Monk thrashed but Lightman sat on her stomach and held her in place.

Wells's eyes flared bile yellow, and she opened her jaws, revealing a sharp set of snowy white teeth that were almost tusks.

Monk thrashed as the jaws descended toward her wrist. Wells's grip remained iron, and Monk felt the wind of her breath on her soft skin. She watched, shaking, in a cold sweat, as Wells sank her sharp canines into her wrist.

Monk screamed as Wells snapped her jaws together and tore away a chunk of meat. Hot, molten agony flowed up Monk's arm as Wells convulsively swallowed. Soaked in hot, sticky blood, she grayed out.

Her cheek stung from a slap.

She opened her eyes. She was lying on a thick carpet in a

sumptuous drawing room full of rich, gilded furniture, polished wood, and expensive knick-knacks.

Wells sat comfortably on a luxurious antique sofa, looking down at her.

"Get up," she said coldly.

Monk's arm felt as though it was on fire between her wrist and her elbow, and the healed gouges on her chest throbbed dully in accompaniment.

Wells lashed out her foot and connected with Monk's ribs. Monk yelped, and Wells smiled. "I said, get up."

Monk slowly and awkwardly got to her knees with tears in her eyes. She was breathing heavily, and felt slightly nauseated. Her wrist still trickled blood and her hand was virtually useless. She tucked it against her school uniform, hissing in pain at the stinging sensation and hot throbbing of the open wound.

She turned at a sudden commotion behind her, and a large dog threw her against the edge of the sofa. She held out her hands to catch herself and yelped as her left arm collapsed underneath her. She fell awkwardly to her knees. She glimpsed Kilkenny behind her, moving toward her, shaking with fear.

Lightman leaned forward, grabbed Monk's good arm, and pulled her to her feet. She gave Lightman a puzzled look, and then glanced back at Kilkenny.

Kilkenny's complexion was milky, her eyes wide with terror.

"Monk," she said. "What?"

"Kilkenny! Run!" Monk screamed, lunging toward Lightman and narrowly missing her.

Wells leaned forward, casually making shooing gestures toward Kilkenny.

Kilkenny turned and ran to the doors. Monk lunged at Wells, as Wells casually got up from the couch, growling.

Kilkenny put on a burst of speed and slammed into a tall figure at the doors. Monk gasped. What was Coopersmith doing here? Coopersmith grunted and stumbled backward. Kilkenny fell to her knees, yelping in pain.

Coopersmith leaned through the doorway and pulled Kilkenny to her feet, seemingly oblivious of Wells moving toward her with bared teeth.

"Kilkenny!" Monk screamed. "Go! Fucking go!"

Wells moved with shocking speed toward Kilkenny.

Coopersmith zeroed in on Monk and backed away as Kilkenny hared past her and shot out of the door.

Monk leaped forward, desperate to catch Wells and give Kilkenny enough time to hide. She ignored the pain in her wrist as her grasping fingers closed around the collar of Wells's shirt. Monk went down, dragging Wells with her and tearing her shirt. Coopersmith lunged at them. Lightman leapt across half the room and shoved Coopersmith back with all her might.

Lightman grabbed Monk under the arms, interlaced her fingers behind her head, and pushed forward. Monk's grip barely slipped, and she pulled with her bad arm, shrieking in pain but tugging for all she was worth. Wells staggered off balance, coughing and twisting so they were face to face.

Coopersmith was on the floor, wide-eyed and scrabbling backward as Lightman, Wells, and Monk squared off.

Wells glared at Monk, panting. Her bile yellow eyes were wild and unhinged.

Monk grimaced, and before Lightman could stop her, levered her feet off the floor and kicked out with all her might. Her feet hit Wells's stomach, and the air left her lungs in an explosive whoosh. Wells stumbled backward, and Monk grunted in pain as her abused body twisted off balance. Lightman pushed forward with her fingers, seemingly intent on separating Monk's head from her neck.

"What are you waiting for, Mitch? An invitation? For God's sake, get out of here," Monk snarled, bracing herself for Wells, who had gotten smoothly to her feet.

"No, Mitch, you stay put," Wells said.

Monk wriggled against Lightman's iron grip as Wells casually approached them.

Wells's eyes shone with good humor and amusement. "Not bad, Therese, not bad."

Coopersmith remained frozen in place. She watched them with round eyes.

"Maybe I should have some fun with her. Is she the real thing, do you think, or is she an illusion?" Wells smiled, seeming genuinely interested in the answer. "Do you want to find out?"

Monk kicked backward as hard as she could and struck Lightman's kneecap. Lightman grunted in pain, stumbled, and loosened her grip.

Monk pulled free and lunged at Wells.

Monk used her larger and heavier body to knock Wells backward. Wells pulled a fist back and punched Monk in the stomach.

The breath left Monk's body in an explosive rush, and tears spurted from her eyes.

Coopersmith finally seemed to come to her senses long enough to take a step toward Monk. The pain in her eyes was almost palatable, and Lightman lunged at her and pushed her sideways toward the French doors and closer to escape and freedom.

As Monk crumpled forward, she bit whatever part of Wells's body she could reach. She was rewarded with a hot spurt of metallic blood in her mouth and a quick, lupine yelp of pain as her teeth sank into Wells's left breast, just above the nipple.

Monk shoved for all she was worth, threw herself out of the doors, and ran. Blood pattered down into the long grass around her.

She bolted into a stand of trees just as Lightman exploded from the drawing room, Wells on her heels.

Monk cursed and hared through the crushed undergrowth, following Coopersmith's and Kilkenny's trail.

She caught up to them a moment later. Kilkenny was bent over with her hands on her knees, breathing heavily. Coopersmith had her hand on Kilkenny's shoulder.

"Get out of here," Monk gasped without preamble. She couldn't look at Coopersmith.

"Monk?" Coopersmith asked softly, reaching for her.

Monk quickly stepped out of her reach and shook her head. She turned to Kilkenny. "Stay away from me. I'll hold her off. She's a werewolf using me to get to you. Hide all of them. Understand?"

Kilkenny nodded.

"What do you mean she's a werewolf?" Coopersmith asked.

Monk looked up at the sound of breaking undergrowth. "Go, Kilkenny. Go."

Kilkenny nodded. She grabbed Coopersmith's hand, but Coopersmith protested and reached for Monk just as they became translucent. Monk felt the whoosh of cold air across her hand and shivered.

Lightman was on her a second later. She crash tackled Monk, and they rolled in the undergrowth. Lightman came to a stop on top of her, eyes glowing bright and virulent red. Her chest heaved with exertion.

"Don't try to run," she said softly, glancing at the slowly approaching Wells.

"I have to," Monk said.

"Trust me," Lightman said. "Trust me."

Monk stared at her, wondering why she should do it. Desperation washed over her in a cold tide.

Wells came to a halt beside them. "Entertaining," she said to Lightman.

She pulled Monk up off the ground with negligent ease. She held Monk by her shirt and slapped her. Monk's vision went grey, and the ground rose up to meet her face as she blacked out.

ϹHAPTER EIGHT

"Wakey, wakey, Miss Therese," Wells said, slapping Monk lightly on both cheeks.

Monk blinked. She sharpened her gaze and pulled away from Wells in revulsion. She looked around. She was once again lying on Lightman's bed. Lightman lay beside her, out cold.

Monk grimaced at the pain of her torn wrist, the sticky wetness of her blood.

Wells smiled at her. "Rise and shine, Therese."

"Fuck off."

"Wish granted. I just need one minute."

"What for?"

"This," Wells replied with a friendly smile. She grabbed Lightman, pulled her fist back, and swung it at the unconscious girl.

Lightman grunted as her eyes fluttered open. Wells dropped her, and Lightman sagged back on the bed, clutching her face. "Fuck, what did you do that for?" she mumbled.

"You've been a bad girl, haven't you, Vanessa?" Wells purred, folding her arms and staring at Lightman with glittering yellow eyes.

Lightman stared at her in confusion. "Wha—?" she began, but stopped at Wells's unfaltering cold stare.

"You know," Wells said.

Monk opened and closed her mouth several times. She wanted to ask what was wrong with Wells but her courage failed her. Wells shot her a cold glare, as though reading her mind.

"If I knew I wouldn't ask you," Lightman said coldly, attempting to sit up. Wells rested her hand against Lightman's chest.

"I loved you," Wells said softly, eyeing Lightman. "With everything I am."

"What do you mean, loved? What the hell is the matter with you?"

"You don't love me anymore," Wells said, sounding much less arrogant than before.

"What the bloody hell are you talking about?" Lightman asked. "Of course I love you."

Monk watched, spellbound, as they seemed to have forgotten she was sitting there.

"I saw more in Therese's mind than I wanted to," Wells said. "You were planning on killing me. You still are, aren't you?"

Monk was shocked to the core. Lightman told her the bond was not telepathic.

Lightman silently bit her lip. Her guilty look, Monk thought sourly, was enough to convict her.

"So it's true," Wells said.

"Oh, use your fucking head, rocket scientist," Monk piped up, dismayed her mouth had taken off without her permission. "If you die, she dies. Great idea for her to kill you, don't you think?"

Wells swung around, fastened on her with her yellow gaze, and drilled her back onto the bed. "Shut up, Monk," she said with a horribly morose note that set Monk's teeth on edge.

"No," Monk said, willing herself to be quiet. "Well? You gonna answer the question or keep barking idiocies at her?"

Wells snarled, grabbed the front of her shirt, and pulled her up off the bed. Her breath washed over Monk in hot, carrion waves. Monk was almost sick.

"I thought I just told you to shut up?" Wells said. "Or do you want to keep throwing up all over yourself and calling it communication?"

Monk shut her mouth with a snap.

"Better," Wells said. "You're up next. I know you lied to me. I know you knew Coopersmith would turn you down."

Monk felt her face flush with humiliation and could not stop her grimace.

Wells smiled and turned back to the silent Lightman. "Well, Vanessa? You have nothing to say for yourself?"

Lightman shook her head. "I have plenty to say, fuck face, but now's not the time." She shot a guilty look at Monk. "Why the hell don't you answer Monk's question? Tell her how you knew."

Wells shook her head. "I'm not going to tell her anything, lover. I'll leave that to you. You want to fuck her, fine, go all the way, then. I'm done for now. You'd better pray I don't catch up to you."

"You don't intend to hunt us, and you know it, freak," Lightman said coldly. "You're still going after Kilkenny. You never intended to kill Monk."

Wells smiled. "True." She turned back to Monk and tilted her head, yellow eyes shining balefully. "Although now things have shifted a bit. Therese is a walking corpse."

"Blah, blah, blah," Lightman snarled. "That was true all along. The last five minutes haven't changed that outcome."

"Tell me," Monk said coldly to Wells. "What the hell is she talking about?"

"You've been fun to play with, Monkhouse," Wells said callously. "But you're really not all that appealing. What interest would a secretive, repressed, socially inept twat like you have for me? You like to think you have courage and can stand up to me, but in reality you do all of your best living in your mind because you really don't know how to interact with other people."

Monk flinched and worked her jaw. Wells had struck a nerve. "Bitch," she muttered. The worst thing was that she suspected Wells was telling the truth.

"Truth hurts, doesn't it, Monkhouse?"

"Truth is totally relative, lover," Lightman broke in coolly. "You can lose the sermon now. What do you intend to do?"

Wells stared at her. "That's for me to know, and you to work out." She smiled and lunged at both of them.

God, I hope Kilkenny has taken the others and run, Monk thought as Wells's fist slammed into her face. Her vision went black.

"Monk. Monk. C'mon, wake up, Monk."

The strident voice, and the pain in Monk's cheek drove her to open her eyes. "Yeah, I'm with you," she said, blinking her eyes.

"Thank God," Lightman said, sounding genuinely relieved.

"What is it?" she asked, looking around. She felt Lightman jerking around behind her. "Are we tied together?"

"Yes," Lightman said. "For God's sake, will you please get up?"

"Uh." Monk was lying down, and she felt Lightman's hands jammed into her back and their ankles tied together. "All right."

She moved around, and felt Lightman shift behind her.

"I can get us off the bed," Lightman said, "but I need you to try and sit up a little more. Can you do that?"

Monk nodded. Her face was throbbing. "Where's the fire?"

"You fucking pike," Lightman snarled. "Look above you. We're going to burn to fucking death unless you decide to move your fat arse quicker."

Monk frowned and looked up. She felt as though she had two bean bags stuck to her face around her eye, and she could barely see. The room felt stuffy, and it was hard to breathe. The air was hazy above them.

Burn to death? "She set the house on fire?" she asked.

"Fucking genius. *Move!*" Lightman bellowed.

Monk strained against the ropes holding them together, felt Lightman's muscles tense along with her. They sat up, and Monk choked in the smoke and hot air above them. Her eyes stung.

"Lift your feet and lean back," Lightman said.

Monk gritted her teeth and lifted her feet. The ropes rubbed painfully against her wrists, and she yelped as it slid against the tear in a warm wash of blood.

Lightman hissed and grunted in pain and hopped toward the window. Monk's face throbbed, and she groaned. The glass in the window shattered and she felt a sick, stomach turning downward motion as they landed on the grass below. Flames jetted out of the open window with an authoritative cough.

She landed on top of Lightman, and they both yelped.

"I'm going to break the ropes," Lightman said.

Monk nodded, and she felt the ropes tighten unbearably for a second around her abused wrists. The skin on her injured arm tore a little more, and she moaned in pain. She was dimly amazed that Lightman had not torn off her hand.

"Are you nearly done?" she ground out through gritted teeth.

"Just a sec," Lightman said.

Monk let loose an unabashed scream of pain as the ropes ground into her flesh—and then loosened.

"Crap," she muttered, finally disentangling herself from Lightman.

"I know," Lightman said, and a few seconds later the ropes around Monk's ankles loosened. She heaved a gusty sigh of relief. "Better."

Monk slowly sat up, clutching her sticky wrist. Blood seeped through her fingers.

"We're going to have to wrap that up," Lightman said. She glanced toward the front of the house. "But we're going to have to get the hell out of here first."

Monk looked back. The entire house was engulfed in flames, and in the distance they could hear approaching sirens.

She didn't need any more prompting. She awkwardly clambered to her feet and clutched her wrist to her chest, trying to stem the flow of blood.

Lightman glanced back at the house. "Fucking brilliant," she muttered.

Monk looked at her.

"My car was in the garage," Lightman said, gesturing at the inferno. "Wherever we go now—and I'm not sure where that is—is going to be on foot."

Monk nodded. "I think we should get the hell out of here. I don't want to talk to the police. I don't know anything, and I don't want them to hold me up."

"Hold you up from what?" Lightman asked, trailing behind Monk as she began to walk down the road.

"I'm going after Wells," Monk said. She felt like hell. She thought about her friends and felt sick. An image of Coopersmith flashed through her mind, followed by a blast of intense pain that was strong enough to make her footsteps falter.

She pushed the thoughts to one side. She focused on Kilkenny and keeping her promise.

"You're crazy," Lightman said. "You've got to be kidding me."

"No," Monk said. "I have to."

Lightman pulled her to a halt. "For God's sweet sake—why? She let you go. Make the most of it and run like hell."

Monk shook her head. "Can't."

"Do you understand any of what's happened to you?"

Monk looked deep into Lightman's eyes. "I understand that I dared Wells, and I did it to keep my friends safe. I understand that all it's done is piss her off. She dismissed me. She's going to kill my friends anyway." She pulled her arm out of Lightman's grip. "I also understand that you recruited me to kill her. These goals work very nicely together." She smiled. "I understand I need your help. I don't know how to find Wells by myself."

"What if I won't help you?"

Monk stared at her, struggling to relax. She had not considered the possibility.

"All right, all right," Lightman said, waving her hand. "I'll help you."

"Good," Monk said. "I'm glad."

Monk kept walking down the street, and Lightman jogged up next to her, keeping pace with her. "Where are we going now?"

"We're going back to my place," Monk said.

"Why?"

"Wells is a werewolf and can be killed by silver, right?" Monk asked.

Lightman nodded.

"Good. Good. We're going back to my place. My mother loves silver, and I'm pretty sure she has a silver letter opener—or two—hanging around the place."

Lightman snorted a bitter laugh. "Really? How coincidental."

"I know," Monk said, as the fire engines rushed by them. Police cars followed closely behind. Monk glanced back up the street at the milling neighbors and stopped cars. "What happens now?"

"How do you mean?" Lightman asked.

"Wells. How do we find her? You know her better than anyone."

"Knowledge has nothing to do with it. She's not human. She's a werewolf, and a powerful one at that. She's the mistress of dreams. There's nothing she can't do when she—and her prey—are asleep." Lightman smiled without humor. "I have an empathic bond to her. I can feel her around. She's masking her side of the bond, so I don't have a sharp awareness of her."

"Empathic or telepathic? She knew what we were planning, after all."

"Empathic. She can't read minds."

"You could have fooled me."

Lightman shrugged.

"Are you ever going to tell me the truth about your bond to her?" Monk asked.

Lightman gave her an enigmatic grin. "I *did* tell you the truth about my bond to her."

"Then how did she do it?"

"She got it out of you. She *told* you that. She *wasn't* lying. She put a controlling bond on you, which *is* telepathic. It has to be. Otherwise it's not a controlling bond, is it?"

Monk glared at her. "You could have told me, you know." She sighed. "So your bond is empathic."

Lightman nodded.

"How does that work?" Monk asked.

"It means I would be able to give you a general direction she was in but not point to her in a room full of people."

"Do you know where she is now?" Monk asked.

Lightman shook her head. "I can't feel her. The best I can tell you is that she's not here right now."

"Is she on the dreamscape?"

Lightman shrugged. "I'm not sure, but I'm guessing probably yes."

"Well, at least we have some clue where she is," Monk said. "It's something we can use. What about the dreamscape? The only way you can get there is by sleeping, right?"

Lightman shook her head. "Wells is a mistress of the dreamscape. She can go there without being asleep."

"How does that work?"

"When you fall asleep and dream the normal way, that's one way in. That's the way almost everybody uses. You leave your physical body behind, and something else that's a part of you enters the dreamscape. The other way is for a master or mistress of the dreamscape to pull you in by your physical body. That's very dangerous. If you go in with your real body, and something happens to you, it stays with you when you leave again."

"How do you know when she's pulling you there when you're awake?"

"You can't tell. Only when things start to go weird. Feels strange, believe me."

Monk glanced at Lightman, too shell shocked and frightened to ask. She stared at the road ahead of them, feeling overwhelmed, tired, and hungry. She felt as though she were falling apart and pushed it to one side. She pulled Lightman to a halt.

"I have to ask you something," she said.

Lightman stared at her, brown eyes without mercy. She looked tense, and had a smear of ash on one cheek. Monk wanted to wipe it away.

"You said you wanted me to help you kill Wells," Monk said.

Lightman nodded.

"I wanted to ask you if you would do something for me, then."

"What?" Lightman asked.

"If anything happens to me, will you keep my friends safe?"

Lightman blew out a gusty breath, sighing and shaking her head. She looked up the street, arms folded across her breasts. She looked back at Monk. Her eyes seemed reddish in the midday sunlight. She studied Monk with a reflective expression. "All right," she finally said. "I don't promise that I can do it, but I can certainly try."

Monk nodded. "Good enough."

Forty-five minutes later, they were walking up the street toward Monk's home. Monk grimaced when she saw the car parked in the carport. She looked down at her tattered and filthy clothing, and her mouth tightened.

Her mother would be even angrier than ever with her.

"What?" Lightman asked with a touch of impatience as Monk faltered in her steps.

Monk stared at her. "I don't want to go in there."

Lightman put her hands on her head and tilted it. "Pardon? Are you *kidding* me?" She stared at Monk. "Look, we can't go to my place. Last time I looked it was in the process of burning to the ground. Even if it hadn't, we still wouldn't be finding any silver in there." She snorted. "Besides, don't you want a bite to eat and a shower?"

"No," Monk said, anxiety putting a fine edge on her temper. "What I want is to have my friends back."

"Chill," Lightman said, easily pushing Monk back. "What's the matter?"

Monk stared at her, amazed at her almost complete lack of empathy. "The last time I was in there, my mother beat the shit out of me, remember? The woman hates my guts."

"Is that all?" Lightman asked. "That's all you're worried about?"

"Isn't that enough?"

"No," Lightman said. "It's not. You said you wanted to rescue your friends. You implied—and probably said—that you would do what it took to make that happen. Now you're hesitating at the first step?"

Monk flinched at the disgust in her tone. "You make me sound like such a loser."

Lightman glared at her. "C'mon."

She grabbed Monk by her shirtsleeve and tugged her toward the house.

Monk was at the limit of her coping skills, and her temper spilled over. She slapped at Lightman's hand and shoved as hard as she could. Lightman took a step backward and tripped over her feet but regained her balance.

"Fuck off, Monk," Lightman said coldly. "Fucking move."

Monk glared at her, shaking with rage. Lightman had no idea about how truly evil her mother was. No one did.

"What's the worst thing your mother can do to you?" Lightman asked.

"She can do the same thing she did to me the other night. I'm lucky I didn't end up in hospital. I'm still fucking sore from that."

"Relax," Lightman said. She smiled. "Let me put this into perspective for you. You're willing to take on my lover, a blooded werewolf. You're willing to fight her to the death. She's faster, stronger, and more cunning than you, and she's not human. She's much harder to kill. Yet you're happy to deal with all of that. We come to your house, and you baulk at one, tiny, human woman who's probably half your size, at least twice your age and physically weaker than you. Doesn't that strike you as totally ridiculous?"

Monk nodded warily. "Doesn't make it any easier, though."

Lightman regarded her steadily, face mask-like. "Then you're screwed. You're not ready to take on Wells."

"Fuck you, Lightman," Monk said, pushing past her. She stopped and looked back. "Coming? Or are you just going to stand out there?"

Monk strode toward the front door, heart hammering, not wanting to open the door. She prayed it would be unlocked. She had lost her backpack in the destruction of Lightman's house. She twisted the knob, amazed when the door opened. She strode into the house, Lightman close behind her, and hoped that her mother wouldn't be there.

She didn't know what her mother would say to her. She fleetingly thought of Coopersmith on the previous evening and felt depressed. Images of Coopersmith with Warland flittered into her mind, and she pushed them back. It was stupid to be distracted when her mother was around scouting for blood.

She stopped in the foyer and listened for a moment. Nothing. She couldn't hear her mother.

Forty minutes later, they had showered, and Lightman was dressed in a pair of Monk's shorts and a tee shirt.

They were in the bathroom, washing off Monk's burning wrist under the cold water tap. Monk hissed in pain and looked closely at the wound. It was inflamed and a dark pink. The inside looked whitish, and it smelt sick. It ached and stung where the water touched it.

Lightman shook her head. "Ugly."

"Okay, let's just get the disinfectant on it and wrap it up," Monk said. "It'll be good."

"Yeah," Lightman said, nodding. "Yeah, sure."

Lightman held Monk's wrist over the sink and poured peroxide directly on the cut. It fizzed and bubbled furiously.

"Gawd," Monk ground out, eyes squeezed shut and watering with the pain.

"What the hell is going on here?" a dry, cold voice asked.

Monk jerked in shock and turned to face her mother.

"Mum," she said.

"I told you not to call me that," her mother said, glaring at her. "What are you doing here?" She looked them both up and down. "Not going to school, I see. Figures."

Monk bit her lip and looked in the sink. She didn't want to fight with her mother, but the glint in the older woman's eye told her that there would be hell to pay later, when they were alone.

"Well?" her mother asked as the silence played out.

"We were just on our way to go back to school," Lightman said, mustering a smile for Monk's mother.

Mrs. Monkhouse ignored her. She reached out and jerked Monk's shoulder. "Well?"

Monk didn't know what to say. Her mother would humiliate her in front of Lightman. She had always hoped that if worst came to worst, and her mother threw her out, she could stay with Coopersmith until the end of the school year. Now she didn't think she could do it even if Coopersmith was still an option.

"We were just on our way back to school," Monk said. Her mind felt frozen—a vicious light danced in her mother's eyes. She was spoiling for a fight.

"Can't you think for yourself?" her mother asked. "If she said she was going to jump over a cliff would you go off after her?"

"I can think for myself," Monk said slowly, after a moment. She felt herself slipping toward panic.

"No, you can't. You can't think for yourself. You need someone to tell you what to do." Her mother tilted her head and studied Monk in an infuriating smug manner.

"Let me put this on your wrist," Lightman broke in quietly.

Monk turned toward her, saw the rage in her eyes. She willed Lightman to keep her mouth shut. Lightman's hot gaze bored into hers as she wrapped Monk's wrist under Mrs. Monkhouse's cloying gaze.

Monk knew she was whey-faced when Lightman finished, and her wrist ached like a rotten tooth under the bandage. She felt slightly ill.

"You want to get a bite to eat?" Monk asked.

Lightman nodded.

"Not here. Your friend is not welcome here," her mother said.

Monk flinched and turned to her mother.

"In fact," her mother continued, "I don't like the influence this . . . girl . . . has on you. She makes you rude to your mother. I want you to tell her to leave and never come back."

Monk stared dumbly at her mother, felt Lightman shift beside her. She thought of Jackie, Kilkenny, Coopersmith, and Warland. Her wrist hurt.

"No," she said softly.

"What did you just say to me?"

"I said no. We're leaving." Monk met Lightman's hot eyes, saw them go pinkish in color. She willed Lightman not to argue with her.

Lightman's mouth tightened, and she gave a curt nod.

"I'll be waiting for you when you get home," Mrs. Monkhouse said.

Monk began to shake. Her mother gave them one last, unpleasant smile and left the bathroom.

Monk still shook as she felt the invisible, black cloud over the bathroom lift.

"Are you really going to stand for that?" Lightman asked.

Monk shushed her and pulled her out of the bathroom. She had the beginnings of an impressive headache and felt exhausted enough to fall asleep on her feet.

She helped herself to two silver letter openers from her mother's special cutlery drawer as they left. She listened carefully for any further signs of her mother but there were none.

They were at the end of Monk's street when Lightman pulled her to a halt. "What the fuck was that, Monk?"

"Me staying alive," Monk said. "What the hell else can I do? I have nowhere to go. I don't have any family besides these guys. I don't have anyone but me. I have to do exactly what she tells me to do, or I'm fucked."

"What about your friends?"

"I don't have any," Monk said, walking forward again. She was hungry. "Do you have any money? I don't have any."

Lightman nodded. "Sure. Where are we going?"

"There's a really good hamburger place in Autumn Park Plaza. Should take us about twenty minutes to walk there."

"Sure," Lightman said.

They walked along in silence for a few moments.

"Do you really not have any friends?" Lightman asked.

Monk shook her head. "None of the people I hang around with I'd really call friends."

"What about all the people that we're putting our necks on the line for? Why are we doing that if they're not really your friends?"

"I'm not talking about them. Whatever happened to them is my fault. I have to fix that."

"Get a grip," Lightman said. "You have to stop feeling so fucking sorry for yourself all the time."

Monk clenched her jaw.

Fifteen minutes later, they were in the hamburger joint, biting into hamburgers with the lot, hot, greasy chips, and cold cokes. Monk sighed in pleasure, feeling better for the first time in what felt like years.

"You said you could feel Wells," Monk said. "Do you know where she is now?"

Lightman's eyes flared red, and Monk looked around hurriedly to see if anyone noticed. The dining room was almost empty, and the chef making burgers was looking the other way.

"I can feel something pulling me," Lightman said slowly. She shook her head. "Feels strange."

"Where is it coming from?" Monk asked.

Lightman pointed over Monk's left shoulder. She took another bite of her burger. "God, this is good." She sighed.

"I know." Monk nodded. "Good. I guess we know which direction we're heading in, then." She chewed for a moment, studying Lightman. She still couldn't quite understand what Wells's lover was doing with her. She felt her pocket for the letter openers, feeling dim comfort at their presence. "Do you know what her next move will be?"

"I'm not sure," Lightman said after a moment's thought. "I'm assuming your *not* friends are in hiding. Do you know where they would have gone?"

Monk thought about it. Jackie and Kilkenny couldn't just disappear without telling their parents, and Coopersmith wouldn't just disappear in general. She would face whatever was coming. They would also know that it was pointless to run or hide. Wells would find them, unless Kilkenny developed some defense mechanism in the dreamscape so she could hide them.

That seemed unlikely since Wells was a master of the dreamscape, and Kilkenny had only just discovered its existence.

"No," Monk said. "I seriously doubt any of them are hiding. None of them can without attracting a huge amount of attention. And if they tried it, they would have to explain they were being chased by a werewolf, and *that* would end up with them in the nuthouse, I think." She carefully chewed a chip. "Besides, I don't think they've had enough warning."

"I don't know that it matters," Lightman said with a sigh. "Wells is after Kilkenny. She's not interested in fighting with you. I'm sure she's keeping a lookout for you, just to see you suffer."

Monk grimaced and fought down her temper. Why did Lightman insist on making her feel completely inconsequential? "Okay, so let me see if I have this. Wells is after Kilkenny, not me. She's dismissed me as an opponent, but she wants me to chase her so that she can kill the people I care about in front of me. The people in question didn't have enough warning to be able to hide from her in time. So she's probably already got them. If I want to find them, I should go looking for her. Sound good?"

Lightman nodded, a cold smile playing about her lips.

"All right," Monk said, leaning forward, smiling pleasantly. "How about this as a strategy? I don't know where they are. I know Mitch well enough to have an idea of what she's going to do, but not so with the others. I know Wells is after them, because she wants me to suffer and so on and so forth. So we could chase Wells to find out where they are. We tackle Wells when we actually find her. We hope that we find her before she finds them."

"That's quite a strategy, Monk," Lightman said. "So in other words, we gamble with their lives. We throw them to the wolf and hope we can actually help them as she prepares to eat them."

"Fuck, Lightman," Monk said, fighting down her temper. "Do you have any better ideas? Where the fuck do we start?"

Lightman shook her head. "We really don't have any better place to start, do we?"

Monk leaned back in her chair, idly fingering her wrist. It still hurt abominably, and was stiff. She felt a little better—a little stronger—after eating, although her head was still throbbing. "Are you ready?"

Lightman finished off the last of her chips. "I'm as ready as I'm going to be."

Monk nodded. "Fine. Let's go, then."

Lightman nodded. "Works for me."

CHAPTER NINE

"There," Lightman said. "She's through there."

"Figures," Monk said. "It just had to be through there, didn't it?"

They stood down the road from Lightman's destroyed house. They watched the last couple of police walking through the debris, saw clusters of residents pointing toward the ruins and talking.

Lightman nodded.

"Do you know where we have to go?" Monk asked.

Lightman scanned the wreckage. There, in the midst of the charred wood, blackened steel, and melted glass was a sooty fireplace. It was unnaturally warped and buckled, twisting toward the sky with a malevolent aspect. She pointed straight at it, and Monk shivered.

"What is this, exactly?" Monk asked. "Is it the entrance to the dreamscape?"

Lightman gave her a brief smile. "It's *an* entrance to the dreamscape. There is no such thing as *the* entrance."

She walked toward it, Monk trailing after her.

Monk tried to fight down a surge of fear. If she didn't walk into the dreamscape, she may never see her beloved Mitch again. Despite all the things that had happened to her and her still uncontrollable jealousy, she couldn't imagine life without Coopersmith.

They stolled along casually, Monk a little behind Lightman, trying not to attract any attention.

They were almost at the edge of the charred shell when one of the police officers spotted them.

"Hey!" he called. "Can I help you?"

Lightman and Monk exchanged a glance and walked faster. The police officer took a step toward them.

"Stop, girls," he said. "Stop!"

Monk and Lightman broke into a dead run. They bolted through the rubble, Monk staggering as Lightman bounded gracefully over it.

Monk reached out blindly for Lightman, felt her take her hand. They ran into the fireplace.

The world shifted beneath Monk's feet. She felt a wrenching sensation, and was tugged forward. She stumbled and fell to her knees, dragging Lightman downward. Lightman tensed and pulled her upright.

Lightman stopped, and Monk bumped into her. She staggered backward, amazed at Lightman's solidity and strength.

Monk peered around and blinked uncertainly. The sky was a brilliant and pitiless blue above them, and they cast short and sharp shadows in the bright sunlight.

"Are we in the dreamscape?" Monk asked.

Lightman nodded. "In our physical bodies."

They were in a green, grassy field strewn with rocky, mossy detritus, suggesting they stood in what had once been a house. The foundations were the same as the house in the physical world, but while that one was in a suburb, this one was in a stretch of wilderness that looked like it had never been touched by a human hand.

A road was close by, and Monk walked toward it, Lightman close behind her.

It was a pitted and scarred dirt trail, and looked long disused.

Monk turned and surveyed the ruins. They had the same forbidding aspect as the ones in the physical world.

"Can you feel her?" Monk asked softly, glancing at Lightman.

Lightman looked all around. "I'm trying to memorize landmarks," she said in response to Monk's questioning look. "This is the entrance we used to get onto the dreamscape. We may have to use it again to get back."

Monk nodded.

"Okay," Lightman finally said, gazing at Monk. "In answer to your question, yes, she's here." She pointed to their left, at the slim path meandering through a thick stand of ancient trees. "That way. We have to go that way."

Monk nodded. "All right, let's get moving. We probably don't have much time."

"Time," Lightman said. "Yes. Right. There's one more thing I should tell you. Time passes differently here. Forty years here may be only be a couple of minutes in the real world. Minutes here can be days there." She sighed. "This could be one hell of a long trip."

Monk remained silent for a moment, digesting this. It didn't surprise her. "Can't help it. Let's just get this done," she finally said.

Lightman nodded, and they began to walk.

Monk stared left and right off the road. There didn't seem to be any wildlife in the forest, not even insects. The silence was eerie and unnerving. They went through a thick, untamed forest, almost the backdrop for a fairy tale. Monk half expected to be dive bombed by a fire-breathing dragon. The ground was hard and dry beneath their feet, and they barely left any trace of their passing in the dirt. The air itself was the most alien of all. It had no taste or smell, a jarring counterpart to the riotous greenery surrounding them.

Monk felt uncomfortable. The quiet and isolation played on her nerves.

"Are we going to meet anyone in this world?" Monk asked, breaking the silence.

Lightman laughed softly. "I think so."

"Who are the people of this world? Are they real people or are they ones Wells made up?"

"Probably a mix of both," Lightman said. "You can't really tell the difference, except constructs can be more one dimensional than real people."

Monk nodded. "How far away is Wells? Can you tell?"

"She's a long walk away." Lightman glanced at Monk. "Are you tired?"

Monk had not gotten any sleep the previous night and not much the night before that. She was exhausted. She nodded.

"You want to stop for a while? Get some rest?"

Monk looked around at the forest. Her wrist was a blaze of pain and throbbed dully from the swinging motion of her arm. She clutched it against her chest. She felt hot and light-headed. She shook her head.

"You look done in," Lightman said.

"I'm fine. Let's just keep walking." Monk was too tired to sleep and in too much pain physically and mentally to get any rest. She felt consumed by worry for the others. She hated the thought of them by themselves in the dreamscape. She wondered what they were doing.

"Look," Lightman said, pulling Monk off the path and into the dense undergrowth. "I'm really tired and I need some sleep." They stopped at the base of a wide tree, sheltered from the empty road and any prying eyes that may have been watching them. Lightman sank down onto the earth, drawing Monk with her.

Monk felt trapped and uncomfortable in the circle of Lightman's arms, yet she was asleep within minutes.

Monk awoke what seemed hours later. The ground around them was damp with dew, and the quality of light reminded her of early morning. She looked up into Lightman's brown eyes and felt empty. Her arm felt stiff and the wrist raw.

She disentangled herself from Lightman and stretched, dimly aware that she was also a little hungry. Lightman helped her to her feet.

"Sleep well?" Lightman asked as they made their way to the road.

Monk nodded. "I wasn't really expecting that, but yes."

Lightman laughed softly. "I know. Weird."

"Do you have any idea how far the closest town is?" Monk asked, looking around. The world seemed as deserted as it had the previous day. The forest had given way to open space, fields of bright, golden wheat swaying gently in the soft breeze. The sky above was just as blue.

"No," Lightman said. "This place doesn't have geography in the way you're used to. No cartographer has ever been here to make a map, and even if they had it would probably be meaningless by now." She pointed to the ground. "But look—this road is used to more traffic."

Monk looked at the ground. The ruts in the path seemed deeper, and there was less vegetation. She looked at her watch. It had stopped.

They kept walking, and Monk saw her first farm on the dreamscape. It looked like a normal farm, in that there was a wooden farmhouse with smoke curling from the chimney and a barn close to it. She could see a dooryard with chickens pecking idly in the dirt. That was where the resemblance to a modern farm ended. The people in the distance looked as though they had come straight from the Middle Ages, complete with rustic, homespun clothes and grizzled hair. The woman wore a bonnet and long skirt, the children rough shirts and shorts. A placid-looking horse hitched to a wagon completed the picture.

All around were confusing twists of metal that Monk realized were intended to be farm machinery, but looked more like modern sculpture. She could not identify one single piece.

"Looks weird," she said to Lightman's questioning glance.

Lightman snorted a laugh. "It doesn't have to make sense. This is the place you go to when you dream. It's built from memories."

Monk nodded. *So Wells really doesn't understand everything after all*, she thought, staring at the twisted metal. It made Wells seem less God-like.

They headed on down the road, seeing more and more people as they went.

"Do we really have to go into this town?" Monk asked, casting furtive glances at the other travelers who steadfastly ignored them.

"It's going to be quicker than going around it," Lightman said. "Trust me."

Monk pressed closer to Lightman as they approached the gates to the large town.

The strangest collection of people Monk had ever seen largely ignored them. Rustic families straight out of a fantasy story jostled with women and men in business suits. Some people rode horses or bicycles, while others walked. Her head began to spin and her wrist ached. She idly fingered the bandage covering the wound.

They finally reached the guard who was wearing armor and colorful jerkin, complete with senseless coat of arms. The animal on it looked like a cross between a rhinoceros and a crane.

"State your business," he said without preamble.

"We're passing through," Lightman said.

"Relativist or absolutist?"

"Relativist, I think," Lightman said, staring at Monk.

Monk struggled to remain expressionless. She felt confused. She didn't understand the question. "Me too," she said when the guard raised an eyebrow at her.

"Go in peace," he said, waving them through. "Next."

Milling people in the main street swept them along. Monk could not fathom the town. It was a bizarre and astonishing mix of shops and housing. The familiar theme of old and new dominated with a blacksmith beside a car dealership—complete with toy cars. It didn't look like it sold the larger models.

Uniformed guards were on patrol everywhere, carefully watching the crowd.

"Whoa," Monk said.

Lightman nodded. They made their way up a cobblestone street—complete with traffic islands—through the largest assortment of refuse and garbage that Monk had ever seen. She was pleased that her nose seemed to be tuning out the stench.

"This place is a shit hole," she muttered to Lightman.

"I agree," Lightman said. "Why the hell doesn't anyone collect the trash?" She looked a little pale.

"Can't do that, young miss," an old man said, bumping into them, courtesy of a slowly moving coach pushing people to the sides as it made its way down the street.

"Why ever not?" Monk asked.

"Well, what happens if someone wants their possessions back?" he asked.

Monk picked up a discarded wrapper. "This isn't a possession, it's junk."

"Hey," Lightman said. "Put that down before you—"

"You're under arrest," a uniformed guard said, appearing out of the crowd who were forming a careful circle around them.

"Pardon?" Monk asked. "What for?"

"Theft," the middle-aged man said, eyeing them severely.

"How the hell could picking up garbage be considered theft?" Monk asked.

"What garbage?" the guard said. "There is no garbage here." He waved a finger in her face. "Everything you see around you is owned by another person. If you touch it—remove it—you are guilty of theft."

"Right," the old man said. "Theft is taking something that doesn't belong to you."

"Whoever had this, threw it away," Monk said, feeling faint from the heat, smell, and pain in her wrist. "It's not owned by anyone."

"When does ownership cease, then, young lady? Do you have the papers that prove that object was signed over to the town and the town is the new owner? Either way, it is illegal to take something that is not yours," the guard said. He gestured toward his comrades, who had magically appeared by him. "Take her away." He turned back to her. "Save your arguments—poor as they are—for the judge."

Monk did not have time to protest as the guards grabbed her arms and began dragging her away. Lightman yelped as they took her alongside Monk, ignoring her mighty protestations of innocence.

They were thrown into a jail cell, complete with straw-covered floor and flushing toilet.

"Nice going, Monk," Lightman said, standing and brushing off her clothes.

"How the hell was I supposed to know we were in a city of madmen?" Monk asked.

"We're on the dreamscape. Nothing makes sense, and it doesn't need to," Lightman said. "Idiot. Next time keep your fucking mouth shut."

"How was I supposed to know that was going to happen?" Monk asked. "Did you know? Have you been here before?"

"God, this is so like you," Lightman snarled. "Whiny as always. 'How was I supposed to know that was going to happen?'" she savagely mimicked. "Use your fucking head, for the love of Christ."

"Stop dumping shit on me," Monk said coldly, pushing Lightman back with her good hand. "This *isn't* my fault."

"Yes, it's your fault. Didn't you listen to the question you got asked when we walked in here? He asked if we were relativist or absolutist. Dummy."

"What the bloody hell is that question even supposed to mean?"

"It means that you *think about* and *watch* what's happening around you. That's what it means."

"In other words you don't know either." Monk sat on the lone cot and shook her head. "You aren't making sense. What do you mean?"

"I mean that you can't just do things on impulse. You have to watch what's happening around you and take your cues from that. Learn to keep your mouth shut and watch what you say."

"You're a fine one to talk," a new, cool voice broke in.

"Oh my God," Monk said, feeling her entire being unclench. She turned toward the speaker, an extraordinarily beautiful woman with dark copper hair. "Mitch."

"Monk," Coopersmith said, approaching the bars of her cage, opposite theirs. Her hands curled into fists around the steel.

"How the hell did you get in here?" Monk asked, tears of relief slipping down her face.

Coopersmith's hands twitched on the bars. "The same way you did, I think. I violated some obscure, opinion laden point of moral law."

Monk nodded. "I gathered that part. The question is how did you come to be in this town at all?"

"Wells came after us," Coopersmith said. "Kilkenny was too late in trying to protect us. We got separated." She bit her lip. "I have no idea if the others are all right."

"Where's Wells now?" Monk asked.

"I'm not sure."

"I can answer that question. She's on her way back here," Lightman said. She shot a look at Monk. "Before you ask, I can feel her."

Monk nodded. "Take Mitch," she said to Lightman. "Get the hell out of here. Keep them safe."

"Look, stop talking about me like I'm not here," Coopersmith shot back. Her eyes flashed. "Half the reason we're in the shit like this is because you didn't tell anyone what was going on, Monk."

Monk's patience snapped. "Don't blame this crap on me." She folded her arms and stared down Coopersmith. "I didn't consciously drag you into this. I did everything I could to keep you the hell out of it. It's not my fault my chemistry teacher turned out to be a barking mad werewolf."

"I'm sure this is charming," Lightman cut in. "I'm also sure this is a conversation you need to be having. Really. I do. I only have one issue." Her hot gaze swung between both of them. *Not fucking now!"*

Monk and Coopersmith quieted. They exchanged a glance. Coopersmith remained expressionless, and Monk sobbed inside.

"That's much better," Lightman said with a smile. Her eyes flared bright, vicious red, and she rubbed her hands together. "We have to get the fuck out of here. Wells is closer, and she's pissed."

"How do you know?" Monk asked.

Lightman shook her head. "Doesn't matter." She wrapped her hands around the bars of the cell and tugged with all her might. The bars bent a little. She fell back, panting.

Monk leaned forward. "Nice. Little bit more, and we should be good. Can't you just break the lock, though?"

Lightman glared at her.

Monk held up her hands and took a step back. "I'll just shut the fuck up now, all right?"

Lightman's eyes narrowed. She snorted as she pulled on the bars, muscles bulging. The bars suddenly groaned and gave way. She fell to her knees, panting, and gestured toward the break. "Go through."

Monk quickly crawled through the break in the bars. She grabbed the door to Coopersmith's cell and opened it.

Lightman and Coopersmith stared at her. She shrugged. "Now who's not paying attention?" she asked Lightman.

Lightman growled.

"Let me guess," Coopersmith said. "Since this city has gone overboard on morals and questions of ethics, it makes sense they would hesitate to lock people up. It does, after all, violate another person's freedoms, right?"

Monk nodded. "Arse up but true. They're probably worried about whether or not we would sue them."

Monk and Coopersmith exchanged a glance and laughed.

"C'mon. Let's get out of here." Lightman sounded less ragged.

The prison was deserted, and the few guards they saw ignored them. It didn't take long until they were back out into the street again.

Lightman looked up at the sky and cursed. One horizon was covered in a layer of black clouds. They roiled furiously, and lightning flashed from them.

Lightman grabbed Monk's bad hand and pulled. Monk screamed at the pain that tore through her damaged wrist. Lightman faltered and released her. Monk felt Coopersmith's hand slip into her good hand, pulling her forward, behind them both.

They ran through the city, avoiding citizens, guards, and piles of refuse. After what felt like an hour, they reached the gate on the far side of the city. A crush of frantic, shoving citizens, trying to leave the city, overran the guards. Lightman pulled them into the throng. They were swept away and out of the city.

Coopersmith kept them all together as they jogged along the main road. The black cloud almost reached it, and an ominous silence descended. Lightman pulled them to a halt, looked back, and waited to see what would happen.

All was silent for a moment. Then, in the distance, they heard the baying from a pack of dogs.

"Oh, God," Lightman moaned, paling.

"What?" Coopersmith asked.

"Death hounds. These are the ugliest, scariest, and nastiest dogs you have ever seen in your life."

Monk squashed the urge to shrink into Coopersmith. She couldn't look at Coopersmith without feeling a stab of pain and jealousy, despite herself. She tried to push the feeling to one side. "Are they looking for us?"

Just at that moment, the baying increased in volume and the screaming began. A man howled in agony, a long drawn out sound that left Monk weeping and shivering.

Soon a multitude of voices lent themselves to the hellish music of the evening.

They stopped to listen to the blood bath in the town behind them. Men, women, and children, all screamed in the final extremities of agony, each one howling for mercy, begging and pleading for their lives. It finally became a cacophony of pain, as individual voices were lost.

Monk, Lightman, and Coopersmith remained frozen as the cries increased, decreased, and petered out all together. Once the baying died down, an eerie silence descended over the town.

"Is it over?" Monk asked softly.

A single bark sounded, as though on cue.

"Crap," Lightman breathed as another dog took up the call.

The baying began again, but this time it moved toward them.

"Fuck!" Lightman cried. "Run. Run!"

Monk stumbled along the road behind Lightman and Coopersmith. Her legs felt full of cement, and her lungs burned. She could barely put one foot in front of the other but both Lightman and Coopersmith looked as though they could run forever. She clutched her injured arm to her chest, grimacing in pain each time her arm jolted.

They slowed down a little, and Monk sank to her knees, chest heaving.

"I think we should be—" Lightman began, and then stopped dead. She tilted her head.

"What?" Monk gasped.

Coopersmith glanced at her, and her eyes widened. She took a step toward Monk, but Monk scrabbled back. Coopersmith flinched and looked away.

"The dogs are coming this way," Lightman said.

"They're already here," Monk said softly and despairingly. She could hear the thud of paws on the hard-pressed ground. "Run." She lurched to her feet.

Coopersmith and Lightman easily outpaced her.

"Can they climb?" she gasped out.

"No," Lightman said.

"Trees," Monk said, heading for the closest stand of trees.

Lightman and Coopersmith leapt up into the nearest trees, clutched at bark, and pulled themselves up with soft grunts of effort.

Monk glanced down at her wrist and felt sick. She had to try. She forced herself to back up and take a run off toward Coopersmith's tree. Coopersmith perched comfortably in the branches, watching her with concern.

Monk jumped and wrapped her fingers around a thin branch. A stab of pain tore through her wrist. Her fingers unlocked as she screamed in pain. She landed in an awkward, bone-jarring heap and clutched her wrist to her chest. Tears of pain leaked out of her tightly closed eyes, and she grunted.

"Monk!" Coopersmith screamed. "I'm coming down to you."

"No. Stay up there," Monk ground out. "No time. I'm gonna have to take my chances." She eyed Coopersmith who stopped moving and reseated herself on the branch. Her eyes were hot as she stared back at Monk.

Monk lay back in the leaves, waiting for the hound, terrified beyond comprehension. She wondered how it would feel to have teeth sunk into her unprotected neck. She wanted to scream and cry but bit her lip. No one could help her now.

The hounds padded up the track, trawling for them, scenting the air, and baying balefully.

Monk saw one of them and gasped. It was the largest black dog she had ever seen, a little larger than an Irish Wolfhound. It had a wide, wedge head and unforgiving, furnace red eyes. Evil smelling saliva dripped from sharp, tusk-like fangs. It saw her, and slowly approached, scenting the air. She looked into its alien, unknowable eyes, resigned to her fate.

She closed her eyes and swallowed, forcibly relaxing her body. Her heart was beating so hard she was sure it would explode. She felt the warmth of a body, the gentle brush of whiskers, and she opened her eyes. A wet nose snuffled her, snorting at her.

Monk shook, but held her position for all she was worth.

The dog lipped her neck, and she gasped. It growled, low and deep, shoving her with its nose. She reflexively raised her arm, wanting to ward it off.

She cursed her weakness.

Suddenly the dog fell back on its haunches, and let out an ear splitting, unearthly howling.

Monk moaned softly, grimly clinging to whatever was left of her rational mind. She lifted her wrist, and the dog took another step back.

She sat up, holding up her damaged arm, watching as a wall of canine faces appeared in a circle around her. Each one of them took up the first dog's call and howled in eerie synchronicity.

Monk's head pounded, and she slowly shifted to her haunches.

"Shut up!" she screamed as she stood. The first dog took a cautious step backward, dropping its head and whining. It groveled on the ground before her. She held out her arm and took a step toward it. It cowered, splattering the leaves of the forest floor with acidic urine, filling the air with an acrid stench.

"Go away," she said, relaxing as she realized they would not touch her.

The dog whined and backed up another step.

"Go!" she yelled, and the dog took off as though burned.

One by one, the dogs ran back the way they came.

Monk collapsed on the forest floor, breathing hard, exhausted. She shook in the aftermath of her terror.

"My God, Monk," Coopersmith said as she dropped to the ground and stumbled to her.

"Mitch," Monk gasped.

Coopersmith reached for her, and Monk struggled not to flinch. She fell into Coopersmith's arms, feeling their strength and softness.

"Don't you *ever* do that to me again. I can't watch it," Coopersmith whispered.

"Okay," Monk said. The words she had spoken to Coopersmith echoed and rang in her head, as did the image of Coopersmith's disregard for her feelings.

Coopersmith hesitantly put her hand on Monk's forehead and cursed softly. "You're burning up."

Lightman dropped to the ground beside her. "Let me see your wrist."

Monk hissed in pain when Lightman gently extracted her arm.

"Shit," Lightman muttered, and Coopersmith grimaced.

Monk's arm was dark red with infection from her elbow to her swollen fingers. The bandage around her wrist was soaked with dark blood. The skin around it was stretched and shiny.

"I'm going to take the bandage off," Lightman said.

Monk shook her head. "I'm all right."

"No you're not, you dope," Lightman said. "You're hurt. Why didn't you tell me? Christ, that was stupid."

Monk narrowed her eyes as a flash of anger tore through her. "Fucking let go of my arm, Lightman," she shot back coldly. She slapped their hands and rolled to her knees. She felt dizzy and nauseous. She slowly got to her feet, stood, and waited for the black spots to leave her vision. She straightened and sighed.

Lightman and Coopersmith were staring at her. Lightman's face was cold, cruel, and beautiful. Coopersmith's eyes showed her pain and concern.

Monk felt her heart twist and pushed the uncomfortable sensation aside for when she could deal with her roiling emotions.

"Lightman," she said. "What was up with the dogs, and why didn't they chew me to pieces?"

Lightman shook her head. "They're death hounds. They're Wells's. They kill people and chew up souls. Very nasty, and one hundred percent fatal."

"And why am I alive?"

"It has to do with your arm. You saw that yourself."

"It's where Wells bit me. What was in her bite?"

"What's in any werewolf's bite, Monk?" Lightman gave her an unpleasant smile. "Lycanthropy."

"You're kidding?" Monk exploded. "I'm turning into a *werewolf?*"

Lightman nodded. "Oh, yeah. That bite is fatal." She threw up her hands and kept walking up the road. She turned back. "Are you both coming, or are you just gonna stand there?"

Monk groaned, allowing panic to race through her system. She felt overwhelmed. She knew nothing about being a werewolf and didn't know how this transformation would take place.

"You knew all along, and you didn't tell me?" she asked.

Lightman shrugged. "You should have known yourself. You've seen werewolves in the movies."

Bitch, Monk thought. "Why did she do it? If she hates me and doesn't trust me, why would she do the one thing that—" She stopped and fell silent for a moment. "She wanted to turn me into one, didn't she?"

Lightman shook her head. "I don't think so."

"Why not?"

"Why?" Lightman asked. "If she makes you a werewolf she's going to have to kill you before you become a pest."

"Either that, or she never intended me to live long enough to go through the transformation. I was supposed to be dead, yes?"

Lightman gave her a single nod, staring at her warily.

Monk shook her head, fighting nausea. "Fucking *bitch*."

Lightman remained silent and immobile, and Coopersmith looked saddened.

"Monk," Coopersmith said softly. "Just take it easy. We'll deal with this. You're not alone."

Monk regarded her steadily for a moment. "You don't have to deal with anything. This is my problem, not yours." She began walking. "And yes, *I* have to deal with this. Not you. You can walk away any time you want."

Coopersmith put a hand on her good arm and pulled her to a halt. She tugged Monk around so they were face to face. Her green eyes flashed. "Okay, I've now officially had enough. What the hell is your problem? I'm just trying to help you, and I sure as hell don't deserve this."

"Deserve what?" Monk said. "Just what is it? You keep making out like we're glued together. Like I can't make it through this without you. Well, I'm really sorry, but I sure as hell can. *I* chose my path. I'm sorry that you got involved but it's not my fault."

"I could say all the same things to you. I thought we were friends."

"Oh, don't go and throw that in my face."

Coopersmith's mouth tightened. "I get it now. We do things on your timetable, or you tell me to get stuffed, right? Your feelings matter more than anyone else's, right? This entire ordeal is completely your problem, and the rest of us are supposed to just hang around and wait for you to come galloping up on your white charger to rescue us? No. No, that's *not* the way it works."

Monk had no idea how to respond to Coopersmith. She had so much she wanted to say, but couldn't. She felt her heart twist, and the fight went out of her at the anger in Coopersmith's eyes. She wanted to say something that would fix the damage between them.

"I'm sorry, Mitch," she said quietly. "I just can't do this. I never meant for you to get involved in this, and for that I'm so sorry. I don't expect you to stand back and watch me deal with Wells. Just try to take any breaks I can give you and use them for yourself." She took a deep breath. "As for my feelings . . . they matter to me. Your feelings matter to me as well. I'm trying to back off. All I do is make you angry and uncomfortable and I don't want to do that."

Coopersmith looked a little mollified. "Do you really think I can sit back and watch you get butchered by Wells?" She tilted her head. "And you don't make me angry or uncomfortable. Do you want to know how I feel?"

Monk knew where Coopersmith was leading, and had no desire to talk about her humiliation. "I can't deal with that either. Your eyes said it all. You don't have to use words as well. I get it." She felt herself blush, and nibbled her lip. She couldn't speak and begged Coopersmith with her eyes to drop it.

Coopersmith nodded. "All right. For now. But you have to deal with my feelings as well, one day." She held out her hand. "Friends?"

Monk nodded. "Friends." She squeezed Coopersmith's hand.

Before she knew it, she was tangled in Coopersmith's warm embrace, feeling colder and lonelier than ever.

CHAPTER TEN

Monk, Coopersmith, and Lightman walked for another few hours until Lightman finally called a halt for another night. The sun was low in the sky, a bloated, alien ball of deep red light.

"I'm hungry." Monk sighed, glancing at Lightman.

Lightman nodded. "I know, so am I. We'll try to get a bite to eat in the next town." She looked at Coopersmith. "How are you doing?"

Coopersmith regarded her warily. "I'm all right. I'm not hungry. I am a bit tired, though."

Lightman nodded. "Okay." She veered off the road and into a thick stand of trees. They found themselves in a clearing, sheltered on all sides from prying eyes. "Sleep," she said, lying down and curling up into a ball.

Monk lay down, and as bone weary as she was, sleep would not come. She was too aware of Coopersmith close to her, and the ground was too hard. She lay and listened as Lightman's breathing even out to a soft snore.

The sky was covered in a thick carpet of stars, alien and unknowable, and she looked for familiar patterns in them.

"Can't sleep?" Coopersmith asked, rolling over and staring at her.

Monk shook her head. "No." Her arm and her aching heart kept her awake in equal measures.

"You tried counting sheep already?"

"I've always wondered—how the hell does that help? If you pay attention to what you're doing, you wake up."

"But numbers are fun," Coopersmith said.

"Uh, huh," Monk said, nodding and smiling. "I don't expect much out of you, you're a maths teacher."

"And you're my best student. Why don't you give an old bag a thrill and count, will you?"

"I already count, Mitch," Monk whispered with a sad smile.

Coopersmith looked as though she wanted to say something, but she remained silent as she reached for Monk.

Monk found herself tangled in Coopersmith's arms. Coopersmith stroked her hair, a soothing rhythm that began to chase her ghosts away.

"Despite what you seem to think, I'm not oblivious to the way you feel. I *know* you count. Trust me. I care," Coopersmith whispered as Monk hovered on the borders of sleep. "We don't have to deal with anything now. Just relax, and let us sort out our problems later, okay?"

Monk nodded and drifted off.

Monk felt as though she had only just closed her eyes when she opened them the next morning. She still lay snuggled in Coopersmith's arms, feeling every ache in her stiff and sore body.

She gently extracted herself and sat up. Her wrist throbbed, and she wiggled her fingers experimentally. Lightning bolts of pain shot up her arm, and she grimaced.

"How's the arm?" Lightman asked, glancing at her. She sat across from them and tied the laces of her shoes.

"Hurts like hell," Monk replied, swallowing against the burning pain in her throat. Her head throbbed dully, and she could feel infection and illness tearing through her body. She hoped she would last long enough to dispose of Wells.

She felt Coopersmith shift behind her, as she sat up and yawned.

"Hey," Monk said, struck by her sleek beauty and grace.

"Hi, Monk," Coopersmith said softly. She frowned. "You look horrible."

"Thank you, Mitch. You're a sight for sore eyes first thing in the morning as well," Monk said sourly, awkwardly cradling her damaged arm to her chest as she tried to stand up.

"I mean it," Coopersmith said, gently touching her forehead. "You're white, and you're burning up."

Monk pulled away from her. "I'm fine," she said with a sigh. "I just need to wake up and get some food into me. I'll be right after that."

Coopersmith looked at her doubtfully. She ignored Lightman's proffered hand and got to her feet.

"You ready?" Lightman asked without preamble.

Monk nodded. "Lead the way."

Coopersmith remained silent as Lightman led them back to the road. She stayed beside Monk, ready to help her if needed.

They walked down the road for an hour in silence, each immersed in her own thoughts. Monk felt dimly pleased that for the first time in days she was able to push aside her pain over Coopersmith. She focused on Jackie and Kilkenny, wondering where they were and hoping they were all right, feeling clearer than she had in days. She snuck a sideways glance at Coopersmith and wished mightily that she could go back in time and change what had happened.

"Penny for your thoughts, Monk," Coopersmith said, glancing at her.

"They're not worth that much," Monk said slowly. She scanned the road ahead of them.

"That's why you have them, I suppose," Coopersmith said with a grin.

Monk mustered a smile. She still felt as though she were chasing away sleep cobwebs.

Coopersmith glanced at her, and her smile faded.

The forest became sparser, as it had before, and was losing some of its lush aspect. The trees seemed shorter and stunted, and the grass surrounding the ruts in the path was yellowish and desultory.

Coopersmith looked down and grimaced. "This can't be good."

"Nothing here seems to be," Monk said.

Lightman stopped and waited for them. Her eyes flared red. "This is a bad place, coming up. It's one of the deserted cities."

"One of the what?" Monk asked.

"Deserted cities. This world is a plague world. It's winding down."

"And it's someone's dream," Coopersmith said softly.

Monk followed the direction of her gaze. The road ahead of them evened out, becoming gravel and then cracked, sun-bleached asphalt. She waved a hand. "Let's just go. Plague world or no, I'm hungry. I need something to eat. I'm about ready to drop."

Coopersmith nodded. "I don't know what we're going to find down there."

Monk held her arm against her chest, coughing and grimacing at the ache in her head and arm. She shrugged. "Doesn't matter."

"Yes, it matters," Coopersmith said, eyes flashing.

Monk sighed. It seemed too much effort to explain that they had to walk through the city to find Wells, and it really didn't matter what was there. "Whatever. I'm too tired."

They continued to walk, and about half an hour later, they were on the outskirts of a deserted town. Unlike the previous town, this looked completely modern but didn't resemble any city they knew.

They passed a small convenience store, and Lightman pulled them to a halt.

"You have any preferences?" she asked Monk.

Monk shook her head. "Just food and drink."

Lightman nodded and walked away from them.

"Nothing for me in case you were interested," Coopersmith said with a dangerously smooth smile.

"No. I wasn't," Lightman said coldly.

Coopersmith glared at her.

Monk stepped between them. "Go. Go, Lightman."

Lightman shot one last glare at Coopersmith.

"Bitch," Coopersmith muttered as Lightman moved away from them.

"She's a werewolf's offsider. I don't think she's meant to be nice."

Coopersmith nodded. "I suppose that's why you're letting her use you as a doormat."

"I'm not," Monk said. "I have my reasons. You have to trust me for the moment."

Coopersmith nodded. "I don't like it."

Lightman shot a brief, unfriendly glance at them and strolled into the store.

Monk felt a second of exhilaration that they were alone for the first time in what felt like days. "I have something I have to say to you, Mitch." She glanced at the door.

Coopersmith gave her a neutral look and nodded.

"I'm sorry. I should have told you what was going on." She glanced at the door again. "It was really stupid of me not to. And now look at what's happened to us. It's all my fault."

"Monk," Coopersmith began.

"No," Monk said. "Please don't say anything. I just can't handle it."

"Monk, look at me," Coopersmith said, gently taking Monk's chin with her hand and forcing her to look at her. "I'm not your mother. I won't hurt you."

Monk's eyes swam, and she flinched. "Thanks," she whispered.

Coopersmith gave her a sad smile. "I won't give up on you."

"Charming," Lightman said, striding toward them with water, potato chips, and jerky strips. The packaging was dusty but the contents weren't. "Are you going to swap spit?"

"Christ," Monk muttered, shooting her a frosty look. "You're fucking disgusting, you know that?"

"At least I'm not an emotionally constipated wimp."

"Shut up."

"Coward. You can't even face the woman to deal with what's happened, can you?"

"Shut up."

"You really think she hasn't noticed that Wells has basically chewed you up and spat you out? And that Kilkenny, despite being a child, has successfully hidden from her, unlike you? And that your basic motivation to become a hero to impress a girl you had a crush on fucked up? You're an immature shit for brains, you know that?"

"Shut up."

"Why the hell should I? You're angling for sympathy. You're doing the martyr thing. You're a fucking loser, Monk."

Monk clutched her potato chips in a white knuckled grip. They burst open and scattered all over the ground. Lightman laughed, and Monk took a step forward.

"Knock it off," Coopersmith said quietly, stepping between them. She glared at Lightman until Lightman looked away. She turned to Monk. "You want more food?"

Monk shook her head, humiliated and fighting tears. "I don't think I can eat. I just want something to drink."

She twisted the bottle lid and yelped as she lost her grip and the bottle jammed her bad arm.

Coopersmith flinched and reached for the bottle. "Let me—"

"No!" Monk screamed in pain as she savagely twisted the bottle lid. Her arm throbbed and tears of pain leaked from her eyes. "I got it."

Coopersmith glared at the smirking Lightman. "Are you happy? Did that feel good?" She turned to Monk. "She's playing you, Monk."

Monk growled, and she flicked away the tears flowing down her face. "She's not doing anything to me. I'm not a fucking victim. I'm not a child. I can look after myself." Her chest heaved as she struggled to find the right words to express how she was feeling. She turned to

Lightman, fighting down the razor sharp edge of her temper. "Damn you. I'm not a coward, a wimp, an idiot, or a loser. My feelings are not public domain. I have a right to my privacy." She turned back to Coopersmith, temper expended but shaking from the adrenalin coursing through her system. "I know you're not my mother. I don't want you to be. I want you to be my friend and to treat me like I'm your equal, not a little sister you have to look out for and protect." She looked down at the potato chips on the ground and the bottle of water in her hand. "I'm not hungry. Just thirsty."

Coopersmith leaned forward. "That works both ways. Treat me like I'm an adult."

Monk nodded. "I know. I know."

Coopersmith nodded. "Okay, let's start again. You need some help with the bottle?"

Monk's hands shook. "Please," she said, handing Coopersmith the bottle.

Coopersmith opened it, took a swig, and handed it back to her. She put a steadying arm around Monk, and they walked to the edge of the town.

They walked for another half hour, Coopersmith close by Monk's side. Monk snuck a couple of glances at her and saw the flash of pain and concern in her eyes.

"How are you doing?" Coopersmith asked softly. "I mean *really* doing?"

"I don't feel all that well," Monk said, trying to choose her words carefully. "I'm all right for now, though." She tried to give Coopersmith a reassuring smile. "What happened to Terri, Jackie, and Kilkenny? How did you get here?"

"Are you changing the subject on me?"

"I have to," Monk said. *I feel fucking rotten. I need you to distract me.* "Tell me."

Coopersmith sighed, her eyes turned toward the cracked and pitted road. They were in an industrial area, and the vast parking lots surrounding vacant factories were empty save for some scattered rusted cars. The chain link fences seemingly begged for crucified victims to hang from them.

Monk felt anticipation in the air and was mildly disappointed that nothing seemed to be happening.

"Well, after you and Wells left, Kilkenny and Jackie told us what was going on. I went with Kilkenny into the dreamscape to look for you, and we found you with Wells. We got blasted out of there. We came back in the next night, all four of us, to look for you, but Wells found us first. We ran. I ran one way, Terri was with me, and then suddenly she wasn't. I found myself in that town with all the garbage. I was there for a day before I got arrested, and the next thing I knew you were there."

"Did you go to sleep, or did Kilkenny bring you through a gateway?"

Coopersmith gave her an odd look. "What's a gateway? From what I know we all fell asleep in the living room of Terri's house."

Monk gritted her teeth and stared at the road ahead, focusing on Lightman's broad back.

"Terri and I aren't dating, and we're not lovers. My car had nails in the tires, and she drove behind me to the tire place. Then she came home, and we had coffee. It was a kiss between friends. That's all we are," Coopersmith said softly. "I just wanted you to know."

Monk clenched her jaw, fighting tears and jealousy. "Thanks." She nodded, and was quiet for a moment, studying the houses that had taken over from the factories. The city felt deserted and cold, claustrophobic and terrifying. She shivered.

"This is horrible," Coopersmith muttered, staring at a red brick house. It looked like an older style, well built and neatly kept. Monk couldn't imagine the gardener who kept the lawns so neatly manicured.

She stopped to stare at it and felt a distant tug in her mind. She couldn't stop studying the dark front door, the heavy curtains, or the rocking chair on the wide porch. It felt as though something lived there, an invisible denizen of a strange world, and Monk had to go to it.

She broke into a shambling run toward the house, ignoring Coopersmith's cries from behind her. She held up a hand, indicating she would not be long. She made it to the front doors. She touched the handle, and it felt as though a lightning bolt tore through her. She dropped to her knees, clutching her screaming wrist and fighting nausea. Her vision blurred, and her head swam. Her control slowly returned. She finally felt well enough to stand, and did so.

What the fuck just happened?

She looked around and found herself alone. She understood Coopersmith was no longer with her and looked up the road in the direction she had last seen Lightman.

It was empty.

She haltingly jogged out onto the road, cursing the dizziness and weakness that threatened to drive her to her knees. She fought down a rising wave of panic.

She felt torn in equal parts between Lightman, Coopersmith, and the house behind her. She forced herself to still her trembling body, and then called for them.

"Mitch! Lightman!" She cocked her head and listened for a moment to the silence. "Mitch! Lightman!"

She listened carefully, but heard nothing over the steadily rushing breeze.

She heard a soft creak and a thud. She jumped, heart hammering, and spun around.

The house's front door swung open and bumped against the wall. Darkness lay within, and Monk's feet itched from the urge to run. Her legs began to move on cue, toward the house.

Adrenalin flooded her system, and her forebrain screamed itself hoarse, begging her to stop moving, yet her feet carried her toward the door. She paused on the top step of the porch, feeling the invisible miasma of misery and evil pouring out of the open front door.

She went inside and paused just inside the foyer.

The sheer normality of its appearance was striking—the neatly dusted small hall table, the scrupulously clean floor, and the perfectly hung pictures at odd intervals on the walls.

She held her breath and tried to still her shaking body. She was distantly aware of the throbbing in her arm, which ratcheted up a notch, and the way the colors seemed to bleed into one another in quick flashes.

She halted, cocked her head, and listened.

There! Her mind screamed as she gazed riveted down the hallway toward the back of the house. *Again!* She heard a soft scraping sound and a chair leg shifting on a wooden floor.

She went as quietly as she could toward the back of the house, her skin crawling with anticipation, and unseen eyes boring into her back.

She widened her eyes as she slowly entered the kitchen. Despite her suspicion that something was in there, the reality of seeing Terri Warland tied to a chair, her wide, light gray eyes eating up her face in fear, caused her to jerk with shock and clutch her chest. The sensation of colors bleeding together in her vision increased, and she glanced around the kitchen.

"Monk," Warland moaned softly. "Is it really you?" She yelped as invisible hands slapped her face, leaving red handprints in their wake.

Monk couldn't see anything, but she could feel the drafts of air from the passage of bodies around her and followed movement out of the corners of her eyes.

"Yes, it's me, Terri," she replied. "Really me."

The colors kept flashing and bleeding into each other, and she tried to focus on them. She felt the sensation as a key twisting inside her head.

"Your eyes, Monk," Warland said.

Monk looked at her. "What about them?" she asked, seeing another aura flash. It formed a crude outline of a human being.

"They're going yellow." Warland's eyes were wide with terror, and she looked as though she wanted to throw herself backward and out of Monk's reach.

Monk flinched. She felt the sting of adrenalin, and was distantly amazed she could feel anything at all anymore.

The auras flashed, and she concentrated on them, harder than ever, and the wavering forms of four human outlines stayed in her vision.

"I'll explain later, Terri," Monk said, as one of the auras reached out a twisted hand to pinch Warland. Warland focused in another direction but avoided the hand that tried to touch her.

Monk went toward the auras, watching them carefully as they recoiled from her.

She quickly knelt behind Warland, untied her, and helped her to her feet.

"Take my hand," Monk said urgently, blindly reaching for her. She felt Warland's hand slip into hers. "Good. Let's go."

She took a step toward the auras, but they suddenly swam together and blocked the way to the door. She touched the first aura and was hurled back along with Warland. They collided with the sink and landed on the table. It shattered like a bomb, leaving them tangled in a bruised heap on the floor.

"Monk?" Warland asked, sitting up and pulling Monk with her. "Can you see what this is?"

The auras weren't wavering for her anymore. Now they were solid, and her aching stomach wanted to expel its contents.

Four figures stood before them, a man, a woman, and two teenage children. The resemblance to anything human stopped there. They had light, mottled gray skin, blackened veins, and listless, straw-like hair. Their eyes were milky and horribly aware.

"Don't worry about what's in front of us, Terri," Monk said. "Worry about how we're going to get out of here."

She took a step forward, and the man thing reached for her. Monk avoided his hands, and he gave a low, chilling moan. Warland shrank into Monk's back as he opened his mouth. Monk's mind recoiled as his mouth opened wide—wide enough to encase her head with rows upon rows of sharp teeth.

Monk pushed past him, and his jaws snapped shut with a click, snagging her shoulder. She yelped as the teeth tore through skin. Warland pulled in closer to her, trying to avoid things she could not see.

They tore up the hallway, out of the house, and into the street. The family of ghouls stayed close behind them.

Monk hesitated and blinked at the raw, bleeding color before her eyes.

Warland tugged her hand, urging her forward. "C'mon. We gotta go."

Monk stumbled along behind her, her aching wrist clutched to her chest. She had the beginnings of a terrible headache. She could hear the ghouls in the street behind them, and Warland kept glancing back.

They ran toward the end of the street, and Monk paused and looked behind them.

"Oh, Jesus," she moaned.

"What?" Warland asked, turning to follow her gaze.

"Can't you see that?" Monk asked.

Warland shook her head. "What do you see?"

"They're coming after us. We have to get out of here."

They turned in unison and ran. The sound of sliding, scraping, and slapping flesh and bodies close behind them tormented Monk.

Monk felt as though she had been running all day, and by the time they had gone maybe a hundred meters down the street, she was ready to collapse. She pulled Warland to a halt and looked at the ghouls behind them.

They slavered and ran after them.

Suddenly, one of them, the leader, skidded to a halt and stood still.

One by one, they all followed suit, blind eyes riveted to a point behind Monk's shoulder.

"What?" Warland asked. "We gotta move."

Monk shook her head, cradling her aching wrist in her good hand. "I can't. I can't. I'm done." Black flowers bloomed before her vision. She fell to her knees.

"Get up, Monkhouse," an icy voice said from behind them.

Warland yelped, and Monk slowly turned to face their attacker.

Wells stood not ten meters from them. A cold, cruel smile played about her lips. "Monkhouse."

"Wells," Monk replied, desperately trying to regroup and reclaim some energy.

Wells took a step forward until they were eye to eye. She casually grabbed Warland by the neck and tossed her into the shattered remains of a car. Warland landed heavily and lay still. Monk felt her insides twist as she tore her eyes away from the sight.

"How's the wrist, Monk?" Wells asked, her bile yellow eyes monstrously jovial.

Monk shook her head, unwilling to tell her the truth and not knowing what to say.

"You're sick," Wells said conversationally. "How about I give you a cheap shot? You want to take a swing at me, go right ahead." She held out her arms.

Monk remained terrified and motionless.

"How about a little incentive, my apprentice?" Wells strode toward Warland before Monk could move. She grabbed Warland and swung her toward the ghouls.

Monk shook in fear but forced herself to move.

She dove at Wells, pushed her backward, and yanked Warland out of her grip.

Wells caught her easily and laughed in her face. "You don't have what it takes to kill me, Monkhouse. You just don't have it in you."

Monk mustered some of her former bravado. "Fuck you, Wells. I have what it takes to get rid of you."

"No," Wells said, smirking. "You don't. You're too much of a coward. You don't like confrontations but you can't stay out of them because of your big mouth. This is a prime example. You never wanted to fight me but now you think you can't do anything else. You're afraid of me."

"So what the fuck did you bite me for? You knew it was going to make me a werewolf."

"Who said I intended for you to live that long? You're already like me, minus the yellow eyes and fangs."

"I'm *nothing* like you."

"You're *everything* like me. You don't want to be but you are."

"Hey. I am *not* cruel, shallow, or insane," Monk screamed.

"Maybe not," Wells said, almost conversationally. "But you *are* strong, arrogant, and driven. The main difference between the two of us is that I'm not a control freak." She burst into a round of loud, rude laughter and shoved Monk who landed on her behind on the road.

Monk shook with fear and anger, but remained silent, watching her carefully. She tensed when Wells pressed her claws against her unprotected belly. She began to sweat—one swipe, and she would be no more.

"Give up, Monkhouse," Wells said coldly. She mock lunged toward Warland, grabbed her by the neck, and dragged her to her feet. Warland began choking.

Wells flexed her claws and they dimpled Monk's skin. Monk filled with panic.

Wells laughed, loudly and rudely.

Monk kicked out as hard as she could and caught Wells in the stomach. She pushed with her feet.

Wells let her go, and Monk fell to the ground, and Warland landed on top of her. She pushed Warland out of the way so she could move.

"Like I said, Monkhouse," Wells said. "You don't have what it takes." She turned to the empty street. "Mitch. Lightman," she screamed in Monk's voice.

Monk recoiled.

" . . . Monk! . . ." The sound floated to them on the steadily rushing wind.

"Arsehole," Monk said. She stood between Wells and the groaning Warland.

Wells snarled, leapt onto Monk, and pinned her to the ground by her shoulders, snapping at her neck. Monk yelled and struggled wildly in raw panic.

Wells snorted a laugh, leapt off her, and ran back down the street. "You're done!"

"Monk." Warland leaned over Monk and swayed. "We have to get moving."

Monk awkwardly got to her feet, her wounded arm shooting white hot bolts of agony into her body.

Warland grabbed her by her good hand, and they ran. Monk glanced behind them and cursed when she saw the ghoul things running after them. They kept pace despite their ungainly movements.

"This doesn't look familiar," Monk panted, dismayed. They bolted up a residential street. Houses were on one side, a decaying sports field on the other side. She could hear doors open behind them, but she didn't dare to look.

Black spots flowered in Monk's vision, and her chest heaved. Her lungs felt full of ground glass. She halted and leant over with her hands on her knees.

"I can't. I can't," she said. "I can't make it."

"I'm not leaving you," Warland said, putting a hand on her back.

"You have to go, if you don't, they're going to tear both of us apart."

"Your eyes go yellow. Like Wells. Can't you use that?"

"I don't know how," Monk said as the second mob of ghouls closed on them.

Warland cursed as a ghoul snapped its jaws and pounced on her. She hit the road, rolled over, and held it off as its jaws snapped close to her neck.

The pack reached Monk and clawed at her.

She screamed in agony as ragged fingernails tore off the bandage around her arm and clawed the suppurating bite.

The ghouls hissed, quieted, and shrank back away from her.

Monk threw up strings of bile as she held up her arm, warding them away. She staggered closer to Warland, scaring the ghoul away.

"Can you stand?" Monk asked, focused on the ghouls and not looking at Warland.

She heard Warland shift behind her.

"I'm up," Warland said. "Let's get out of here."

Monk turned, and they began to walk quickly up the street. She glanced over her shoulder. The ghouls remained in position, staring at them with cold, calculating eyes. After a moment, they scattered and ran back the way they came.

Monk and Warland walked to the end of the street and turned right. Monk could see the tall buildings of the city centre in the distance.

"Where the hell are we?" Monk could feel the blood and pus from her damaged arm soaking through her tee shirt.

"I don't know," Warland said, looking around. "Before we do anything else we have to get some bandages on your arm."

She gently took Monk's hand. It was swollen, hot and dark, shiny red.

"Jesus," Warland breathed. "What happened to it? Can you move your arm?"

"Wells bit me, and I can hardly move my fingers. It hurts," she said, pulling out of Warland's gentle grip.

Warland nodded. "All right. We'll try and find a chemist." She touched Monk's forehead. "Quickly."

Monk nodded. Her headache thumped and snarled, and she felt nauseated.

They walked up another old and cracked street.

"How did you get there? What happened?" Monk asked.

Warland expelled a deep breath. "We were all in my house. Kilkenny put us to sleep, and I dreamed Wells came for us. We all scattered, and I remember falling through the sky and ending up here. I landed in the middle of the street, and something I couldn't see came for me." She shuddered. "I got pulled into that house and tied into a chair. It felt like there were people around me. What the hell was that, Monk?"

"You couldn't even see them at the end?" Monk asked.

Warland shook her head.

"Then you don't want to know." Monk glanced at Warland. "They weren't pretty. Let's just leave it at that."

Warland was silent for a moment. "All right." She paused. "Have you seen any of the others?"

"I was with Mitch and Lightman," Monk said. She tried to stop the flare of hostility inside her as an image of Coopersmith and Warland embracing shot through her mind. "I got side tracked by you."

Warland nodded. "What happened to them?"

"I don't know, really," Monk said. "When I saw the house you were in, they seemed to have disappeared. I know they could hear me. They called for me."

"Are you sure it was them?" Warland said. "Listen. Michelle!"

They waited for a moment.

" . . . Terri . . ."

Warland gave Monk a bitter smile. "It's always that far away. It never gets any closer."

Monk sighed. "Figures." She felt sick. She didn't trust Lightman, even though she had asked her to look out for Coopersmith.

Warland pulled her to a halt. "Here." She pointed to a chemist. "We try there."

Monk nodded and allowed Warland to lead her inside. The fully stocked store was as dusty and devoid of life as all the other buildings they had seen. They took bandages and disinfectant, plus some of the snack food at the front of the store.

"Let's get out of here," Warland said, juggling her load of goods and glancing around.

Monk nodded. "I hear you."

They went back out and sat cross-legged in the middle of the street.

"Let me see." Warland reached for Monk's hand.

Monk held it out for her, and Warland grimaced.

"I hope the disinfectant is really disinfectant and nothing different," Warland muttered. She looked into Monk's eyes. "This is going to hurt like hell."

Monk nodded, paling.

"Ready?" Warland asked.

Monk nodded.

Warland hesitated for a moment and then poured the disinfectant onto Monk's wrist. Monk screamed in agony, feeling as though wave after wave of fire was burning into her arm. Her fingers twitched uncontrollably, and she fought not to snatch her hand out of Warland's grip.

Warland quickly wrapped up her wound in fresh bandages, and Monk sagged against her, exhausted.

Monk felt herself being pulled into Warland's arms, breathing in the soft scent of her perfume.

"You say Wells bit your arm?" Warland asked.

"Yeah," Monk said.

"You're turning, aren't you?" Warland asked. "It would explain the yellow eyes."

Monk nodded, convicted. "I think so."

She felt Warland's arms tighten, felt the gentle movement of Warland's hands on her back, offering her silent comfort. "One thing at a time, Monk. We have to deal with Wells first. After that, you."

Monk nodded, allowing herself precious moments of relaxation in her gentle embrace.

CHAPTER ELEVEN

Monk and Warland walked through deserted residential streets, lost, alone, and no closer to finding the others. It felt like they had walked for hours, yet the sky overhead remained overcast and the steadily rushing wind did nothing to dispel the clammy air.

Monk could not get her mind off Coopersmith, Jackie, and Kilkenny. So many questions whirled through her mind: where were they? Had Wells caught them? Were they alive? Were they dead?

Warland, for her part, remained silent and grim.

They walked down deserted streets, making left and right turns by mutual, silent decision.

"God," Monk muttered after they made another turn down a nameless street. "This is really starting to get on my nerves."

"You reckon?" Warland asked pleasantly. She put a hand on Monk's back and rubbed as Monk leaned forward.

Monk nodded. "I reckon."

Warland looked around at the houses. "Does this look any different when your eyes go yellow?"

Monk shook her head. She stared at the closest townhouse. It was of the nameless variety that lined the streets of Newtown in Sydney. A layer of brick covered the tiny front yard, and the porch looked dusty but sturdy. A brass knocker, begging for use, hung on the dark brown front door.

She tried to look inside, through the ruined curtains that outlined dirty windows.

"Monk?" Warland asked, peering at her.

"Shh." Monk looked at the house.

Warland stood beside her, gaze alternating between Monk and the house.

"Enough," Warland said quietly. "What's going through that mind of yours?"

Strange auras swam before Monk's vision. She could see more bleeding color inside the house.

"I have to go in there," she said.

"Why?"

"I don't know. I just do."

Warland snorted. "All right. Enough of this elliptical bullshit of yours. What the hell are you seeing in the house?"

Monk felt her temper flare. She had more than enough of people telling her what she should think and feel. She glared at Warland. "Either you come with me or you don't."

Warland's eyes flashed. "No way."

"What?" Monk stared at her in shock.

Warland leaned forward, arms crossed. "I said, no way."

"Thanks, I got that part. What the fuck is the matter with you?"

"I'm fucking sick and tired of you standing in front of me like I'm a child in need of protection. I'm not. I'm a grown woman who doesn't really like being sheltered by a know-it-all teenager."

Monk gaped at her. "I'm not a know-it-all."

"You are. You have to learn how to communicate. If you had leveled with me about all of this before it happened, I would have had a choice in whether or not I wanted to be involved."

"What the fuck are you talking about?"

"I'm saying that if there's something in the house, you should tell me what it is. Then I can decide whether or not I want to go in there. Unlike you, I'm not a victim."

"What the hell is that supposed to mean?"

"Jackie and Kilkenny filled us in on what happened before we all ended up in this godforsaken place," Warland said, studying her. She still looked angry but more in control over her emotions. "They told us that you volunteered to be meat for Wells. That you would shield them until Kilkenny could take care of herself. Do you have any idea how stupid that was? How self destructive? You should have told us from the start that's what you were doing. We would have decided whether we wanted to help you or back away. You would have given us a choice. Before you ask, my choice would have been to go with you. You're my friend." She blew out a gusty breath. "You should have had a little more consideration toward the people that care about you."

"Like fucking who?" Monk asked bitterly. "My mother uses me for target practice and Mitch . . . I think if I died tomorrow Mitch would be upset but she'd get on with her life quickly enough."

"Knock it off with the self pity. Goddammit. Michelle's life doesn't revolve around you. You should be happy that she'd be strong enough to go on without you."

"I'm not wallowing in self pity. And Mitch is my friend."

"Hello, Monk? Hello? What about your *other* friends?"

"Oh, yeah? Like who?"

"Like me. Like Jackie. Like Kilkenny," Warland yelled. "Remember us? Stop treating us like shit. Stop ignoring us and rely on us. Care about us and what we think. Enough with the poor me routine." She paused and then looked closely at Monk. "You really just don't understand, do you? Not everything in life has to be temporary, including our friendship. I have no idea what we're going to do about Wells but we'll do *something*. But that doesn't really matter to you because you're more interested in losing than winning, aren't you? Well, stop doing that. Focus on winning." She folded her arms. "You're worth something, Monk, in and of yourself. *You* matter. Your *life* matters. You can't just squander it. Take it and make it yours. Own it."

Monk clammed up. She felt embarrassed and angry.

Warland waited for a few minutes and then shook her head. "Just think about it," she said with a sigh. "All right, what's in the house?"

"I don't know, and that's the truth," Monk said. She avoided Warland's eyes. "I only know that I want to go inside. I don't know why."

"Do you see anything with your yellow eyes?"

Monk shook her head, looking straight ahead. "Not this time."

Warland took a step toward the house. She turned back to Monk. "Well? Are we going to have a look?"

"I have no idea what's in there," Monk said. "You sure about this?"

Warland nodded. "I get to choose. I choose to go into the house."

Monk followed her closely to the front door. The atmosphere of the house was frightening. It felt as though a black miasma hung over it. Monk felt waves of horror washing over her. She shrank into Warland.

Warland pushed the door open with a shaking hand. Her lips were pressed into a straight line, and she looked pale and grim. The door didn't move, and they both almost sagged with relief.

"Well," Warland said. "Looks like we can't—"

The door swung open. Warland's mouth opened and closed several times. Monk nodded. She felt herself break out in a cold sweat.

"I don't really want to do this but I feel like I have to," she said as she pushed past Warland and walked through the door. She almost screamed as she felt Warland's long body press into her from behind. Her heart was beating so hard it felt as though her chest were about to explode.

Her mind shied away from the fractured geometry of the house. Corners met at an angle that was not quite ninety degrees; flat floors seemed longer than hallway ceilings; doors that could not possibly close were sensibly shut. Worse still, the house seemed wider on the inside than it did on the outside. She looked around, forcing her mind to accept what her eyes were telling her.

A darkened sitting room was to the left, and ahead were a hallway and set of stairs leading to an upper level. The doorway to the right looked like it led into an office.

"Geez," Warland breathed, pointing over Monk's shoulder and down the hallway.

Monk felt her vision bleed auras and the throbbing in her damaged wrist slid up a notch.

She could see movement at the end of the hallway in the kitchen. It looked like twenty or more silhouettes, and they walked back and forth, seemingly oblivious to their presence. She narrowed her eyes and took another step down the hallway. She thought it looked like a city street, and the normality of the scene made her hair stand on end. She was grateful for Warland's close presence, and drew strength from her proximity.

Warland gasped, and Monk felt her shift. Suddenly Warland's hands closed around her arm in a death grip.

Monk turned to the left, in the direction of the sitting room. The air inside the room was shimmering, and there seemed to be wavering outlines of people inside it. Monk blinked with uncertainty, stomach roiling from the pain in her wrist and the bleeding auras before her vision.

Warland took a step back, dragging Monk with her. Her hand was sweating and shaking. A silhouette that had been in the sitting room was moving toward them and had taken a step out into the hallway. It radiated coldness, and something so dark and unsettling that Monk's mind almost froze under its onslaught. Wave after wave of cold terror washed over her. Her vision flickered again, and the silhouette resolved into the shape of a handsome, dark-haired man with flaming red eyes. He radiated hatred and malevolence, and balanced on the balls of his feet, prepared to lunge at them.

Warland grabbed Monk's good hand. She tried to move toward the front door, but the man suddenly stood in the way. He smiled, revealing snowy teeth filed into sharp points. He shut his mouth with a gristly snap and blood, bone, and flesh splattered them.

Monk moaned, tugging Warland toward the stairs. She took them, two at a time, adrenalin giving her sorely abused muscles enough strength to function. She paused at the first landing, allowing Warland to hare past her, and stared down the stairs at the man. His smile remained firmly in place, despite rivulets of blood leaking down his chin and staining his white shirt. He met her eyes and took a gliding step forward. Monk whimpered as he floated up the stairs in eerie silence.

Warland quickly backed down the steps again, grabbed Monk's tee shirt by the shoulder, and tugged her up the stairs. Monk's shirt tore with a soft, purring sound. She ran on Warland's heels toward the front of the house, toward what looked like the master bedroom.

Warland tore the door open, and they stumbled inside. Warland slammed the door behind them and sagged against it, panting.

"Christ, Monk," she said. "What the bloody hell was all that?"

"I don't know," Monk moaned. "What is it with all the fucking shadows and miserable air? And what the bloody, fucking hell is that?" She pointed at the window.

They were one floor above ground level, but the window showed them a view onto a Victorian street, complete with cobbled road, carriage, horses and milling men, women and children. They were all rugged up against the cold in bright, sunny air. Their breath frosted in front of their faces.

Warland squeaked, and dove away from the door, and backed to the windows, her huge eyes eating up her face.

"What—?" Monk hissed in shock.

A solid arm and hand stuck out of the door, grasping blindly. The hand found the handle and pushed downwards. A low howl of triumph sounded from behind it.

"Window?" Monk asked urgently.

"No!" Warland exclaimed, backing away from the window toward the closet.

Monk stared as she took in the view outside the window with a sinking heart. It was full of faces, pressed against the glass and peering in at them. The faces belonged to every person that had been walking along the street. They were unblinking, with unkind eyes and cold expressions on their faces.

"Here," Monk said, pulling Warland toward the closet.

She tore open the door, and inky blackness spilled out in a frigid flood. She stumbled and lost her footing.

Monk couldn't have said how big the space was. Her eyes were useless. It was so dark there was no difference between open and closed eyes. She felt Warland close to her, frantically reaching for her, gasping for breath.

Their fingertips brushed, and suddenly Warland was yanked away, shrieking.

Monk screamed in terror, sickened at the sensation of freefall and the vast, cavern-like space all around her.

She felt heat from below and brought up her hands to protect her face. She hit the ground before she had time to scream.

Hands grasped her and held her still.

She thrashed and screamed in raw panic, and slowly a sound penetrated the haze surrounding her.

"Monk," a familiar voice said. "Monk. Open your eyes."

Monk did as the voice said.

She blinked against the suddenly brighter light, and she darted her gaze back and forth between Lightman and Coopersmith. "Get off me, Lightman. I'm all right."

Lightman did as Monk asked.

"Monk," Coopersmith said with no small amount of relief.

"Oh, God, Mitch," Monk moaned, tears of relief leaking out of her eyes. "Mitch."

She cautiously reached for Coopersmith, who slipped her arms around her body. She leant into Coopersmith, closed her eyes, and sighed. She shook from the aftereffect of adrenalin in her system.

"What's the matter?" Coopersmith asked.

Monk felt disorientated and exhausted. "What the hell just happened?"

Coopersmith gave her a sad smile. "You fainted, I think. You were staring at that house and you went over." She brushed Monk's shaggy hair back from her forehead. "I thought I'd lost you."

Monk finally began tracking and looked around. She was lying in the street outside the residential house that she thought Warland was in. Lightman stood a small distance away from them, watching both ends of the street.

"I'm all right," she said, gazing into Coopersmith's emerald eyes. She remembered what Warland had said to her. *You have to learn how to communicate.* "Actually, something weird just happened to me." It felt awkward to say, but it felt good not to bottle up her experience with Warland.

"What?" Coopersmith asked.

Monk took a deep breath and told her everything about Warland, the ghouls, wandering through the city and the strange house they had gone into, including falling into the darkness and Warland torn from her grasp. "How long was I gone for?"

"You weren't gone at all. You fainted," Coopersmith said, nibbling her lip.

"That can't be right," Monk said. "It was so real." She held up her damaged wrist, studying the clean bandage. "Look."

Coopersmith's eyes widened. "This looks different."

"That's because Terri put more antiseptic on it and a new bandage." Monk leapt to her feet. She glanced back at the house. "I'm going in there. I have to see if Terri's back in there."

"I'm coming with you," Coopersmith said.

"Are you sure?"

"Yes, of course I'm sure. I can't let you go in there by yourself."

"If you want to come in there with me, do it because you think Terri's in there. Not because I need protection," Monk said carefully, without her customary heat. "Please, Mitch."

Coopersmith gave her another sad smile. "That's what I meant. I'm also doing it because you're my friend. I don't want to lose you. I don't want to lose any of us."

Monk nodded. "Mitch, I'm sick. I'm turning into a werewolf."

Coopersmith gently stroked her face. "I know. I know. But you're always going to be my Monk." She studied Monk for a moment with sad eyes. "Besides, you know how to stop being one, don't you? If it's really something you don't want?"

Monk felt the sting of tears. She nodded. "I know." She patted her pocket, feeling the almost forgotten outline of her mother's silver letter openers in it.

"I don't want it to come to that." Coopersmith's eyes shone with unshed tears. "Shall we go?" She held out her hand, and Monk levered herself up.

Monk leant over, struggling against a sudden bout of dizziness. Coopersmith helped her stand upright.

"You're going into that house?" Lightman asked. Her eyes flared red.

Monk nodded. "We have to."

"Beware," Lightman said. "That house is an intersection."

"Between what?" Monk asked.

"Between worlds. Or places in this world."

Monk nodded, as if this made sense. She was too tired to puzzle it out but had seen the results when she traveled with Warland.

Monk led the way into the house, Coopersmith close behind her. She kept a firm grip on Coopersmith's hand and pushed open the door.

The inside of the house looked different to the first time Monk had gone in there. The house had a cold, deserted feel. A thick layer of dust covered the floor, and it looked as though no one had been in there for years. Monk extended her senses, but all she could feel was the emptiness of a long abandoned house.

She led the way to the back of the house, into the kitchen. The kitchen table lay in splinters on the floor, and a lone chair sat in the middle of the room, ropes lying around its base.

Monk shook her head. "Terri was here. Now she's gone."

"Yeah," Coopersmith said. "And it looks as if all of that happened years ago."

Monk looked more closely at the ropes, seeing the same layer of dust covering them as in the rest of the house.

They searched through the house but found no sign of anyone or anything. Monk was almost relaxed when they left. Lightman sat on the front brick fence, waiting for them. Her eyes were furnace red.

"Couldn't find her, huh?" Lightman asked.

Monk shook her head. "She's gone. Do you have any idea where?"

Lightman shook her head. "I don't even really know what happened to you."

"We're in a living dream," Monk said. "Nothing really has to make sense."

"You ready to keep moving?" Lightman asked.

"Don't you think we should have a look around for Terri?" Coopersmith asked.

"Did you see any footsteps in the dust?" Monk asked.

Coopersmith thought about it for a second and then shook her head.

"Neither did I," Monk said. "And if she walked out of there recently we would have seen them." She held up her hand to forestall any arguments. "I don't want to leave here either."

"Look, dipshit," Lightman said almost kindly. "I can tell where this is heading. You want to camp out here for a while, make sure that Warland doesn't really turn up, right?"

Monk nodded.

"No," Lightman said.

"No?" Monk asked. "What do you mean, no?"

"Exactly that," Lightman said coldly. "In case you hadn't noticed, your friend, a child, is still running around in here somewhere trying to escape my lover. She doesn't stand a chance if you're not with her."

"So what do you propose?" Coopersmith asked.

Lightman pointed over her shoulder, back toward the left. "We go that way. We find Wells. If we find Wells, we find your *not* friends, Monk. Remember?"

Monk blushed. "I remember."

"You're a vicious little thing, aren't you?" Coopersmith asked, staring coldly at Lightman. "You want us to just dump Terri? Well, I'm not in that."

"You're not dumping her," Lightman said. "Monk came back to the same place she left from. Warland is probably going to do the same thing. Chances are it won't be here." She gave them both a nasty grin. "Or that she's even alive, really."

"Why wouldn't she be alive?" Monk asked. "Wells wants to torture me."

Lightman shook her head. "That's the one thing you've just never internalized. Wells isn't after you. She's after Kilkenny. She's always told you that she wants to kill your friends in front of you, but she's lying. You mean nothing to her or in the grand scheme of things."

"Then why did she bite me?" Monk asked. "Why did she try and turn me into a werewolf?"

"She didn't. That, I think, was just coincidental. You're not supposed to be alive anymore. It happens."

Monk felt humiliated and sick to her stomach. Wells had told her the same thing. It was probably the truth. She felt Coopersmith's hand on her shoulder.

"Look, Lightman," Coopersmith said coldly. "If anyone means nothing in the grand scheme of things, it's you. You're nothing more than a glorified delivery girl. You're still watching Wells's back, just like a good little dog."

Lightman growled and took a step toward her.

Monk saw auras and blinked, keeping her eyes carefully away from Coopersmith.

Lightman nodded approvingly. "The change is happening. Good. It's going to make it easier to kill Wells if you're the same."

"Change?" Coopersmith asked.

Monk looked directly at her, watching the colors surrounding her flare and melt into one another.

"Monk," Coopersmith moaned.

Monk nodded. "I am. It's speeding up." She turned to Lightman. "I want to talk to Mitch privately for a second."

"I'm not listening," Lightman said, walking away and sitting back on the low, brick fence in front of the house.

"Look," Monk said to Coopersmith. "We can talk later if you want about lycanthropy. For the moment, I'm not worried about that. I care more about Terri." She fell silent for a moment, afraid to speak. She cleared her throat, gathering her courage. "I think we should go."

Coopersmith's mouth tightened, and she opened it to speak.

"I think Lightman's right," Monk said, cutting Coopersmith off. "I think Terri was here a while back but she's not anymore."

"If you came back to the place you started from, why wouldn't she?"

"If she did she would be here. Paradox." Monk felt the sting of tears. "I have to find Wells. It's all my fault you're in this mess. If what Lightman said was true, and Wells was never interested in me, then you're all in this completely needlessly. My arrogance dragged us into this mess. Everything that's happened to all of us sits right on me."

"Monk," Coopersmith said. "Wells hated you from the start, remember? You have no idea what either one of them wanted from you, or for you. Lightman and Wells aren't telling you the truth. I don't know if we can assign blame to anyone for any of this." She studied Monk for a moment. "We're in this together now, and if you keep talking to me like you are now, we have a fighting chance."

Monk bit her lip and felt the sting of tears. "I'm afraid for Terri, Jackie, and Kilkenny. My gut tells me Terri's not here and won't be back. We have to keep pushing forward."

Coopersmith was silent for a long moment, staring at the house. "All right," she said, grim and pale as she turned back to Monk. "We go." She shook her head. "I don't know if I'm ever going to forgive myself for this."

Monk nodded. "I know." She turned back to Lightman. "Let's go."

Lightman nodded approvingly. "Good. We move out."

They walked for another hour or so through deserted city streets. The city was unfamiliar to all of them, so they navigated by Lightman's bond to Wells. They made their way into the city center, looking up at tall, crumbling skyscrapers and down at the rubble on the ground, in a place so devoid of life, Monk wondered who had built it to begin with.

"Monk," Coopersmith said, breaking the comfortable silence that had sprung up between them. "There's been one thing that I've been meaning to ask you."

Monk glanced at her, and then continued her study of the buildings around them. "Shoot."

"We all fell asleep. I'm assuming you fell asleep as well. Where? When I wake up I'm coming to get you."

Monk sighed. "I didn't fall asleep. I was brought through a doorway created by Wells."

"You're awake?" Coopersmith asked, horrified.

Monk took in the shock on her beautiful features. "Yup."

"So if you get hurt here you won't just wake up like we will?"

Monk shook her head. "No, but it doesn't matter now."

Coopersmith stopped and stared at her. "Yes, it matters. Of *course* it matters."

"How?" Monk asked. "I'm turning into a werewolf. What difference does it make? If I don't die here, I'll die there, and either way I'm going to be howling every full moon. You really think I want that?"

"I don't care if you're turning into a werewolf. I care about *you*. There's no guarantee that you're going to turn out the same way Wells did."

"And there's no guarantee that I won't, either," Monk said. "Let it go. Whatever happens, happens."

"Why don't you care? Don't you know I . . . God, Monk." Coopersmith threw up her hands and turned away from Monk.

"Oh, I care, all right. I care an awful lot. There's just not much I can do until all of this is over." Monk gently took her by the shoulders so they were facing each other. "I can't deal with this right now. I don't know how long the transformation is going to take before it finishes. We have bigger worries than my hairy palms." She fell silent for a moment. "One thing that's been bothering me are the ropes I took off Terri and the house she was in."

"Why?" Coopersmith asked, impatiently wiping the tears from her eyes.

"The house that I untied her in and the one we went into, that took me from her, were both doorways." She turned toward the avidly listening Lightman. "Weren't they?"

Lightman nodded. "Yeah."

"Tell me more about it."

"It was a doorway into other places in the dreamscape. Everyone, when they dream, creates their own reality. The realities can either bubble around each other—like what's happening now, since you're all sharing the same dream—or they can just intersect. That house was an intersection."

"So where did she go?" Monk asked. "Obviously another dream, but whose dream?"

"Whose dream are we in now, Lightman?" Coopersmith asked, giving her a measuring stare.

"We're in Wells's dream. Her world," Lightman said. "She's a master of the dreamscape so she can make things intersect or overlay, depending on how she feels."

"Do you think Kilkenny took Terri?" Monk asked.

Lightman shrugged. "I don't know, and it doesn't matter. All I know is that we have to get to Wells. All this ends when she ends, and I *want* to end."

Monk nodded. "I agree that it should end. But it's going to end on my terms."

They continued walking for another hour until it started to get dark. Monk detected the scent of brine in the air.

She was struggling to put together all the things she had seen and learnt when she had entered the netherworld.

First, Lightman and Wells were both liars. Monk didn't trust Lightman, and deep down didn't believe that Lightman wanted to dispose of Wells.

Second, she didn't know if Wells was in the dreamscape as a dreamer or in her physical body. If they were lucky, she was in her physical body. They would not have to go and look for her in the real world. They could end things on the dreamscape.

Third, they had lost Kilkenny, Jackie, and Warland. There was no guarantee they were in Wells's dreamscape. The doorways between dreams gave Monk the idea that perhaps they were hiding in their own dream, waiting to rescue whoever remained in Wells's dream.

That meant that they were all perfectly safe split up as they were. She was free to take on Wells.

The only problem was Coopersmith. She couldn't tell Coopersmith that her plan had not changed. Coopersmith wouldn't understand and would be furious. In addition, Lightman was around them, and would undoubtedly relay any plans they made in her presence to Wells.

Underneath her roiling thoughts was simple fear of what she was becoming. She didn't want to be mad like Wells, or arrogant like Lightman. She was simply herself, and deathly afraid to her core. She felt isolated and alone. Her source of strength—her friendship with Coopersmith—had radically changed, so she had to rely on herself, something she hadn't done before. Yet something deep inside of her awakened in response to cradle her with gentle strength.

"C'mon, guys," Monk said as they turned down another city street, which wound along a vast, open, and flat sea. "Let's stop for the night."

Lightman nodded and looked up at the sky. "Good idea." She pointed at a crumbling hotel to the left. "There. That looks good."

Coopersmith and Monk exchanged glances and nodded.

"Works for me," Monk said as Lightman led them into the building.

CHAPTER TWELVE

Monk woke up the next morning snuggled in the still sleeping Coopersmith's arms. She rolled over and gazed at Coopersmith's perfect features, relaxed in sleep. She tried to memorize every line and curve. She thought about what Warland had tried to tell her.

She hadn't given a thought to what would happen to them when she told the others she would take on Wells. She had made a decision for all of them without asking any of them what they thought.

Now she found herself in the unenviable position of turning into a werewolf—a gift she didn't want. From what she had gathered from Lightman, from the weariness in her eyes, they had both been alive for a very long time. The prospect of an unending future terrified her, and she wanted to cling to Coopersmith, but knew that was selfish and unfair to both of them.

Coopersmith drove her thoughts in another direction. Her confession had damaged their friendship. She hadn't considered how awkward it would make things between them if Coopersmith didn't feel the same. *I would give everything I have to take that back. It was stupid to blurt it out like that. I never really thought about how I felt about her until then. It was all academic until I opened my big trap. I guess I really did want more from her but all I'm going to get is her friendship—if she's even interested in having me as a friend after this. But now that it's out there, can I really settle for* only *her friendship?*

She felt naked and a fresh bolt of pain and humiliation shot through her as she remembered Coopersmith's expressionless face.

All her secrets were exposed, her inner world torn out for others to see.

She *hated* the loss of her privacy and the resulting scrutiny and name-calling from Lightman and Wells.

She *hated* it. She *loathed* it.

Coopersmith was right. She *did* matter. She *was* worth something, if only to herself. She had survived death hounds; had walked into a haunted house; had shoved a werewolf. She was sick but she still had enough to move on. That was *worth* something to her. She had done more here than she ever had in the real world, in full possession of the knowledge that what happened to her here could have disastrous consequences to her. She now understood she had the ability to face everything in her life in the physical world.

She felt the strength that had begun to diffuse through her the previous evening and wondered how to make it come out and shield her. She wanted to face Wells and the future without the paralyzing fear that had plagued her for what felt like forever.

"Good morning. Penny for your thoughts," Coopersmith said, opening her eyes. She blinked, trying to focus.

"They're not worth that much," Monk said with the ghost of a smile for the old joke. "You want to go outside and breathe in some of that fine, brine air?" She looked pointedly at the still sleeping Lightman.

Coopersmith nodded.

Monk held out a hand and helped Coopersmith to her feet. They went outside, blinking in the crisp, cool air under an overcast sky. The sea ahead of them was as smooth as glass, the acrid scent of the seawater heavy in the air.

They sat on a bus seat, incongruously placed in the middle of the road.

"What's up?" Coopersmith asked.

I can't lie about anything anymore, Monk thought. "I think we're going to meet up with Wells soon, and I don't want you around when that happens."

"I know you don't," Coopersmith said after a moment. "Tough. I'm not letting you do this without me. You might need my help."

Monk sighed. Coopersmith was making decisions for her the same way she had done for Coopersmith. "Terri and I disagreed about whether or not we should go into the doorway house. She told me that I had to tell her what I thought it was, since it let her make up her own mind about what she wanted to do. She also pointed out that I suck at communication. I agree with her on both points."

Coopersmith remained silent.

"I'm turning into a werewolf. I'm a lot stronger than I was even a week ago. I can give Wells a run for her money, so I'm sure that I'm as safe to be around as anywhere else in this world. I also think I can do a better job of protecting Kilkenny than I did before."

Coopersmith nodded. "You still want to protect me?"

Monk shook her head. "No. That's not what I want. What I want is for you to decide whether or not you want to be here. I want you to know that you can back out if you want to. If you want to stay, stay, but you have to stand back and let me do my thing."

"I don't really have a choice now, and I don't think I ever did. Wells can do whatever she wants to me, and she knows it. She knows that your weakest spot is me, and that's why I'm still here."

Monk recoiled. "You think I can't live without you? You're staying because you think you're *stuck* with me? You really think you have no better option?"

Coopersmith shook her head. "No. That's not it. You have a self-destructive streak a mile wide. I know you intend to take both of you out when you fight her."

Monk flinched. No more secrets. "No. Not anymore." She felt herself blush. "You remember what I told you? At school just before you ended up here?"

Coopersmith nodded. "I remember."

"Secrets are amazing things, aren't they? You have them, and you think they're yours, but there's always someone out there who sees them as a banner over your head. You eventually collapse under the weight of them."

"Meaning?"

"It's just easier not to talk and not to admit to anything vaguely personal because it means you don't get hurt. I never even admitted to myself that I felt that way about you because I knew you could never return my feelings. You'd always find some reason to say no. It would be my youth, my big mouth, my temper, or now I know, my self-destructive streak." She gave a small, bitter smile. "I've done some amazingly stupid things during all of this shit, and I want you out of here not because I want to protect you, but because I have enough faith in myself to get out of this mess without help. I can guarantee that you'll live. I have what it takes. I'm strong, I'm smart, and I want to live. That's enough. Nothing else matters." She looked deep into Coopersmith's emerald eyes. "I don't want you to stay with me because you think I need you. I don't. I want you to *stay* with me for purely selfish reasons—because I love you. I want you to *leave* because I know you don't, and it hurts me to be around you. That's what's distracting me."

Monk turned and studied the gray water ahead of them, smooth as glass, cold and deep. She couldn't detect any sign of life there. The wind rushed around them in a steady stream.

"Monk," Coopersmith said. "I don't know what to say."

Monk watched her wipe the tears from her eyes. "Say nothing. Just tell me what your decision is when we reach another doorway."

"God, do you really care so little about what I think and how I feel?" Coopersmith asked. "Or is it that you just don't have the guts to face me?"

Monk gathered her courage. She had made that decision for Coopersmith as well, she now realized. "I care. Very much so. I want to know. Shoot."

"I've been seeing a shift in you over the past couple of days. Everything you just told me is pretty much what you meant every time you yelled at me to treat you like an adult and an equal, right?"

Monk nodded. Coopersmith looked tense and helpless. Monk could see pain in her eyes.

"You blindsided me at school. I was mad at you for doing that to me then, but I figured out why you did it. That was when I started misjudging you." She gazed deep into Monk's eyes. "I care about you. More than I should. I don't see a teenager anymore when I look at you—I see an adult. That scares me, especially now." She stared out at the ocean for a few moments as the wind dried her tears. "When we reach the next doorway, I leave. You're right—I'm distracting you by staying. It's not helping. I have to believe in you, just like you have to believe in me." She captured Monk in a gentle, green gaze. "Come back to me. I can't lose you. Promise me."

Monk smiled and gently wiped away Coopersmith's tears. "I promise."

Coopersmith pulled Monk to her and sank into her embrace, as if drawing comfort from her strength, as Monk had done from her so many times in the past.

"Now you have to promise me something," Monk whispered.

"What?" Coopersmith asked.

"You have to promise to trust me. No matter what happens, have faith in me."

Coopersmith nodded against Monk's neck. "I promise."

They were companionably silent for a moment.

"You told me I was letting Lightman use me as a doormat," Monk said. "I disagree. Just because I'm not blowing my cookies at her doesn't mean I agree with her or think I deserve the way she talks to me. I don't on either point."

"Then why are you letting her do it?" Coopersmith asked.

"A simple thing called diplomacy."

Coopersmith stared at her. "There's a difference between diplomacy and letting someone wipe their feet on you."

Monk nodded. "I know. I need her to think she has me cowed. That's how I have Wells focused on me. She's enjoying the fact that she thinks she's terrorizing me. Let her do it. She can call me as many names as she likes, they mean nothing to me."

"You can't tell me it doesn't hurt."

Monk gazed at her. "I *can* tell you that and I do. I know all about name calling. I've been subjected to it for years. So that doesn't hurt. I've already told you what hurts me."

Coopersmith blushed.

"Are you two love birds done?" Lightman asked from behind them.

Coopersmith slowly sat up and turned toward her, raising an eyebrow and giving her a cool stare.

Monk turned and glared at her. The colors started to bleed around Lightman, and she forced herself to see more of them.

"Very impressive, Monk," Lightman said with a happy grin. "You're almost a werewolf."

"I know." Monk held up her arm. Her wrist no longer hurt as badly as it had, and she could move it further.

"Monk?" Coopersmith asked.

Monk turned to her.

"I miss your blue eyes," Coopersmith said, pointedly ignoring the grinning Lightman.

Monk forced the color bleed and auras out of her vision. "Better?"

Coopersmith nodded. "Thanks." She turned to Lightman. "You want to keep being an arsehole for a while, or are we going to move out?"

Lightman glared at her. "You're lucky I promised Monk I'd protect you."

"Aren't you glad that's a promise you don't have to keep?"

Lightman and Coopersmith stood nose to nose, glaring at one another, and Monk stepped between them and gently pushed them apart.

"All right, ladies, let's just move out, shall we?"

"You know where we're headed?" Lightman asked.

Monk closed her eyes and extended her senses. The ocean to her right felt like a gently moving blanket, the clouds above like cotton balls. Every one of the buildings felt like children's blocks, and if she looked to the left in her mind, she could feel a block that she wanted to visit.

Wells was probably nowhere near it. It didn't matter to her. If it was a doorway, there was a way for Coopersmith to leave.

"That way," she said, pointing further into the city. "We go that way."

Lightman nodded. "Wells is in that general direction, I guess."

"Then let's go." Monk began walking. She cautiously hung her wrist by her side and for the first time in days, it didn't feel as though someone were cutting into it with a rusty hacksaw.

"You really do look a little better, Monk," Coopersmith said softly as they walked along a wide, deserted city street.

Monk glanced back at Lightman walking behind them. She was gazing up at the buildings and at the gray ocean behind them.

"I really feel a little better," Monk said. "Pity I'm a fur face now." She felt a little sick at the prospect, despite her jovial tone.

Monk and Coopersmith turned at a crash behind them. The ocean had woken up. A line sat on the horizon, solid white, and it looked to Monk as though the horizon itself had risen at least a foot. A closer wave came in and flooded the road beside the ocean. The bench Monk and Coopersmith had been sitting on was soaked.

"This isn't real good, is it, Lightman?" Monk asked.

Lightman shook her head. "No, I reckon not."

Monk groped blindly for Coopersmith's hand. She squeezed it, and they began to run.

"Don't look back," Monk panted.

Coopersmith, whey-faced, shook her head. They bolted up the street, Lightman on their heels, heading in the direction Monk wanted to go.

Monk heart hammered with grim intensity, and she tightened her mouth. She wanted Coopersmith through the doorway before the wave behind them broke.

"There," Lightman said, pointing over Monk's shoulder.

"Got it," Monk said, pulling the panting and stumbling Coopersmith toward the building.

It was a mammoth skyscraper, about a hundred stories tall, of glass, concrete, and steel. A sign reading *HOSPITAL* hung over the doors.

Monk and Lightman burst through the doors, trailed closely by Coopersmith. She collapsed in the foyer, while Monk and Lightman held the doors closed.

Foam from the ocean wave washed over the bottom two inches of the door, leaving behind tendrils of strongly-scented brine just in the doorway.

"Crap," Monk muttered, trying to gain some control over her breathing.

Lightman nodded. "Wells has found us."

"We have to get moving," Monk said, peering around the foyer, wondering where they should head next. The foyer was immense. On the far wall were a set of lifts. The up arrow lights above and to the right of each set of steel doors were on, green shining dimly through a thick layer of dust.

Marble stairs on both sides of the foyers led up to another level.

At the back and to the right was a small sign with an arrow beside it. It read:

EMERGENCY >—

Monk stared at it and tilted her head. The weird arrow was as idiotic as the meaningless word on the front of the building. Lightman wrinkled her nose. Coopersmith was bent over, hands on her knees, trying to gain control over her breathing.

"Let's go to emergency," Lightman said. "After all, that's one hell of an intriguing sign, isn't it?"

"No," Monk said, exchanging a glance with Coopersmith. "No. It's not."

"Well, my gut tells me to go that way," Lightman said. Her eyes flared red as she eyed each of them. "Well? Are you coming?"

Monk shook her head. "Yes. I guess so."

Coopersmith muffled a snort of laughter, and Monk grinned at her. Her nerves were on edge, and she couldn't say why.

They walked into the darkened corridor the sign pointed down, and Monk glanced around at each door. They seemed to be passing darkened hospital wards, and she prayed that they were really empty.

A sheet of plastic with a biohazard symbol on it covered the corridor ahead of them. Monk shivered, and Coopersmith pulled in close to her.

Lightman didn't hesitate. She walked straight through the plastic sheeting and held it back so Coopersmith and Monk could go through. Once on the other side, the corridor's appearance radically changed.

Up until then, a thick layer of dust had covered everything. This brilliantly lit corridor was clean, so clean it sparkled. The scent of antiseptic was still in the air. They reached the first junction and found themselves close to a nurse's station.

Monk's disquiet grew. She shot a quick glance at Coopersmith.

Coopersmith leaned over the counter and stared at the desk. She picked up a clipboard with crisp, white paper and began reading. Her eyes widened.

"What?" Monk asked.

Coopersmith handed her the clipboard.

Cliff Jenkins, it read. *Deceased 2:32pm. Gross circulatory distress.*

Monk frowned. "What the hell does that mean? Have you ever heard of such a thing before?"

Coopersmith shook her head. "It can't be real. Nothing in this world is real."

"Do you know where Lightman is?" Monk asked suddenly, whipping around and looking for Wells's familiar.

Coopersmith's eyes widened. "There."

Monk frowned at her tone and looked in the direction Coopersmith was pointing. Lightman stood further down the corridor, arguing with a gown-clad nurse and doctor. She gestured up the hallway and nodded toward them.

The doctor and nurse nodded and began walking to them.

Monk froze, and then she scrunched her face in disgust.

The doctor and nurse both had a grayish tint of incipient gangrene. The doctor, in particular, had thin tears of blood leaking from his eyes, cutting tracks down his cheeks and staining the top of his face mask.

"Can I help you two?" he asked. His voice sounded gravelly.

Monk struggled to control her bile. "No, I don't think so."

"Well, come on now. You came into the hospice for a reason, didn't you?"

"No. No reason. Mistake. We're leaving now," Coopersmith said.

Monk shook her head. "Actually, we have to go that way," she muttered to Coopersmith. "That's where the next doorway is."

"You're kidding," Coopersmith said.

Monk shook her head. She grabbed Coopersmith's hand and led her toward Lightman. She could feel the doorway close, inside a room that stank of suppurating wounds and disease.

Lightman grinned as they approached.

Monk turned and looked down the corridor. The doctor and nurse were standing by the desk, carefully studying the clipboard.

Coopersmith was so pale she was almost translucent. She swallowed. "You're not going to tell me this is the doorway, are you?"

Lightman gave her a smug grin. "No. I won't tell you this is the doorway."

Monk pulled Coopersmith to a halt. "This is bullshit, but we agreed you were going to leave. I hate this." She reached into her pocket and pulled out a silver knife. She was dimly amazed she had managed to keep it. It felt hot in her hand. She gave it to Coopersmith.

"You know what this is," she said. "Take care of yourself, Mitch."

Coopersmith pulled Monk into her arms so they touched along the entire length of their bodies. She breathed a kiss onto Monk's neck and gave her another gentle brush on her forehead.

"Remember your promise," she said.

"I remember," Monk said. "You remember yours."

Coopersmith gently pulled back and then headed toward the doors. She pushed them open, and then glanced back at Monk.

Monk swallowed convulsively. Stinking greenish black fluid covered the floor behind the doors. "God," she muttered.

Coopersmith looked up and strode into the room as though she owned it. She had not gotten four steps before the air shimmered, and she disappeared.

Monk sighed, and a second later, she widened her eyes in alarm when the world lurched and went dark. "What the fuck?" she muttered. She blinked and peered around into the darkness.

The hospital had undergone a complete transformation. Now the corridor and room looked like the rest of the hospital—dusty, long empty of people and things.

Lightman laughed. "That was good, huh?"

"Pardon?" Monk asked, looking for the doctor and nurse, both of whom had vanished along with the new corridor.

"Coopersmith. She's a fucking bitch. I just wanted to pull her chain."

Monk's temper snapped, and she grabbed Lightman and slammed her against the wall, showering them in plaster dust.

"Do *not* fuck with Mitch. You can do what you like to me but you fucking *leave Mitch alone*, you understand me?" She gave Lightman a vicious shake.

"Really?" Lightman asked airily and let out a snort of laughter. "I can do what I like. You're a wimp."

"I'm *no* wimp," Monk said coldly, shoving her against the wall again. "Just because I consciously choose to ignore half the diarrhea that comes out of your mouth does *not* make me weak. You do that again to her or any of my other *not* friends, and I'll fucking kill you." She shoved Lightman into the wall again to underscore her point.

Monk watched the diseased auras swirling around Lightman, until Lightman's eyes finally stuttered away from her face.

"All right," Lightman muttered.

"Good." Monk nodded. "Now, then. What the fuck did you do? I thought you had no control over the dreamscape?" She glanced into the room. It was pitch black, and she couldn't see anything with her shape-shifter vision.

Lightman's eyes flared red. "For starters, let me go. Second, I can't create constructs in this world but I can change what's already here."

Monk felt her blood run cold, and she peered up the corridor.

"Very good, dumb shit," Lightman said. "They're up." She pointed upward.

Monk looked up.

The doctor and nurse clung to the ceiling, skeletons covered in moldy rags and ancient, dried blood. They each had glowing red eyes, a similar shade to Lightman's, but where Lightman's irises were naturally red, theirs were like furnaces in deeply pocketed eye sockets.

They watched Monk carefully, and the one with the rotting facemask snapped its teeth together with a grisly crunch.

"Crap," Monk said, releasing Lightman and backing away. She could barely make out the black color sludge surrounding them.

Lightman let out a loud, raucous laugh.

Monk backed further away from Lightman. The figures clinging to the ceiling above her didn't move. She looked carefully down the corridor, narrowing her eyes as she saw flashes of movement. She focused on one of them, and it slowly resolved into a humanoid figure in the hallway, another skeleton covered in rags. She had the impression it was another doctor. She slowly realized that all around it were more pairs of eyes, some of them flickering in an obscene way.

Behind them was a pair of glittering, bile yellow eyes.

Monk sprang into action and pounded down the corridor toward the skeletons. She was terrified but they looked fragile, so she lowered her shoulder and hit the first with it as hard as she could. It exploded like a bomb, covering her in fragments of dried bone, petrified sinew, and moldy, dusty rags.

The other creatures reached blindly for her, snagging her clothes but unable to stop her forward momentum.

Monk slammed into Wells as hard as she could, and Wells went over backward, carving a path through the dust on the floor as they skidded. The bones of the doctors and nurses Monk shattered, quivered, and vibrated on the cracked tile floor.

"Wells," Monk said coldly. The pain in her wrist was almost gone, and she pinned Wells easily.

"Monkhouse," Wells said, equally coldly. "I see you got rid of your little fuck buddy."

Monk snorted a bitter laugh. "Nice try. Won't work on me anymore."

"Why not? You *still* don't have what it takes to kill me."

"God, you sound like a broken fucking record. You want to make a bet?"

"I don't have to. You want to know how your friends are doing? I found them, you know." Wells threw Monk against a wall. The air went out of Monk's lungs in an explosive rush, and she lay still for a moment, trying to catch her breath. Dread washed over her in a slow, sick wave as Wells's words registered.

Wells leapt to her feet, and before Monk knew what was happening she was sailing through the air again, down the corridor toward Lightman. She crashed to the floor and screamed as her bad arm took the brunt of her impact.

"Doorway, Vanessa," Wells yelled, leaping and bounding toward them with sickening grace.

Lightman grimaced, and her eyes begged Monk for mercy as she leaned down and snagged the front of Monk's tee shirt. Monk grunted as Lightman hefted her into the air and tossed her through the same door Coopersmith had walked through minutes earlier.

The doorway was pitch black, and Monk blinked, trying to make her eyes work as she sailed downward through the air with a stomach turning feeling of weightlessness.

She went into freefall for some fathomless length of time, enough for her to struggle to contain her bile.

She landed on the ground, unprepared for the impact, and the air exploded from her lungs in a forceful rush. She lay, temporarily stunned, as the air lightened and a golden glow filled the room. She looked around, seeing colors bleed and auras form.

It looked like an operating room, but like none she had ever seen before. The operating table was missing, as were the overhead lights. In their place were four chains hanging down from the ceiling.

Her four friends hung on the chains, suspended by their ankles. Their hands dangled toward the tiled floor. They were white and rigid in death.

Monk stared at them for what felt like a hundred years, scalp crawling in shock, in too much pain to scream or cry. She sank to her knees, staring, images of all the time she had spent with them flitting through her mind. She would never again see the twinkle in Warland's light gray eyes, feel the strength of Coopersmith's arms, Jackie's sweet smile, or Kilkenny's laughter.

She felt sick and empty. It was over.

The tears flowed as she thought of her conversation with Coopersmith. She wasn't certain she would win in a fight against Wells, despite her desire to live, and her heightened abilities. Wells was older, cunning, and more experienced. They had spoken about choices, and how to protect themselves, but in the final analysis, it meant nothing. They couldn't hide on the dreamscape, and Lightman had kept Monk distracted from Wells.

"Monk, they're not dead," Lightman said quietly from the doorway.

"Really?" Monk asked coldly. She kept her voice tightly controlled. She felt stretched thin and nailed to a wall.

"Really," Lightman said. "Understand. I'm begging you, understand." She pushed herself off the wall and slowly headed toward Monk, bright red eyes beseeching. "Wells is not interested in you. She's interested in Kilkenny because young Sharp is another shape-shifter. She is a wolf, and she's come to take Kilkenny's territory. You caught her eye and challenged her, and now she's playing with you like a cat plays with a mouse. It's more fun for her to torture you. It amuses her to see all of you run around and try to hide from her." She sighed. "Whatever you tried to do for Kilkenny is pointless. Kilkenny is a werewolf. She can defend herself. Just because she looks like a child doesn't mean she is one."

Monk snorted. "And you? Tell me again why you're here?"

"As proof."

"Of what?"

"That just because you're full of righteous anger doesn't mean you get to win. Sometimes brute force, cunning, and general cruelty are enough to make you lose."

"I don't believe that," Monk said, stepping away from her and looking at the hanging bodies. Her scalp crawled in revulsion, and her mouth felt tinder dry.

"You better believe it. Otherwise you're still going to be full of the idea that you'll win a fight against Wells."

"Tell me one thing," Monk said after a moment. "Why am I a werewolf? Why'd she turn me into one? You lied to me. You knew she wasn't going to kill me before the transformation finished. She had to have known she was signing her own death warrant."

"Werewolves don't die of natural causes. You would always hunt her, and she would always escape you. You would end up being her slave for all time, never able to forgive yourself for letting your friends die. You'd always needlessly blame yourself for it. You'd always be the prey pack leader of her hunts because you would never understand that you can't win a fight against her."

Monk looked at the hanging bodies. She understood at an intellectual level what Lightman was telling her but her emotions simply could not catch up.

"Don't listen to her, Monk," a young voice said.

Monk started and turned to stare at the bodies. Kilkenny's eyes fluttered open, shining a vibrant, bile yellow. She blinked.

"Don't listen to her," she said again. "We're all fine." She bent at the waist and reached for the chain suspending her body from the ceiling. She cut it with a forefinger. Monk dived forward and caught her before she could fall.

Monk stared dumbly at her. She shook as adrenalin and relief coursed through her system. She blinked against tears.

"Come with me," Kilkenny said. "Come back to us. Let Wells follow. I don't want to hide anymore." She bit her lip. "You're my friend. Come with me and help me that way."

Monk nodded. She was sick of hiding as well. If Lightman really was right about Wells, she wanted to be with her friends. She didn't see the point in continuing to pretend everything was fine.

"How?" she asked.

"You have to want to," Kilkenny said. "You're a shape-shifter. Use what nature gave you."

Monk stared at the tiled wall of the operating theatre. Color bled before her vision and auras formed. She stared into the swirling mist, gently pulling it apart with her mind, until a slit was open before her. She gazed through it, and saw Coopersmith, Warland, and Jackie.

They were in a large living room, kneeling around the prone figure of Kilkenny. Light from the dreamscape leaked into the room, and they all turned to stare at it. Their eyes widened when they saw her.

Kilkenny took her hand and dragged her toward the hole. Lightman stayed close behind her.

They stepped through, and Kilkenny's hand dissolved out of hers. Monk felt a wrenching motion and the sickening, familiar sensation of freefall. It didn't last as long as the other times, and she fell to her knees on the carpet.

Coopersmith dived toward her and gently grasped her shoulders. She gazed deep into Coopersmith's emerald eyes, forlorn and aching. Her sense of relief was overwhelming, and she shook.

"Monk," Coopersmith breathed.

Warland dropped to her knees beside both. "Monk?" She pulled Monk into a hug, and Monk returned it.

"I'm all right," Monk said as Warland released her. She sank into Coopersmith's bittersweet embrace. She wrapped her arms around Coopersmith, and a primal part of her quieted.

"What about me?" Lightman asked loudly, sitting on her behind on the carpet, legs stretched out in front of her. "Doesn't anyone care about how *I* feel?"

"Not particularly," Coopersmith said coldly, glaring at her.

"Fucking bitch," Lightman muttered.

"Monk," Jackie exclaimed, ignoring Lightman and bounding over to Monk. Coopersmith helped Monk to her feet, and Jackie pulled her into an enormous bear hug.

"Stop calling her a bitch," Monk said to Lightman. Her sorely abused control over her temper slipped away. "Your sense of entitlement is sickening. All you've done is throw around a superior attitude and call everyone names. What makes you so fucking special, you arse up bitch?"

"If it weren't for me you'd be dead, you idiotic cow," Lightman shot back.

"Thanks to you both they're *all* dead," Wells said dryly, as she climbed out of the dreamscape and into the real world through the hole they had forgotten to close.

CHAPTER THIRTEEN

Monk snarled. She dove at Wells before Wells was able to straighten, and took them through the hole back into the dreamscape. They ended up in the air close to the top of the hospital, and Monk yelped as they plummeted to the ground. Wells clawed at her, but Monk hung on, feeling blood stream out of her arms. An enormous roaring noise filled the air, and Monk twisted toward it.

She gasped. A wall of water, twice as high as the hospital building, roared toward them at breakneck speed, demolishing everything in its wake.

Wells laughed. "Wanna give up yet, Monk?" she screamed. She snapped her jaws, and her canines clicked together, spraying her with spittle.

Monk yelled and wrapped her arms and legs around Wells's sinewy body as the wall of water slammed into them. They rode the wave just ahead of the crest, surfing on a monstrous, curling sheet of foam.

Wells bit and clawed at her, every dig into her flesh a new experience in agony. Brine soaked into the cuts, cleansing them, making her scream.

Yet Monk clung to Wells with grim intensity, accepting the pain and letting it wash over her.

Another cold wave doused them, and Monk spluttered and struggled to control her breathing. She was acutely aware of the rubbery skin that brushed by her. She looked into the water, and quickly looked away. She had no desire to see how she swam with hundred-foot sharks, each more evil looking than the last.

Monk's muscles ached, and she fought to keep them both afloat for another three waves. She was shaking and exhausted as a mighty wave deposited them on top of a limestone cliff almost a thousand meters above the darkened rocks below.

She collapsed back on the sodden grass, hating the smell of the brine that surrounded them.

She had never felt so small and insignificant in her life. She gasped for breath, trembling and exhausted. She looked out at the ocean, knowing that if the waves started again she would not survive them.

She sank to her knees and felt the world go dark.

Monk opened her eyes. Her clothes were almost dry, and it was dark and cool. Wells was gone. A sea breeze flowed over her, making her shiver. Her arms ached. She looked down at her wrist. The bandages had torn off, and the skin was pink and healthy.

She could not control her flinch.

The transformation was complete.

She was a werewolf.

She shifted her vision, and the darkened landscape became a bleeding riot of color, as bright as day. She couldn't help but smile as she surveyed solid ground.

She stood at the large end of a headland. A road lead toward the jutting fingers of rock that marked the tip of the headland. It wound through a small village, curving toward a mighty lighthouse at the end.

The lighthouse remained dark, and Monk supposed it didn't matter. She didn't think that any ships would be passing along the raging ocean any time soon.

She focused on the lighthouse, wondering what had happened to Wells. She began to walk toward the village, more for a place to go than for any real sense of purpose.

She got halfway down the road, and the lighthouse came to life and poured out greenish gray light. She grimaced at the sickly purple hue of her skin where the light touched it.

A shadow passed over her.

She stopped to follow its motion.

It passed over the landscape, a giant silhouette of a crucified figure, hung spread eagle before the corpse light. Monk felt sick. She had to get to the lighthouse. Who was the figure? Had Wells gotten one of her friends?

She ran down the path and into the village. Villagers stood before their houses, looking up at the lighthouse. They reached for her as she passed; they called to her but she didn't acknowledge them. She barely understood them.

She bolted up the path out of the village, pounding toward the lighthouse. The shadow—that now seemed to be moving—washed over the rolling fields around the village in eerie silence.

Monk shattered the heavy, oak door at the base of the lighthouse, tore inside, and hared up the shaky stairs two at a time until she reached the top. She exploded through the doors to the light room.

The light washed over her, hot and blinding, and she groped for the control at the side of the room that would turn it off. She kept her eyes tightly closed as they leaked tears from the visual onslaught. She groped for the button, and pushed it, and the light slowed its rotation until it finally stopped.

She could hear whimpering as it quieted, and she opened her eyes and used her shape-shifter vision to look at the source of the sound.

She did a double take.

She untied it, gently laid it over her broad shoulder, and then onto the wooden floorboards.

Lightman stared up at her, burnt and covered in dried blood.

"What the fuck happened?" Monk asked. "Why?"

"Wells came back. The others refused to leave. She left me for dead for disobeying her." Lightman drew in a deep breath. "She's on this side with the others."

A bolt of terror went through Monk, and she felt sick. "Who? Where?"

Lightman lay still, unconscious.

Monk stood and looked down at her. She felt nothing.

Just at that moment, the light started again, and Monk felt the heat of its passing, heard the hum of the globe.

She stood on the rickety balcony outside the light room, gazing at the thick storm clouds on the horizon. Lightning flashed, and the ocean was dotted with whitecaps in the distance. The corpse light shone out over the land and sea, throwing her into sharp relief as the light passed behind her.

If she were Wells, where would she have gone? Wells had to be close by. She wanted to keep a close eye on Monk. Monk glanced back at Lightman. Lightman said that Wells was on this side with the others.

Wells was a master of the dreamscape, and now that Monk shared her blood, she was one too. She closed her eyes and extended her senses. The dreamscape felt different to the physical world. It almost felt as though strings came off everything in it and fed into Monk. Objects felt more real, as though Monk knew them from the inside out.

A part of herself felt like it was detached from her body and flowed down the side of the lighthouse, clinging to its rough surface with an invisible grip. Every time her hand touched the rough surface, an aura appeared.

She floated through the walls, down to the living areas.

Most of the floors of the lighthouse were deserted and dusty, but the main room the ground floor showed disturbances in the dust, like footprints. They stopped in the middle of the room, and Monk stared at the space where they had stopped. She could feel heat from that area.

Curious, she returned to her body, went back inside the light room, and extended her senses and feeling for Wells. She couldn't find any sign of her.

Lightning flashed in the distance, far out to sea. An immense crack of thunder followed it—one that rolled across the sky from horizon to horizon. Monk winced.

She cautiously made her way down the stairs, listening for Wells or for any sound from the unconscious Lightman above her.

Once on the ground floor, she carefully checked every corner and shadow for Wells, but didn't find any sign of her. Monk shifted her vision and studied the auras, but again found nothing.

She walked into the main living room and tried to take a step beyond the dusty footprints.

"Ouch!"

Monk frowned and rubbed her shoulder. She reached out in front, and felt cautiously over a rough, brick surface. It abruptly disappeared under her fingertips.

Thunder rumbled, and Monk's bones vibrated.

She stepped toward the breach and felt an instant of dislocation. She blinked against a sudden burst of light. She looked around.

Coopersmith, Warland, and Jackie were kneeling, bound and gagged on the floor before her. Kilkenny was not with them. Wells stood behind them, holding a large knife. Her eyes shone a deep and vicious yellow.

"So, Monkhouse, you decided to join us."

Monk nodded. "Couldn't let you have all the fun, now could I?"

Wells snorted a laugh. "No, I couldn't, could I?"

They were silent for a moment. *Mouth shut, Monk,* Monk thought. *She loves hearing the sound of her own voice so I give her about five seconds of silence before she begins another sanctimonious monologue.*

"I—Huh!" The breath exploded from Wells's lungs as Monk crash tackled her. The knife sliced between Monk's ribs, and a warm wash of blood flowed down her side. Monk grabbed Wells's wrist, and held it back and off her for all she was worth. Wells snarled and roiled under her, attempting to dislodge her.

"Shut up!" Monk screamed. "All you've ever done is babble and yack at me. You're a cruel fucking bitch."

Coopersmith, Warland, and Jackie scrabbled to the side of the chamber, out of the reach of the combatants. Warland and Coopersmith turned back to back to try to untie their bonds.

Fuck, Monk thought. *I'm going to have to let go so I can get better leverage.*

She relaxed her grip for a second, and Wells sat up and threw Monk backward. She snarled and dove toward the prone Monk. Monk caught her mid air and used her own momentum against her. Wells sailed through the air and crashed into the wall.

Wells struggled to regain her feet as Monk flipped and landed on hers.

"What I do matters, you bitch! My life means something to me. It's *mine* and I *want* it. I *don't* deserve to die," Monk screamed, advancing on her. "How I live and what I do *matters*."

Monk fumbled in the pocket of her shorts for the silver knife. Her hand closed around it, and the silver felt hot against her skin. Her hand was still in her pocket when Wells tackled her and raked her claws across Monk's throat.

"You mean *nothing*," Wells snarled. "*Nothing* you do matters. You are a complete and utter *loser*, Monkhouse."

Monk's blood spurted and coated the front of her tee shirt, rapidly pooling beneath her. She watched, stunned as the skin closed after a second or so.

Wells got off her and moved toward Coopersmith.

"Mthhllle!" Warland screamed, twisting and trying to push Coopersmith out of the way.

Wells dove toward her.

Monk extracted the silver knife from her pocket, howling at the almost overwhelming heat against her skin, and plunged it to the hilt into Wells's back, through her cold heart.

"I *matter*! I *matter*! I *matter*!" she screamed, punctuating each declaration with another plunge of the knife.

A deafening thunder crack sounded all around them, leaving Monk half deaf from the concussion. The air hummed with electricity.

Wells screamed in agony and sank to her knees. She weakly groped for the smoking knife sticking out of her back. Her eyes flickered, gradually losing their vicious yellow color and sinking back to light brown.

Monk forced herself to move. She clumsily knelt behind Jackie and rapidly untied her bonds. Jackie silently untied Coopersmith and Warland.

Monk turned to Wells and intently watched her. Jackie sobbed and snuck her arms around Monk. Monk leaned back into her.

Wells's skin darkened, and looked wet and shiny. She turned mottled black, decaying rapidly as Coopersmith and Warland knelt beside Monk.

"Monk," Coopersmith whispered into her ear, slipping her arms around Monk's body. "Monk."

Monk gently caressed her hand. "I promised."

"Yes, you did," Coopersmith said.

Monk sank back into her embrace, smiling, as Jackie and Warland added their own love and thanks to hers.

Monk suddenly stiffened, feeling her eyes flaring yellow once more.

"What?" Jackie asked.

"Can you hear it?" Monk asked. "The screaming?"

The others exchanged a glance.

"No," said Jackie.

Monk extracted herself from Coopersmith's embrace and stood. She could feel the bright yellow of her eyes. Coopersmith flinched. *She knows,* Monk thought with a sinking heart. *God help me, she knows. She realized I'm one of them for good.*

Lightman exploded through the door, leapt onto her, and screamed.

There was nothing left of the girl that Monk knew. Wells's death had sent her over the edge into mindless madness. Lightman had warned her about how closely the two were tangled together, but Monk had always assumed she was exaggerating and that Lightman would die the instant Wells did.

Monk was not strong or fast enough to defend herself from Lightman's insane onslaught. Lightman held the silver knife up, a hair away from savagely arcing it down into Monk's unprotected chest.

A gout of blood spurted from Lightman's mouth, washing over Monk in a sickening flood. Lightman hesitated, and the knife fell from her nerveless fingers. She tensed and toppled forward to become dead weight in Monk's arms.

Monk grimaced and threw her off. She sat up and stared at the wide-eyed Kilkenny Sharp.

The girl looked down at her hands, shaking and spluttering. She looked at Monk with a quivering lip as the tears flowed from her eyes.

"Monk?" she asked in a thick voice. "Monk? I think I . . . I . . ."

Monk pulled Kilkenny into her arms. "Shh. It's all right. I'm still here because of you." She held Kilkenny as she shook and raged against the guilt and loathing that coursed through her young body. Jackie's arms joined hers, and they comforted the devastated girl as best they could.

Some unfathomable time later, Kilkenny pulled out of Monk's arms. Monk looked deep into her eyes and felt a moment of regret and dismay.

Kilkenny's eyes were haunted and dark, filled with knowledge of things most adults didn't care to know. Monk felt the ghost of Wells's blood wash over her, saw Wells's eyes grow dark as life fled her body, and understood how Kilkenny felt.

"Let's get out of here," Coopersmith said, touching Monk gently on the shoulder.

Monk glanced back at her and nodded. She stood, pulling Kilkenny with her.

By unspoken consent, Monk cut a hole in the dreamscape that led to Warland's living room. They climbed through, one by one, Monk last of all.

She sealed the breach and turned back to the others. They all stared at her with unreadable expressions.

Well, at least no one but me got hurt. I did what I had to do. Good enough.

She shifted under their gazes, and looked longingly down a

corridor she assumed led to the front door, wondering how to make her goodbyes.

"I don't know about the rest of you, but I really don't feel like going to sleep," Warland said with a sheepish grin that didn't touch her eyes.

Coopersmith shook her head. "I'll second that."

"I don't want to be alone," Kilkenny said. She turned to Monk. "Stay. I know you want to run, but stay."

Monk blushed and wondered how Kilkenny seemed to have the ability to read minds.

"I'm with Kilkenny." Jackie gently squeezed Monk's arm. "Thank you, Monk," she said at Monk's questioning glance.

She cautiously put her arms around Monk and squeezed hard. Monk smiled and returned the hug, amazed at how simple human contact threatened to turn her inside out. She was afraid to look at Coopersmith, afraid of her reaction.

Warland glanced between Monk and Coopersmith. "C'mon, guys," she said to Jackie and Kilkenny. "Let's go see if we can find something to snack on."

The girls nodded, and they headed toward the kitchen.

Coopersmith's gaze remained on Monk, and the expression in her eyes made Monk shift from foot to foot. The intensity in them was almost palatable. Monk watched Coopersmith, dimly amazed that she was not afraid of the older woman. She *wanted* Coopersmith to talk. Not talking about things didn't make them any less real or important. She had no control over what Coopersmith thought and felt and didn't want it anyway. She felt a strange peace suffuse her.

"You kept your promise," Coopersmith began quietly. "You came back."

"I came back." Monk gave her a half smile. "I've always tried to keep my promises to you."

The silence played out for another moment as they simply gazed at each other.

"Are you going to just stand there and look at me or are you going to put your arms around me and hold me?" Coopersmith asked softly.

Monk's reserve broke, and she took a step forward. Coopersmith met her half way, and they tangled together so tightly they touched along the entire lengths of their bodies. Monk stroked her hair, breathing in her perfume and the gentle scent that was Coopersmith herself.

"We have to talk about us," Coopersmith said after timeless moments. She had tears in her eyes, and she gently traced Monk's prominent cheekbones with her fingers.

Monk smiled, leaned forward, and gently claimed Coopersmith's lips. She craved Coopersmith and couldn't stop herself. She had never kissed another human being before, and she was a little hesitant until Coopersmith responded with fiery passion.

The kiss lasted for some time, and when they broke, Monk felt as though she had been turned inside out and upside down. Her body didn't seem to know what to do with the barrage of emotion hammering her from all sides.

"Wow," Coopersmith muttered, resting her forehead against Monk's.

Monk nodded. "I know." She took a deep breath. "You never told me how you felt. I *want* to know. I want to know *everything* about you." *I want to be inside you the same way you're inside me.*

Coopersmith smiled and pecked her on the lips. "I'm glad you finally asked me. I love you."

"I love you, too. We have so much to talk about." Monk felt buoyant. "So much we have to sort out. But I don't want to talk about that right now. I just want you to be mine for an evening."

Coopersmith laughed softly. "It's not just for one evening. I hope you know that."

"I do know," Monk said, gently picking her up and looking at her. Coopersmith's arms snuck around her shoulders.

"I want *all* of you, all the time," Coopersmith whispered. She gazed down at Monk, fire in her eyes.

"So do I," Monk said. "You changed *everything* for me."

"You kept your promise. It was the most important promise anyone has ever made to me."

"To come back to you? How could I not? Don't you understand what you mean to me?"

"Everything, I know. You mean the same to me," Coopersmith said, closing her eyes against tears.

She settled Coopersmith back onto her feet, and they stayed tangled together until Terri Warland cleared her throat close to them.

Monk glanced at her.

"Sorry," Warland said. She smiled at them. "I saw nothing, I see nothing, and so it shall remain."

Coopersmith nodded. "Thanks."

Monk grinned. "Works for me."

"Are you guys interested in some coffee?"

Monk nodded. She had not eaten properly in what felt like days, and her stomach grumbled loudly.

"I'll take that as a yes," Warland said with a grin. "Monk, you obviously want something to eat. How about a toasted cheese sandwich and some soup or something?"

"I'm sold," Monk said. "Thanks."

Coopersmith trailed Monk into the kitchen. Monk internally winced when she saw Kilkenny's expression. She seemed lost, and had a haunted look in her eyes.

The kitchen table had six seats, and Monk settled herself in beside Kilkenny, Jackie opposite them, and Coopersmith at one end on the other side of Monk.

"Hi," Monk said softly to Kilkenny.

Kilkenny glanced at her.

"You want to talk about it?"

Kilkenny shook her head. She was silent a moment. "How come you've still got yellow eyes?"

Monk suddenly felt very aware of all the eyes on her. She focused on Kilkenny. "I don't know. The movies always say that if you're a werewolf and kill the head of the bloodline, then the curse disappears." She gave a small, sad smile. "If that's true, then Wells wasn't the head of her own clan."

Kilkenny nodded. "Do you feel any different?"

"If you're asking if I feel like a psychopathic bitch, the answer is no. I don't. If you're asking me if I feel different overall, then yes, I do." She glanced at Coopersmith. "But that's a whole other story."

"Why, Monk? Why am I like this? Did Wells tell you anything?"

Monk shook her head. "No, we never talked about any of that kind of stuff. Nature made you like this. You were born that way. You are part of the natural order of things."

"What about you?"

Monk was quiet for a moment. "I still feel all the same things I did before. I still care about all the same things as before. I don't feel like there's a wall of malevolence hiding inside me. I feel like a regular person." She paused. "But I also feel sharper and stronger than I did. I know I'm not human anymore."

Kilkenny sighed. She looked haunted. "I don't know what it feels like to be human."

"Don't say that," Jackie said.

"Why?" Coopersmith asked.

"I've always been like this. I've never known any different. And today I killed someone. I'm not like you. I wasn't made. I have it in me because of what I am." Kilkenny's voice wavered.

"I don't know what to say." Monk put a hand on Kilkenny's shoulder. "You did it to help me. I'm not going to get on my high horse about it. I'm also not going to worry about what's inside you. I know better than that."

Kilkenny looked doubtful.

Monk exchanged a helpless glance with Coopersmith, who smiled.

"So, Kilkenny," Coopersmith said conversationally.

Kilkenny looked at her.

"Felt good, did it?" Coopersmith asked.

"What felt good?" Kilkenny asked.

"Sinking the knife into her body. You know, something really sharp that feels like it's trying to stab through rubber. Suddenly everything gives way and there's blood on your hands. Kinda warm, huh? And tough to get out. Pain in the butt, really."

Kilkenny glared at her. "What's that supposed to mean? You think I liked it? Well, no, I really didn't. If I never go through that again it's going to be too soon. How would you know what any of that stuff feels like anyway?"

"If that's how you really feel, what makes you think you're suddenly going to turn into Jack the Ripper?" Coopersmith asked dryly. "Either you have it or you don't. What you did was out of self defense."

Kilkenny looked annoyed. "No it wasn't, and you know it. Lightman wasn't attacking me, she was attacking Monk. I killed someone because they were hurting Monk. Self defense is just that— self defense. You defend yourself, and sometimes hurt other people in the process. What I did wasn't the same thing."

"I'd be dead if you hadn't done it," Monk said quietly. "Would that have suited you better? And *I*, by the way, *do* know what it feels like."

Kilkenny went white. She opened and closed her mouth several times.

"Look, Kilkenny," Monk said. "The yellow eyes are a part of you, just like they're now a part of me. There's a big part of me that hasn't changed. I don't like killing or hurting things. Do I regret killing Wells? Hell, yes. Do I wish things could have gone another way? Hell, yes again. Do I think Wells would ever have *let* them go a different way? Hell, no. I had no choice on any of this because I wasn't given one. It wasn't because of something inside me that snapped and turned me into a murderer."

"So you think the same applies to me?" Kilkenny asked with a terrible, anxious hesitation.

Monk stared deep into her eyes, willing her to believe. "Yes."

Kilkenny's stare gained a spark of peace and turned inward as she tried to understand Monk's words.

Monk let the silence play out for a few moments. "Keep thinking about it, Kilkenny."

Coopersmith gave her arm a gentle squeeze, and she smiled.

"We're up," Warland said cheerfully, and Coopersmith got up and helped her dish out food to everyone.

"So what happened to you in the dreamscape with that house thing?" Monk asked Warland after everyone was seated. "One moment you were there, and we were falling through a closet, the next you were gone."

"I don't completely remember because it was all just a dream for me," Warland said. "But I do remember that it felt like I'd been wandering around for days before that family got me. Then you came. We traveled together for a couple of days, and then ended up in that house."

"What I find weird is the way it looked like she hadn't been there for months when you tried to tell us Terri was in the dream," Coopersmith said.

Monk ate her soup quietly for a moment, relishing the wonderful taste. She put down her spoon and rubbed her wrist. "Remember what Lightman told us? *Time moves differently here.* The house Terri was in, and the house where we both fell through the closet were *both* doorways. That first one was a place doorway, the second one a gateway to the physical world."

"The time dislocation doesn't really make sense, though," Coopersmith said. "I still don't quite get it. How can we walk past a house that Terri was in right then and still be standing outside it months later?"

"You're assuming that's what happened," Monk said with a grin.

"You're assuming that you waited outside for months. You're assuming I stayed outside the house the whole time. That's wrong. The house was a *gateway*. So when I walked into the house to find Terri, I took a little trip backward through time. Everything that I did after that happened months earlier from your perspective. Terri and I traveled together in the past, and then I came back to the present. The dust wasn't disturbed, right? If I had walked into that house at the moment you thought I'd fainted, I would have had to have levitated across the floor." She grinned wider. "I could probably do that now but not then. When I fell through the second doorway, Wells wasn't quite ready to let me leave so she pulled me sideways back into the present I was sharing with you and Lightman."

Coopersmith stared at her. "Wow."

Monk nodded, and they all ate in silence for a little while.

"What happens now?" Jackie asked.

"Life goes on," Warland said.

"And we go back to school and finish our final year," Monk said.

Jackie looked disappointed and vaguely dissatisfied.

"But," Monk continued, "there's no reason we can't keep mucking around on the dreamscape."

Kilkenny's eyes shone with hope. "Really?"

"Sure," Monk said. "We *both* have to learn how to use our werewolf powers."

"What about Sister Constance, Michaels, and all the others?" Jackie asked.

"Let's scope it out. I'm hoping it will all have gone away once Wells left but it's hard to be sure."

"What do you think happened to them?" Warland asked.

"Wells was able to slip inside people's minds and watch what was going on. She did it to me a couple of times," Monk said, feeling her blush. Coopersmith took her hand and gave it a comforting squeeze. Monk returned it. "Maybe that's what she was doing, and if it was, then maybe it's just not a problem anymore."

They finished the rest of their meal in silence and helped Warland clean up afterwards.

"Believe it or not, I'm just whacked," Jackie said when they were done. She followed this up with a bone cracking yawn.

Warland grinned. "No worries. You can either sleep in the guest rooms or here in the living room. Your call."

Jackie and Kilkenny exchanged glances.

"I want a real bed," Kilkenny said.

Jackie nodded. "Works for me. You want to stay with me for the night?"

Kilkenny nodded. "I'd feel better. Thanks, Jackie."

"No worries," Jackie replied, leading Kilkenny to the ground floor guest room.

Warland shot a questioning look at Coopersmith. Coopersmith glanced at Monk. Monk shook her head.

"You have no idea how much I want to stay here tonight," she said. "But I haven't been home in days. I should go there. What day is it anyway? And what time is it?" She lightly slapped her wrist. "My watch got busted."

"It's nine o'clock on Saturday night," Coopersmith said.

"Then to hell with it," Monk said. "What's one more night? It's not a school night. I'll go home tomorrow."

Warland glanced at Coopersmith. "All righty, then. Come with me. There are more guest rooms upstairs." She led them upstairs and pointed to the first doors on the right. "Knock yourselves out. Each has an ensuite, and towels are there. I've got the master bedroom at the end of the hallway. I'll catch you both tomorrow morning."

Warland went down the hall and into her room.

Coopersmith pushed Monk into the first guest room. They stared at each other for a second or so, and then Monk was flat on her back tangled together with Coopersmith, and they were kissing for all they were worth.

"I'm still your maths teacher until the end of the year," Coopersmith said when they broke, "so we can't really pursue this now. You understand?"

Monk nodded. "I don't like it but I won't give you a hard time about it. We have to think long term."

Coopersmith smiled and nodded. "Right." Her smile slipped away. "You're going back to your mother, aren't you?"

Monk grimaced. "I have to. I don't really have a choice on that one. I can't stay with you because that'd be career suicide for you." She paused, studying Coopersmith's beautiful features. "I'm not worried about it. She can't torture me the same way she used to."

Coopersmith nodded. "All the same, if anything happens, come to me. We'll worry about my career then."

"I know we can't be together until the end of the year," Monk said, gazing deep into Coopersmith's eyes. "But for this evening, you're mine."

"Are you sure?" Coopersmith asked. "We don't have to do anything if you don't feel ready. We can stop whenever you want. I'll wait."

"I'm not sure I can stop," Monk said. "And I trust you."

Coopersmith rolled on top of her, her gaze predatory. "Then, yes. Tonight you belong to me." She lightly trapped Monk's arms over the top of her head and began to feast on her neck.

Monk smiled, and her heart rate picked up. She felt a deep surge of love for Coopersmith, saw it returned in Coopersmith's eyes.

"I need a shower," Monk said breathlessly. "I'm pretty gross."

"So do I," Coopersmith said. She slowly stood, holding Monk's fiery gaze. She unhurriedly stripped off her shirt and held out her hand.

"Are you coming?" she asked, pulling Monk to her feet and stripping off her tee shirt. Her slow, appreciative gaze took in Monk's full breasts and muscular torso. She ran her hands over Monk's smooth skin, tracing her muscles and cupping her breasts.

Monk nodded, breathing unsteady. "Where you go, I go," she whispered, kissing Coopersmith and unclasping her bra. She filled her hands with Coopersmith's flesh and smiled at Coopersmith's soft moan.

CHAPTER FOURTEEN

The next morning, at around ten-thirty, Coopersmith pulled up at the end of Monk's street.

Monk glanced down at the hand she had unconsciously rested on Coopersmith's thigh, thinking about the previous night. Coopersmith was a wonderful friend and a better lover. Monk had always lived her life from day to day, had never really looked forward to tomorrow. Nothing had ever really felt worth it to her.

She glanced at Coopersmith.

Now she had more than one reason.

"Are you sure you want to do this?" Coopersmith asked, looking carefully at her.

Monk nodded. "I have to. I don't really have a choice."

"There's always a choice," Coopersmith said. "I'll do anything to get you out of there, love."

Monk smiled. "Anything?"

"Hell, I'll even move you in with *my* parents," Coopersmith replied. "My sister. Anybody. It rips me apart to know you're going to go in there, and your mother is going to use you as a punching bag." She paused. "And it's all for my sake. I don't think I can do this anymore."

"Mitch, my love," Monk said. "A lot has happened to me over the past few days outside of the species change. I've learnt a lot about myself." She paused. "You're not responsible for any of this. This part is about me and my ability to stand up for myself. I want to know if I can use what I've learned to deal with my mother. I don't want to be afraid anymore. I don't want her to hit me anymore. I'm going to make that very clear to her."

Coopersmith nodded. "Well said."

Monk nodded. "I need you to know. I need you to understand. I have to talk to you about things. I'm so tired of keeping everything inside all the time. I want someone to share things with."

"I'm glad. Because now I really feel like I can tell you any and everything." Coopersmith gently caressed her face. "Why, oh why couldn't all of this crap waited until the end of the school year?"

"Shitty timing?"

Coopersmith laughed and nodded. "You have to go. If you stay here another second, I'm not going to let you go."

"Look, if she turfs me out can I come and stay with you for a while?"

"You really need to ask? Of course you can. That's always been true."

Monk leaned over and stole a kiss. "If things don't work out, who knows? I may be on your sofa this evening. If not, I'll see you tomorrow at school."

Coopersmith raised an eyebrow. "If you're staying with me you can't seriously think I'm going to let you sleep on the sofa? I'd call it a sign from God that we can start now."

Monk felt her blush and grinned. "You're absolutely right."

"Do you want to meet up with me tonight?"

"I'd love to but I can't. I have to try and do some studying."

Coopersmith nodded. "All right."

"I can't believe you'd let me do that," Monk said with a grin. "Of course I'll do something with you tonight."

Coopersmith gave her a broad grin. "You're on. I'll pick you up at around seven."

"Don't worry about it," Monk said, slipping out of the car. "I'll come to you."

Coopersmith nodded and started the engine with a decisive twist of her wrist. Monk waved and watched as she drove away.

A few minutes later, she stood on the sidewalk, looking at both of her parents' cars. A solid feeling of dislike steeled over her. It felt grim. It was a place she could not be herself. She almost glanced back up the street, the way she came. Coopersmith. *She* was home.

Monk steeled herself, hating every second that had to pass before she could be with Coopersmith again.

She walked up the front path and saw shadows shifting behind the living room curtain.

Just as she put her hand on the knob, the front door opened, and her mother stood there.

"Get inside," she said without preamble. Her eyes flashed, and her mouth tightened.

Monk silently strode past her into the living room. There was no sign of her father—he didn't want to know what was happening—or her older sister—her mother forbade her from watching.

"Whatever you want to say, get it over and done with. I'll go after that," Monk said, eyeing her carefully.

Her mother walked toward her with a raised hand.

"Don't," Monk said. "If you hit me, I'll hit you back, and I'm bigger, stronger, and faster than you are."

Her mother stopped and glared at her. "Who the hell do you think you are to talk to your mother this way? After all that I've done for you?"

Monk felt like rolling her eyes, but refrained. She looked down at her mother, a small, grey-haired woman, covered in middle-aged flab, more interested in her older daughter and appearances for her church friends than the wellbeing of her husband and younger daughter.

"What, exactly, do you think you've done for me?" Monk asked. "You only had me to keep Jean company, and you've been calling me an embarrassment ever since you worked out Jean didn't want me for a playmate."

"How dare you speak to me this way?" her mother asked, genuinely shocked. "I love you."

Monk raised her eyebrows. "Really? Could have fooled me." She leaned forward. "You don't love me. You never did. Stop lying."

Her mother swung and delivered a stinging slap to Monk's cheek.

Monk felt the heat in her skin, and for the first time didn't feel anything other than sickened by her mother's reactions. Her mother seemed small and ridiculous, more interested in hitting and damaging anything she could not control. Monk found her repulsive.

"Did that feel good?" Monk asked, honestly curious. "It didn't do anything for me." She smiled. "I also don't think it had quite the effect on me that you want."

Her mother looked confused. "I don't understand what you mean. I love you. I only care about what's best for you."

"You have the weirdest way of showing it," Monk said dryly. "Look, starting from now we're going to institute some new rules. You never get to lay a finger on me again. We avoid each other. I don't like you any more than you like me. You want everyone to think you only have one daughter, be my guest. I could care less. You want me to move out, just tell me. I'm gone."

"Good, get out," her mother said. "You're a waste of space. You eat too much. You stink. Nobody likes you. You have no friends and nowhere to go."

Monk wanted to laugh at the ridiculous insults, but she held back. "Oh, Mother, I think I do have one or two friends."

"Good." Her mother folded her arms and gave Monk a superior look. "Then they can take care of you."

"Fine," Monk said. "I'm going to get my clothes and obey your wishes."

Her mother's unpleasant smile turned into a feral grin. "I said they could take care of you. That means *all* of you."

"Can I at least get my school uniforms and books?"

Her mother shook her head. "No."

Monk's temper flared at her mother's childish behavior. She studied her mother, looking for auras, and found one, beginning at the top of her head. She focused on it, and the world became a bleeding riot of color.

"I'm going to get my books and clothes," she said. "Dare you to stop me, old woman. Double dare you."

Her mother went white with fear at Monk's bright, bile yellow eyes. She made the sign of the evil eye. "That explains it. You're possessed. Get thee behind me, Satan."

Monk couldn't help herself. She threw back her head and laughed, loud and hard. "You have so got to be kidding me." She snorted when she finally managed to contain her mirth. A red aura flowed from her mother, swirling above her head, bleeding into the floor. "I'm just going to grab my stuff and go."

"If you walk out that door, you're dead to us. You'll never be welcome back here again," her mother yelled to Monk's retreating back.

Monk stopped, turned, and held up a hand. "Unwelcome. Dead. Door. Got it." She headed to her room, grabbing her duffel bag from the hall closet along the way. She went into her room and stuffed her duffel bag with all the clothes she could find at short notice.

Her mother stood in the doorway and mumbled an Our Father, several Hail Marys, and a smug, self-righteous Act of Contrition. Monk gritted her teeth, stuffing textbooks into her spare backpack, and tried to tune her out.

When she finished, she slung the duffel bag across her back, and shouldered the backpack.

"You know," she said, "all I ever wanted was for you to love me. Why do you hate me so much?"

Her mother ignored her. Her eyes remained trained on the floor.

Monk shrugged. Her mother had no more answers than before. She felt a surge of relief. It was finally over. She walked quickly out of the house and down the front path. It seemed as though an immense weight slipped off her shoulders, and she was free for the first time in her life.

She smiled and walked toward Coopersmith's flat.

Forty-five minutes later she saw Coopersmith just as she was walking out of the front of her building.

Coopersmith gestured toward the duffel and backpack. "She threw you out, didn't she?"

Monk nodded and grinned. "And I don't care." A shadow crossed her features. "I can only kind of take care of myself. I get money from the government so I can stay in school."

"Well, don't worry about the other stuff. I can take care of us both." Coopersmith held out her arms, and Monk threw herself into them, squeezing for all she was worth and breathing deeply of Coopersmith's perfume.

"Offer still open?" Monk asked hesitantly.

"Um, let me think. *Yes*," Coopersmith said. "And I think I have a solution to our little problem of your official residence."

"Which would be?"

"I'm going to talk to my sister. You can use her address as yours until the end of the year. Sound good?"

"Live here and direct my mail there? That's a fantastic idea."

"Thought you'd like it," Coopersmith said. "I was going to go out and meet her for brunch. You want to come?"

"It kills me to say this, but I can't. I've got homework, and I've got a couple of days of catching up to do."

"Okay," Coopersmith said. "How about we do something when I get back?"

"By then I'll really be ready for a break," Monk said with a grin.

"I'll just let you in upstairs, and I'll be back in a few hours."

Coopersmith gave Monk her security code and a set of keys to her unit and went to meet her sister.

Monk gazed around the empty living room. She felt relaxed for the first time in a long time. She opened her backpack and pulled out books. She had a lot of catching up to do before Coopersmith came back.

Coopersmith returned a few hours later and gazed at Monk as though seeing her for the first time. "You're still here."

Monk nodded. "Of course. Where else would I be?"

Coopersmith blushed. "I don't know. You always seem to disappear on me."

Monk shook her head. "Not anymore. I'm not going anywhere."

Coopersmith encircled Monk in her arms, and Monk felt her nod. She was silent for a moment and then pulled back and gazed into Monk's eyes. "I have a gift for you."

"Really?" Monk asked with a grin as she accepted the small box Coopersmith handed to her. She carefully pulled the lid off. "Oh, wow." She pulled out a brand new diver's watch.

"There's an inscription on the back," Coopersmith said.

Monk turned it over. *Love until the end of time,* it read. Monk strapped it on and wordlessly squeezed Coopersmith.

"I don't know what to say besides thank you," Monk said. "Every time I look at it I'm going to think of you."

Coopersmith fingered her crucifix. "I know." She smiled. "Are you done studying for the day?"

Monk nodded. She was too distracted to think.

"You want to go for a walk along the beach?" Coopersmith asked. "And a nice, romantic dinner later on?"

Monk smiled and nodded. "Sounds like a great idea to me."

"Monk," Jackie said, jogging toward her as she got into school the next morning.

"Hey, Jackie," Monk said cheerfully. "What can I do for you?"

"Nothing, actually," Jackie said with a grin. "I just wanted to ask you if you wanted to sit with me and my friends."

Monk glanced at Fletch, sitting in their accustomed spot by the auditorium. Monk liked Fletch but not any of the girls that surrounded her, seemingly hanging on to her every word.

She turned back to Jackie and smiled. "Love to. Your friends aren't going to have a problem with this, are they?"

Jackie shook her head. "Even if they did, you really mean an awful lot to me. You're *my* friend."

Monk nodded. "You mean the same amount to me."

"Monk!" Kilkenny called.

"Hey, Kilkenny," Monk said. "How are you this fine and bright Monday morning?"

"I'm good." She looked around. "Does it seem different to you?"

"I don't know," Monk said. "We're going to have to see how the day goes."

"How about you just *see*?"

"You want me to do that here?" Monk asked.

Kilkenny nodded. "You're the only one who can see it. And if you can, maybe do something about it."

"And how do you suggest I do that?" Monk asked.

"Look at someone you think is wrong. Let's see what happens."

"Like who?"

"Sister Constance," Kilkenny said.

Monk looked at the faces before her and felt awkward. "Okay, but no one's allowed to look." She began to walk toward the office, Kilkenny and Jackie trailing behind her. As soon as they entered the hallway outside the office, Monk shifted her vision without thinking about it.

She quickly slipped her sunglasses on.

Sister Constance stood outside the office, talking to Warland, and unable to look at her. She spoke quietly and quickly, and then turned and walked away. Warland gave her a puzzled look.

The auras surrounding Sister Constance and Warland, as well as the rest of the hallway, looked normal to Monk. She couldn't see anything that suggested to her that students and teachers were under some kind of external control.

"I think we're good," she said.

Kilkenny, whose eyes also blazed yellow, nodded. "I agree."

"Good." Monk shifted her vision back and gave them both a questioning look. "Let's go out and paddle around in the sunshine before we get stuck inside for another seven hours."

Jackie grinned. "You're on." They walked back to the courtyard. "Wonder who we're going to end up with for chemistry?"

Monk smiled, shouldering her backpack and looking around at the milling girls in the courtyard. The sun shone down on them, a brilliant benediction. She felt a surge of gratitude and liking toward her two new friends. "I have no idea. I only hope she's not a dog like the last one."

ABOUT THE AUTHOR

Jordan Falconer was born in Sydney, Australia, and from a very young age had an interest in ghoulies, ghosties and long legged beasties and all things that go bump in the night. After surviving Catholic school (twice!) she graduated from Sydney University with an honors degree in Psychology. She currently resides in Canada with her other half and three small, demanding dogs.

Jordan can be reached at jfishmael@hotmail.com

www.ingramcontent.com/pod-product-compliance
Lightning Source LLC
Chambersburg PA
CBHW020417180626
46812CB00003B/1023